THIS ARMY DOES NOT RETREAT: THE MEMOIRS OF GENERAL GEORGE H. THOMAS

THIS ARMY DOES NOT RETREAT: THE MEMOIRS OF GENERAL GEORGE H. THOMAS

A Novel by

JACK M. ZACKIN

ISBN: 1537187228
ISBN 13: 9781537187228

DEDICATION

To Freda whose encouragement and support made this book possible.

PREFACE

Headquarters, Department of the Cumberland
Nashville, Tennessee   December 14, 1864

My Dearest Wife,

I swear, Fanny, Grant and Halleck treat me as if I were a boy. They seem to think me incapable of planning a campaign or of fighting a battle. However, I am sure my plan of operation is sound and that we shall whip the Rebels tomorrow.

It is quiet now after another day of unceasing activity, but I cannot sleep. It is not tomorrow's attack that keeps me awake. Having completed our preparations for battle, I have every confidence that the brave men of this army will deal the enemy a decisive defeat tomorrow. It is rather my treatment at the hands of my superiors that makes me sore-at-heart.

Rumors have reached me that General Grant is on his way here from Virginia to relieve me of my command. For over two weeks, Generals Grant and Halleck have bombarded me with telegrams, first urging me and then ordering me to attack Hood's forces at once. I initially explained that additional time was needed to mold the disparate troops of my command into a unified army and to gather the necessary horses to mount the cavalry force essential to victory. All was in readiness for my attack when an ice storm, as severe as anyone has ever seen in this area, necessitated a delay, since neither horses nor men could advance over the ice-covered roads. Despite my advising him of these conditions, Grant continued to insist on an immediate attack.

In fact, Grant, over five hundred miles away in the trenches around Petersburg, seems to have come practically unstrung with worry over the possibility that Hood will bypass my army, cross the Cumberland River and invade Kentucky. I have repeatedly assured him that the disposition of my forces, and the presence of Admiral Lee's gunboats both above and below the city, render such a movement impossible. He refuses to recognize that I have the situation in hand and am prepared to deal Hood a decisive blow as soon as the weather permits.

I have seen too many examples in this war of troops forced into battle by commanders who are ill-prepared for battle. Countless brave men have been needlessly sacrificed as a result. I have therefore refused to allow myself to be pressured into an attack until I was certain that my army was properly trained and equipped to achieve victory with the minimum effusion of blood. I have now reached that point.

However, no one knows better than I that the outcome of a battle is never absolutely certain and that unforeseen circumstances can upset even the soundest plan of battle. If such should occur tomorrow, I will be forced to resign in disgrace and my reputation will be forever ruined. Yet I could have acted in no other way consistent with my sense of duty to my men and to my country. When a general commanding an army is ordered to do what he feels he ought not to do, he should act upon his own opinions and let things take their course. As always, having done all in my power to assure success, I leave tomorrow's outcome in the hands of Almighty Providence.

I am, as always, upheld by your love and unfailing support. I look forward to the time, hopefully in the not too distant future, when this terrible conflict shall be concluded and we can live out our days together in peace and contentment.

With deepest love,
George

George Henry Thomas (Library of Congress)

Chapter 1

I was born on July 31, 1816 in Southampton County, Virginia, about six miles southwest of Jerusalem, the nearest town of any note. My father, John Thomas, whose ancestors had emigrated to Southampton County from England in the early colonial days, was a farmer. My mother was born Elizabeth Rochelle. One of her grandfathers was a Huguenot who emigrated to Virginia in 1609.

My parents were married in 1808 and had nine children, only six of whom survived infancy. I was the fourth oldest surviving child, having two older brothers and three sisters, one older and two younger.

In those days, Southampton County was an isolated country, filled with swamps, bogs and marshes. A few scattered farms were located on the patches of high ground dry enough to grow crops.

At the time of my birth, my father owned about eight hundred acres on which he primarily raised tobacco, cotton and corn. He also owned between twelve and fifteen negro slaves at any one time. We were a prosperous family, but not part of the elite Tidewater planter caste.

My childhood was a happy time. I spent hours every day in the forests and swamps near our farm. Even at an early age, I had a great love of and interest in nature and I gathered and studied the plants and flowers that grew in abundance. This interest has lasted all my life and in army camps around this country and in Mexico, I always made an effort to locate unusual plants, sending particularly interesting species to the Smithsonian Institution in Washington for further study.

My father was a stern man, who seldom laughed or seemed to relax. He had little time for his children, spending each day from early morning until sunset in the fields working with his negro field hands. On February 19, 1829, when I was 12 years old, he was killed in a farming accident.

In contrast to my father, my mother had a happy disposition, and I can still hear her musical laugh which rang out so often in our house. She was also an extremely strong and capable woman who, through her strength of character, kept our farm and our family together after my father's death. I believe I owe to her my ability to remain calm and resolute in the face of a crisis, which has served me so well and so often in my military career.

Three years after my father's death, when I was fifteen, my family and I were caught up in the Nat Turner slave uprising. Turner was a slave on the farm of one of our neighbors. He was known in the neighborhood as being extremely bright, with the ability to read and write. He was also deeply religious, conducting church services for other slaves and free blacks on Sundays. He had run away several years prior to his rebellion but voluntarily returned to his plantation.   As far as I knew, since returning home, Turner had never created a problem for his owner.

On a hot summer night in August, we were awakened by frantic shouts accompanied by a pounding on our front door. Looking out my bedroom window, I saw a group of four or five horsemen who, from the look of their horses, had been doing some hard riding. I descended the stairs in time to see my mother fling open the door to admit the single horseman who had dismounted.

"Mrs. Thomas," the rider said, "the slaves have rebelled. They are slaughtering every white person they can find and it looks like they are headed this way. Gather up your family and head for town. To stay here is certain death."

My mother wasted no time in trundling us into a wagon and setting out toward town. Travelling through the pitch black night on the rutted country roads was slow and difficult. Even with the aid of lanterns, we could not see very far ahead and the horses often missed their steps. After we had traveled about three miles, we stopped and listened to determine whether we were being pursued. We could distinctly hear shouts and the sounds of running feet somewhere off in the distance.

My mother prepared to start the wagon again when I spoke up. "Mother," I said, "they will surely overtake us if we keep to the road. I know this country very well. Let's leave the wagon and set off through the woods on foot. I can guide us to town."

My mother was thinking this over when we heard a loud shout that sounded as if it had come from close by. "All right children. Everyone get off the wagon and follow George."

My brothers and sisters alighted from the wagon, my brother John bringing the lantern with him. "No, no," I told him. "We need to make our way in the dark. They can see the lantern light a mile away."

John doused the lantern and we set off. I had spent my youth exploring the woods and swamps around our farm and was confident I could find my way to town. There was no moon, and I felt, rather than saw, my way forward. Strange noises filled the forest, each of which filled us with dread, but having no choice we pressed on. In about two hours we reached Jerusalem.

The town was in an uproar. No one seemed to have a clear idea of what was really happening. Wild rumors circulated on the night air. Some said that the slaves had been incited to insurrection by abolitionists from the North who had supplied them with firearms and were personally leading the uprising. Others reported that thousands of slaves all over Virginia were involved and had already burned down countless farms and plantations and had slaughtered hundreds if not thousands of whites.

As night turned into morning, the town fathers and community leaders brought order out of the chaos. The local militia units were mustered and regular troops were sent for. As the day progressed, we learned that Turner and a group of slaves had hacked Turner's owner and his family to death and then proceeded from farm to farm gathering adherents and murdering whites. The total number of slaves involved in the uprising was believed to be about seventy. Sixty whites were killed by Turner and his band, using knives, guns and an assortment of farm implements.

Retaliation was swift and harsh. Patrols were formed to aid the militia in hunting down Turner and his followers. In all, over two hundred black men, most of whom played no role in the insurrection, were shot or hanged. Turner successfully avoided capture for two months, hiding out in the swamps. When he was finally caught, he was quickly hanged.

Up to the time of the Turner uprising, I had given little thought to slavery. It was simply part of our daily existence. The events of that August caused me to reflect on our "peculiar institution." The whites publicly maintained that the slaves were much better off than they had been in Africa and were generally well-treated and happy, at least in Virginia. On the other hand, fear of a slave insurrection was always present just below the surface. Somehow, these two disparate views existed side by side.

As a child, I had played with the slave children on our farm and by the time I was eleven I was supervising the field hands. I assumed that our slaves were well cared for and relatively happy. After Nat Turner's Rebellion, I began to question these assumptions.

Chapter 2

In my youth, there were no public schools in Southampton County. Until the age of nineteen, I attended a school run by one our neighbors somewhat ambitiously called the Southampton Academy. The schooling I received, though far from comprehensive, proved adequate to allow me to keep up with my classmates when I entered West Point.

Having little interest in working the family farm, I gave serious thought to becoming a lawyer. My late uncle, James Rochelle, who had died shortly before I finished school, had held the position of County Clerk. I applied to his successor for the job of Deputy County Clerk and was sworn into this position on November 18, 1835. I believed that serving as Deputy Clerk would prepare me for a legal career better than working in the office of one of the local attorneys.

After about three months on the job, a short, rail-thin man with coarse silver-gray hair appeared at the office and introduced himself as John Y. Mason, our area's Congressman. "Are you George Thomas?" he asked in a high, piercing voice. I affirmed that I was and he continued. "Your uncle James Rochelle was a good friend of mine. He spoke highly of you and from what I can gather from your neighbors, they generally share this opinion."

When I thanked him for these sentiments, he waved my words aside with an impatient gesture. "Thomas, I have an appointment to make for the Military Academy at West Point and have come here to see if you have any interest." His words were such a complete surprise that it took me a moment to reply, during which he sat across from me and stared appraisingly into my eyes. I had never considered a life in the military, but now, attending West Point suddenly seemed like the opportunity I had been waiting for.

I was bored with life in Southampton County and longed to see other parts of the country. My duties as Deputy County Clerk had convinced me that the legal profession was not to my liking and there were no other likely job prospects in the area. "If my Mother will assent to my attending West Point," I eventually replied, "I would very much like to accept the appointment."

Mason told me that he would be in Jerusalem until the following afternoon and asked whether I could give him an answer before he left town. I told him that I could and, unable to focus on my work, I closed up the office early and rode home to talk to my mother. She was very receptive to the idea, agreeing with me that, if I remained in Southampton County, my prospects would be extremely limited. Having obtained her acquiescence, I did not delay, but immediately rode back to Jerusalem, located the Congressman and accepted his offer. Thus, in the space of several hours, my future course in life was settled.

In early April, 1836, I left home and headed for West Point. When saying goodbye to my family, my brother John shook my hand and told me, "George, you are a man now and I hesitate to give you advice. But I will tell you this. If you do what you conscientiously believe to be right, you may regret, but should never be annoyed by, a want of approbation on the part of others." With these words I took leave of my family and the scenes of my youth. John's admonition stayed with me, and I have always attempted to do what I thought was right, even when, as was often the case, I knew my decisions would not be popular with my political and military superiors.

On the way to West Point, I stopped in Washington to thank Congressman Mason for my appointment. His response was far from what I expected. "Young man," he said, "no cadet appointed from my district has ever graduated from the Military Academy. I am tired of this humiliating record. If you fail to graduate, I never want to see you again."

Taken aback, I stammered that I would try not to disappoint him and left his office. I do not know to this day whether Mason was serious or whether this was his rather unorthodox method of providing motivation. Whatever the case, I did become the first graduate of West Point from Southampton County.

On June 1, 1836, I enrolled at West Point. Andrew Jackson was President of the United States. I was twenty years old, about four years older than the average entering cadet. I stood about six feet tall, weighed one hundred eighty pounds, had light brown hair and blue eyes.

I was one of seventy-six first year students, or plebes, that entered the Military Academy that spring. I was assigned to a dormitory room in the South Barracks and upon my arrival I found my two roommates already there. One was Stewart Van Vliet, from New York State. The other was William Tecumseh Sherman from Ohio. Sherman was a few months short of his seventeenth birthday. He was filled with nervous energy and seemed incapable of sitting still for more than five minutes at a time. In conversation he jumped from topic to topic and offered opinions and theories on every imaginable subject, assuming that he knew more about whatever was being discussed than anyone else. Throughout my long acquaintance with Sherman, these characteristics never changed.

In July, the plebes and the third year classmen were ordered out of barracks and into camp. This involved moving into tents on wooden floors arranged in orderly rows. For two months we were instructed and drilled in the rudiments of military formations and practices. The days were long, hot and arduous and each plebe was assigned to guard duty for eight hours out of every twenty-four. Despite these hardships, the routine of military life greatly appealed to me, and I determined very quickly that I would make the military my career.

After two months, we struck the tents and moved back to barracks. "Hazing" of plebes by upper classmen was an established part of West Point tradition. One night early in my first year, an upperclassman entered our room without knocking and demanded that we accompany him outside where he would supervise us as we marched at double time around the post. I considered this ritual quite silly and was, moreover, unwilling to take time away from my studies on such a useless enterprise. I therefore advised him that if he did not immediately leave my room, I would seize hold of him and bodily throw him out the window. He stared at me for a minute and, apparently recognizing that I was in earnest, made a quick exit. From that time on, I was left alone by the upperclassmen.

The course of studies at West Point in the 1830's was devoted primarily to engineering and mathematics. There was almost no study of military strategy and tactics, the exception being the course offered by Dennis H. Mahan, entitled Civil and Military Engineering and the Science of War, required to be taken by every cadet in his fourth year. Even Mahan, however, devoted only nine hours of classroom time to the Science of War section of his course. Mahan was a brilliant theorist and had much to teach us. Finding no existing texts suitable, he supplied his students with lithographed notes of his lectures which were later adopted as textbooks by many schools in the United States and abroad.

Practical training in artillery was provided by Lieutenant Robert Anderson, who was destined to gain national renown as the hero of Fort Sumter. From him I gained an appreciation for the proper use of artillery and a special fondness for this branch of the service.

Jacob W. Bailey was professor of natural history, a relatively new discipline at West Point. Bailey's enthusiasm for his subject matter reinforced my interest in nature which has continued to this day. In military camps from Florida to Texas, I relieved the frequent boredom of military routine with a study of the native plant and animal species.

During my fourth year at West Point, I served as one of eighteen cadet lieutenants. Ulysses S Grant was one of the first year cadets. Grant was quiet, though genial and friendly. He was, however, careless and indifferent to his studies, traits that were quite foreign to my nature. I thus found it difficult to befriend him.

I am the first to admit that I was not a brilliant student. But I worked hard, generally avoided the many distractions available to cadets off-post, and, in June of 1840, graduated from West Point twelfth in a class of forty-two. I received my commission as second lieutenant in the United States Army from President Martin Van Buren, was assigned to Company H of the Third Regiment of Artillery and ordered to report to Fort Columbus on Governor's Island in New York Harbor on or before September 30, 1840.

Chapter 3

After a visit home, I reported to Fort Columbus and joined the Third Artillery Regiment. The United States was then engaged in fighting what became known as the Second Seminole War and I learned that my regiment was soon to be transported to Florida to take part in the conflict. Because artillery was virtually useless in the Florida swamps, nine companies of the Third Artillery, including mine, were converted into infantry before being sent south.

The Second Seminole War grew out of President Jackson's' policy of removing the Seminoles to reservations west of the Mississippi River, codified into law by the Indian Removal Act of 1830. Many of the Seminole Chiefs resisted the government's removal efforts and full scale hostilities erupted in 1835.

For about two years, beginning in the Summer of 1838, General Zachary Taylor rose to prominence as commander of the American forces in Florida. In May of 1840, about four months before I reported for duty at Governor's Island, the government acceded to Taylor's request for a transfer and General Walker Armistead was named as his replacement.

My first assignment in the army was training two hundred recruits for infantry service fighting the Seminoles. In mid-November, 1840, after a ninety day training period, my recruits and I boarded ship and arrived in Fort Lauderdale, Florida a week later. Fort Lauderdale was less than an impressive outpost, consisting of a group of cane huts with thatched roofs and a scattering of wigwams. Rations for both officers and men were meager in both quality and variety, consisting mainly of salt pork, crackers and buckwheat cakes.

Despite these rude conditions, I found Florida much to my liking, at least until the sweltering bug-infested days of summer arrived. When not on duty, I was able to explore the surrounding countryside and beaches. I was fascinated by the many unfamiliar species of plant and bird life. I also enjoyed fishing from an open canoe and was able to supplement our meager rations with fish of numerous varieties.

I was not initially included in the scouting parties regularly sent out from the fort to locate Seminole villages. Instead, I was appointed quartermaster, commissary and ordnance officer. Though disappointed at not being allowed to participate in the expeditions against the Indians, my duties taught me valuable lessons about how to supply and feed an army in the field, lessons I never forgot.

In June, 1841, Captain R.D. Wade assumed command at Fort Lauderdale charged with implementing a new strategy designed by Colonel William Jenkins Worth, who had recently replaced General Armistead as overall commander in Florida. Whereas General Taylor had adopted a largely defensive strategy, constructing a series of fortifications in Northern Florida to defend the more heavily populated areas, Colonel Worth determined to actively seek out the Seminoles, destroy their food supplies and canoes and bring them to battle or force their surrender.

Happily for me, Captain Wade relieved me of my administrative duties and appointed me as his second in command on the raiding parties he led in search of the hostiles. Nothing I learned at West Point prepared me for the type of warfare I was now to face. The Seminoles never formed battle lines or fought in fixed formations. Instead, small parties of Indians made quick, deadly hit and run raids on military and civilian encampments before disappearing back into the almost impenetrable swamps.

Now, we were going to take the fight to the enemy. Captain Wade organized raiding parties of about twenty men, equipped with fifteen days of rations. We travelled by canoe when possible and by foot when the water was too shallow, through territory rarely seen by white men. We sometimes encountered small groups of warriors who we killed or took prisoner, but mainly came across empty Seminole villages and campsites, which we burned together with food supplies and canoes. The Seminoles always seemed to know we were coming and slipped deeper into the swamps before we arrived.

On some occasions, however, we met with greater success. In August, 1841, Captain Wade organized an expedition of twenty hand-picked men on an expedition of over one hundred fifty miles by land and water. Once again, I served as second-in-command. The heat and humidity were oppressive, the waterways full of water moccasins and alligators and the air full of mosquitoes and other biting and stinging insects. We stayed vigilant for ambush by the Seminoles, one of their favorite tactics. We knew that if trouble arose, we were on our own, far from any possible help.

About a week after we set off, we surprised and captured a group of twenty warriors, some of whom spoke English. Captain Wade offered leniency to any Indian who would lead us to his village. One of our prisoners agreed and Captain Wade ordered me to march behind him with a loaded pistol pointed at him.

"At the first sign of an ambush," Wade told me, "put a pistol ball into this man's brain. Is that clear, Mr. Thomas?"

"Quite clear, sir," I replied.

Turning to the prisoner, Wade asked, "Do you understand the order I just gave the Lieutenant here?" Assuring the Captain that he did, our prisoner advised us that his village was a day's march away and we set off. As ordered, I kept my pistol aimed at the Seminole the entire march.

Early the next afternoon, we sighted the village consisting of numerous wooden huts, covered with cane and thatch. Quietly, we surrounded the village and, for once, turned the tables on the Indians, catching them completely by surprise. Even so, the Seminoles put up a sharp fight, returning our musket fire with a hail of arrows and musket fire of their own. After about an hour of hard fighting, the Indians capitulated. We captured sixty-three Seminoles, killed eight and destroyed a large number of war canoes and other goods. For my role in this expedition, I received a brevet promotion to first lieutenant.

In February, 1842, my regiment was ordered to New Orleans, and my role in the Second Seminole War came to an end. By that time, Colonel Worth's policy of searching out the enemy in his own country had proven successful, though not without substantial casualties through battle and disease and at great cost to the U.S. Treasury. In November 1842, Colonel Worth recommended that the remaining Indians be allowed to stay in South Florida on a de facto reservation deep in the swamps. The government agreed to his suggestion and the Second Seminole War came to an end.

My service in Florida confirmed my decision to make the army my career. I enjoyed the camaraderie among our small garrison, beset with danger in hostile surroundings, and discovered that I had an aptitude for leading men in combat and for organization and logistics. I also discovered that during the actual fighting, time seemed to slow down for me. I was able to remain cool in the face of enemy fire and to react quickly as the battle ebbed and flowed.

From Florida, my Company was assigned garrison duty at Fort Moultrie in the harbor of Charleston, South Carolina. I enjoyed my stay in Charleston and found the townspeople friendly and hospitable, often staging entertainments for the officers of the Fort. In Charleston, for the first time, I heard stirrings of national discord.

The issue at hand was the admission of Texas, which had declared its independence from Mexico. Southern politicians pressed for admission of Texas to the Union as one or more slave states. At the many soirees hosted by Charleston's residents, there was much talk about the perceived intransigence of Northern politicians and of the need for the

South to secede from the Union should the Yankees block statehood for Texas. Many officers joined in these discussions and I was surprised that many of my fellow Southerners agreed that secession might prove necessary.

I saw no reason to take part in these discussions and generally kept silent. When directly asked for my opinion, I offered the view that secession would never prove necessary because allegiance to the United States in both North and South was too strong. At the same time I was confidently expressing this opinion, construction was beginning on a new fortification in Charleston Harbor. My post at Fort Moultrie was an excellent vantage point from which to watch the boats dumping tons of rock into the harbor to form an island on which the new fort was to be erected. The name eventually chosen for the new stronghold was Fort Sumter.

In December, 1843, I was transferred to Light Artillery Company C at historic Fort McHenry in Baltimore Harbor. This assignment was much to my liking, not only because Baltimore was close to Washington and offered many pleasing amusements, but because it was my first posting to a fully equipped artillery battery. During my stay at Fort McHenry, I was promoted to the permanent rank of first lieutenant.

In July, 1844, I was transferred again to Fort Moultrie. My new commander was Braxton Bragg, a North Carolinian. Like me, Bragg was an artilleryman, a graduate of West Point and a veteran of the Seminole War. With much in common, we became good friends. Bragg was to be my comrade- in-arms in the war with Mexico and my adversary when he commanded the Confederate Army of Tennessee in the War of the Rebellion.

During that war, he gained the reputation of being short-tempered and irascible, and was heartily disliked by his subordinate generals. At Fort Moultrie and in Mexico, however, he was affable and had a cheerful disposition. He was also a stickler for details, no matter how petty, and wasted time and effort seeing to it that everything was done precisely by the book. This quality, which grew worse over time, greatly undermined his effectiveness as a commander.

In May 1845, I left on a one week leave for a visit to my family in Virginia. While home, I received orders to report with my company to New Orleans to rendezvous with General Zachary Taylor who was organizing an army to confront the Mexicans.

Chapter 4

The antagonism between the United States and Mexico was of long standing. A succession of Mexican governments had been keeping a wary eye on their country's expanding neighbor to the North for many years.

After the American settlers in the Mexican state of Texas fought for and won independence from Mexico, the Democrats in the United States Congress, anxious to add Texas to the Union as a slave state, pushed for its annexation. In February,1844, during the closing days of President John Tyler's administration, Congress passed a joint resolution inviting Texas to join the Union. Mexico did not recognize Texan independence, and this resolution greatly intensified tensions between Mexico and the U.S.

Thus matters stood when President James K Polk assumed office in March, 1845. Polk had run on a platform calling for the annexation of Texas and expansion of the Union all the way to the Pacific Ocean, which implied the cession of at least part of Mexican California to the United States. Not incidentally, the idea that a large section of Mexican territory could be seized and also turned into new slave states was not lost on President Polk and his fellow Southern Democrats.

In May, 1845, even before the government of Texas acted on the American invitation to join the Union, President Polk, reacting to Mexico's threats to invade Texas, ordered General Zachary Taylor, the commander of United States forces in the Southwest, to occupy Corpus Christi on the Nueces River in Texas. Taylor's orders were to defend Texas from a Mexican invasion. By August, 1845, Taylor's forces totaled approximately 2,500 men, which comprised the entire American regular army, save for four regiments.

The choice of General Taylor to lead the American forces was a surprise to me since I had assumed that Major General Winfield Scott, the General in Chief and a hero of the war of 1812, would assume command of any force sent to Texas to confront the Mexicans. However, Scott was a Whig with presidential aspirations. The Polk administration feared that if Scott won further renown in Mexico, he would mount a successful challenge to the Democrats during the next presidential election. Taylor, on the other hand, was viewed in Washington as apolitical.

As matters played out, this strategy back-fired. General Taylor scored a string of impressive victories in Northern Mexico, leading to widespread anticipation that he would be a candidate for President in 1848. To the Democrat's chagrin, Taylor seemed receptive to this idea. Therefore, the Polk administration decided that, after his early successes, Taylor would essentially play no further role in the war, and that General Scott would be dispatched from Washington to lead the campaign against Mexico City. This did not, however, help the Democrats' cause, as Taylor was elected President on the Whig ticket in 1848.

Witnessing these events soured my view of politics and politicians, and I determined to steer clear of politics both in the government and in the army. This determination only strengthened as the years went by.

Taylor's election as President was far in the future when my company, commanded by Captain Bragg, arrived in Corpus Christi in August, 1845. The Company consisted of four six-pound cannon, the designation referring to the weight of the projectiles thrown by the guns. We had no horses and our caissons and other equipment were in poor shape, having sustained substantial damage on the voyage from New Orleans. My days were occupied with procuring suitable horses from the Texans and in overseeing the refitting of our equipment. I suggested to Captain Bragg that we also use this time to construct furnaces so that we could hurl incendiary projectiles at the enemy. He declined my suggestion.

In December 1845, while Taylor was gathering troops and supplies, Texas was admitted to the Union. In January, the Polk administration ordered Taylor to march to the north side of the Rio Grande, the river claimed by the United States as the border with Mexico. The Mexican government did not recognize this boundary, claiming that the border was the Nueces River, several hundred miles further north.

General Taylor began the march to the Rio Grande on March, 8, 1845. My company left Corpus Christi on March 11th, accompanying the last infantry brigade to leave the city. Our destination was the northern bank of the Rio Grande opposite the Mexican town of Matamoros. We reached this location, exhausted and short of supplies, on March 28th, after a grueling march of one hundred twenty miles, and began construction of a fort opposite Matamoros. Our battery cited our guns south toward the fortifications being erected by the Mexicans on the opposite bank of the Rio Grande.

On April 25th, Mexican General Arista send a cavalry force across the river and attacked a squadron of American dragoons, capturing or killing them all. As a result of this confrontation, General Taylor notified Washington that hostilities with Mexico had begun.

General Taylor established his supply base at Point Isabel, about fifteen miles from our position on the Rio Grande, at a point where the river enters the Gulf of Mexico. This allowed the army to be supplied by ship. When our fort, which was christened Fort Texas, was nearing completion, Taylor took the bulk of the army to Point Isabel to pick up supplies. He left behind about 500 men, consisting of one infantry regiment and two companies of artillery, including mine. Major Jacob Brown commanded our little force.

The Mexicans had about 8,000 troops across the river. They began shelling our position on May 3rd while our construction efforts were still underway. My company's light six-pound guns were useless against the Mexican artillery, but our bigger eighteen- pounders responded to the Mexican salvos. I was standing near one of these guns, watching its crew in action, when the battery commander asked me what I thought of his unit's prowess "Excellent," I replied, and then added only half in jest, "but I'm thinking that after a while we made need the ammunition you're throwing away."

We succeeded in disabling some of the Mexican's cannons, after which they brought up howitzers and mortars capable of lobbing projectiles into our fort from beyond the range of our guns. For the next seven days we remained under constant enemy fire from three directions. We had constructed bomb proof shelters which protected us from most of the shelling, but on May 6th Major Brown was fatally wounded. General Taylor later renamed the installation Fort Brown in his honor, and the town of Brownsville, Texas is now located on the site.

That same day, enemy infantry was seen approaching the rear of the fort. My company was ordered to drive them off with grapeshot, which we promptly did. Several hours later, we refused a Mexican demanded for our surrender. Although the bomb proofs kept us relatively safe, we were running short of supplies and ammunition. Our horses were being killed and our caissons disabled.

As the shot and shell continued to rain down and nothing was heard from General Taylor, I could not help but think of how, at the Alamo, the Mexicans refused to accept the surrender of the Texans and piled up and burned their corpses outside the Alamo's walls. I was not alone in thinking that if help did not arrive shortly, we would share a similar fate.

Then, in mid-afternoon on May 8th, we began to hear the sounds of battle to the northeast. There was no doubt that this was General Taylor on his way to relieve us. If he succeeded in breaking through the Mexican lines, we were saved. If he failed, our situation was hopeless.

The next day we again heard artillery and musket fire, this time closer to the fort, and late that afternoon we could see the enemy retreating across the Rio Grande. Some of the retreating Mexicans passed under the walls of our fort and we hurried them along, pouring fire down on them from our ramparts. Taylor entered the fort to our shouts and cheers.

The sounds of battle we had heard from the fort were Taylor's victories at Palo Alto and Resaca de la Palma, both fought several days before Congress officially declared war on Mexico. On May 18th, the American occupation of Mexican territory began when we marched into Matamoros on the south bank of the Rio Grande.

With the Mexican Army's retreat from Matamoros, the way was open for Taylor to move on to Monterrey, the key strategic location in Northern Mexico. Several major roads converged on Monterrey, a city of about fifteen thousand, including the road from Santillo, fifty-five miles to west, that reached Monterrey after traversing the Rinconada Pass through the Sierra Madre Oriental Mountains.

In early June, General Taylor began his movement toward Camargo, situated halfway between Matamoros and Monterrey, that he had chosen as his staging point. Although most of the men and equipment travelled by riverboat, I was designated to lead a small advance force of artillery, infantry and cavalry by land along the south bank of the Rio Grande. The march was hard on men and animals with temperatures during the day reaching well over one hundred degrees. After a few days, I determined to march only at night, when the heat abated somewhat.

Leading the first American troops to reach Camargo, I was able to select the most comfortable bivouac for my company, in the shade of the town's plaza. I also commandeered a peach orchard that provided my company with the only fresh fruit available. The roughly 6,000 troops that arrived later were not so fortunate and found little relief from the scorching heat. Contaminated water, poisonous insects and disease made our stay at Camargo a misery and depleted the ranks of effective troops.

After three months of training and refitting in Camargo, General Taylor determined that we were ready to attack Monterrey and, in September, we began the final one hundred mile push toward our objective. We arrived at the northeast outskirts of the city on the morning of September 19th. It was apparent that Monterrey would not be easy to capture.

The city lay mostly on the north bank of the Santa Catarina River. The river and a series of fortified hills prevented an effective attack from the south. Steep hills also flanked both sides of the Santillo Road, the western entrance to the city. Imposing fortifications stood on both of these elevations. The Bishop's Palace dominated Independence Hill on the north side of the road and El Soldado on Federation Hill commanded the south side of the road. On the east, directly in our front, stood a seemingly impregnable fortress named The Citadel. All of these fortifications were connected by an inner ring of ditches and strongly fortified earthworks. An outer ring of works also encircled the city.

In Monterrey, itself, the houses were mostly constructed of thick stone walls with slits for windows. These houses had flat roofs, making perfect perches for snipers. Barricades had been constructed in the streets at key intersections. A total of 7,500 men held these defenses.

it was clear that a frontal assault was impossible. Nor could we hope to reduce the town with artillery, since even our eighteen-pound guns lacked the capacity to batter down the thick walls of the fortifications.

After a council of his senior officers, General Taylor decided to divide his force and send General William Jenkins Worth, with 2,000 men, on a flanking movement to the west to capture the Santillo Road. Taylor, with the remainder of the army, would remain on the eastern edge of town, and, by threatening to attack, hold as many of the Mexican troops in his front as possible. If circumstances developed favorably, Taylor could convert his demonstration into an actual attack.

On September 20th, General Worth began his swing to the west, stopping for the night just short of the Santillo Road. The next day,

Worth attacked and captured El Soldado atop Federation Hill on the south side of the highway.

As Worth's attack proceeded, General Taylor grew increasingly frustrated at his own inactivity. Finally, late in the day, he ordered an attack on the eastern end of the city, but well short of the guns mounted on The Citadel. My artillery company accompanied the infantry in mounting this attack, which consisted of house to house and man to man combat. Because my six-pound gun lacked the firepower to damage the stone walls of the houses, I loaded the gun with grapeshot and poured fire into the enemy to provide cover for the infantry.

At first we made steady progress, capturing several important positions. Then, a combination of heavy sniper fire and barricaded streets slowed and finally stopped our attack. Late in the day, I was halted by a barricade on a narrow street, leaving me no room to maneuver. Seeing my predicament, the Mexicans focused their musket fire on us. In their panic, the horses became entangled in their harnesses and were all shot and killed.

Still under heavy fire, we managed to cut the gun free from the horses, allowing us to train the gun on our attackers. I sent a message to Captain Bragg requesting fresh horses and, firing as rapidly as possible, kept the enemy at bay until the new horses arrived and we were able to get the gun back to our lines. Somewhat incredibly, none of my men was killed and only a few suffered light casualties in this encounter.

Soon after this, General Taylor realized the futility of continuing his attack and ordered a withdrawal, surrendering most of the gains we had made early in the day. It was apparent that for an attack to succeed from our quarter, different tactics would have to be employed.

The next day, General Worth resumed his attack, and after hard fighting captured the Bishop's Palace on the north side of the Santillo Road. General Taylor contented himself with lobbing artillery fire into the city.

That day a group of Texas Rangers suggested a new method of attacking the city. Instead of proceeding through the streets, becoming ensnared by barricades and subjecting ourselves to sniper fire from the rooftops, they proposed that we avoid the streets and break through the walls of the houses with axes, crowbars and similar implements. In this manner, we could take the snipers from behind. Responding favorably to this suggestion, General Taylor ordered the units who were to form the vanguard of the new attack to arm themselves with tools that could be used to batter down the thick stone wall of the houses.

When we awoke on September 23rd, we found that the Mexican commander, General Ampudia, had withdrawn his troops from the outer line of defenses. General Taylor lost no time in ordering the infantry forward to take this line and to launch a new attack on the inner line of works. This time, using the tactics conceived of by the Texans, instead of staying on the streets we entered back yards and alleys, knocking down walls and killing or capturing the Mexican sharpshooters inside. Our company stayed close to the infantry pouring a steady hail of grapeshot into the defenders.

In this manner, we moved relentlessly toward the city center. At the same time, General Worth continued his advance from the west. Nightfall brought a temporary close to our attacks which resumed the next morning at first light. Soon, a flag of truce appeared from the Mexican lines.

Three days later, after satisfactory surrender terms were negotiated, the Mexican Army marched out of Monterrey. We had lost 120 men killed, 368 wounded and 43 missing. Mexican casualties were similar.

On September 23rd, in recognition of my performance at Monterrey, I received a brevet promotion to captain. Bragg was breveted to major and given command of a different unit. I assumed temporary command of my company.

Taylor had won three major victories over the Mexicans and become a national hero. It was at this point that politics reared its head and the Polk Administration determined that Taylor be given no further opportunities for glory. General in Chief Winfield Scott was sent to Mexico and most of Taylor's army was transferred to his command. Scott's plan was to land an army at Vera Cruz, far south of Monterrey on the Gulf of Mexico, and march northwest to capture Mexico City.

The decision to attack Mexico City was strategically sound since it was unlikely the war could be won by simply expanding our conquests in Northern Mexico. But the selection of General Scott to lead the attack on Mexico City was entirely political. General Taylor had demonstrated his ability to win victories in the field, and no military reason existed to deny him command of the Mexico City campaign. Instead, he was left with barely 4,500 men, of whom no more than 500 were regulars.

In February, 1847, despite orders to remain on the defensive, General Taylor, angered by his treatment at the hands of the Polk Administration, marched his reduced army south from Monterrey to Agua Nueva, about twenty miles south of the town of Saltillo. This move placed us in great danger because Mexican President and General Antonio Lopez de Santa Anna had captured a copy of a letter from Scott to Taylor detailing the units of Taylor's army that had been transferred to Scott, describing Scott's intended landing at Vera Cruz and reiterating Taylor's orders to stay on the defensive. Armed with this information, and with an army exceeding 20,000 men, Santa Anna was confident that he could crush Taylor's much smaller army before marching south to repel Scott's landing at Veracruz.

Fortunately, a scouting party of Texas Rangers located Santa Anna's army encamped at San Luis Potosi, about seven miles south of Santillo. Taylor fell back to a more defensible position in a pass through the Sierra Madre Mountains near a large ranch known as Buena Vista. Our new position lay across the road that ran north from San Luis Potosi to Saltillo. To the right of the road, the ground was cut by deep ravines which we supplemented with ditches, making an attack from that direction virtually impossible. Lieutenant John Marshall Washington's artillery battery defended the road itself. To his left, the remainder of the army fanned out toward the foothills. My six-pounder was on the extreme left of the line supporting the Second Regiment of Indiana Volunteers. The other two guns of my company, under the command of

Lieutenant Thomas West Sherman, were placed on the other side of the line next to the road.

From early morning to midafternoon on February 22nd, we watched as the Mexican Army moved into position opposite our lines. When their dispositions were completed, we spotted a horseman under a flag of truce coming from the Mexican lines. It was a simple matter to conclude that Santa Anna was offering General Taylor a chance to surrender. Knowing Taylor, none of us doubted that he would refuse. The Mexican emissary returned to his lines less than an hour later and, immediately thereafter, Santa Anna commenced his attack.

The left of our line was obviously our weakest point, lacking any natural defenses, and the Mexicans directed their attacks on this position. Fighting on the 22nd was indecisive, although the Mexicans were able to capture some positions on the mountains overlooking the road. The night was cold and wet and we slept on our guns, serenaded for a time by music from Santa Anna's personal band.

The next morning was a Sunday and we watched from our entrenchments as the Mexicans celebrated mass with impressive ceremony. This ritual completed, Santa Anna again ordered an attack upon our left. Under intense pressure, the Second Indiana Volunteers broke toward the rear, allowing the enemy to get around our flank. General Taylor, having ridden to Santillo to bring up reinforcements, was not on the field at this time. General Wool, commanding in his absence, refused our left flank, bending our line at a right angle to face the Mexicans who were now on our front and left and in our rear.

The salient of this right angle became the focus of the Mexican attack. Defending the salient was my six-pound gun, a twelve-pound gun commanded by Lieutenant S.G. French, who was soon wounded and carried off the field, and the Second Regiment of Illinois Volunteers commanded by Colonel William Bissell. Loaded with grapeshot, our guns poured fire into the oncoming enemy, blowing great holes in their lines. Nevertheless, the Mexicans kept coming. The air was filled with the sound of bullets and screaming horses. Most of the teams went down.

Many of the officers had their mounts shot from under them. Virtually all my gunners were killed or seriously wounded. With the last few gunners and officers who could still stand, we fired at the enemy continuously at point blank range.

General Taylor now arrived on the field with the reinforcements he had brought with him from Santillo. Bragg came up first without infantry support and took up a position on my left. The Mexican attack was slowed but not stopped. Without infantry support, we would be overrun in a matter of minutes.

At this critical juncture, Taylor ordered Colonel Jefferson Davis and his regiment of Mississippi Volunteers to advance to our assistance. Coming in range of the enemy, the Mississippians delivered a murderous fire that broke the Mexican attack and forced the enemy back.

If not for Davis' timely appearance, I would most likely have been killed that day at the salient at Buena Vista. Ironically, twenty years later, in the closing days of the War of the Rebellion, I commanded the forces that captured Davis, then the fugitive President of the so-called Confederate States.

Although fighting continued late into the afternoon, the repulse of the Mexican forces at the salient seemed to sap the enemy's spirit and the Mexicans, despite their numerical superiority, never again came close to breaking our lines. About four pm, after I had been under fire for over ten straight hours, Santa Anna called off his assault. That night he withdrew his army from the field. We had survived a very close scrape.

Buena Vista marked the close of active operations for Taylor's army. Thereafter, the focus of the war shifted to General Scott's campaign against Mexico City. Much to my regret, my company was not transferred to Scott's command, but remained on garrison duty at Monterrey. Not being on campaign, I had ample free time to indulge my interest in natural history by exploring the Northern Mexican countryside. As I had done in Florida, I sent what I considered to be new or interesting plant specimens to the Smithsonian Institution in Washington. I also learned to speak Spanish and, while not fluent, I could generally make myself understood.

Scott's operations against the Mexicans proved a triumph and, when I learned that he had captured Mexico City on July 14, 1847, I was optimistic that the war would soon be over. Negotiations over the terms of the peace treaty dragged on for months, however, and it was not until February 2, 1848, almost a year after the battle of Monterrey, that the treaty of Guadalupe Hidalgo was signed, formally ending the war.

By this time, my company was back at Fort Brown, in Texas, the site of my first action in the war. In October, my company was ordered to leave Texas and report to Fort Adams in Rhode Island. I was greatly looking forward to rejoining my wife on the East Coast, but, instead, I was placed in command of a supply depot at Brazos Santiago, a small island off the Texas coast. It was not until five months later, on February 1, 1849, almost four years after the siege of Fort Brown, that I was relieved of this command and given a six month leave. I left Texas for my family farm in Virginia.

I was extremely proud of what my artillery company had achieved in Mexico. Withstanding the bombardment at Fort Brown, improvising street fighting tactics in Monterrey and fighting off repeated infantry attacks at Buena Vista were notable achievements. On a personal level, I gained valuable lessons in the use of artillery and in the art of command. I also began to understand the character of the American volunteer soldier.

Chapter 5

I greatly enjoyed my long leave. I spent most of my time on my family farm but also visited my brother John in Norfolk and my brother Ben in Vicksburg, Mississippi. While in Southampton County, the citizens presented me with a ceremonial sword in recognition of my service in Mexico. It was quite a handsome sword, as I remember, although I have not seen it in years. I left the sword in Virginia with my sisters, intending to retrieve it at a future date. When the Civil War commenced, and I elected to stay with the Union, my sisters viewed me as a traitor and never spoke to me again. After the war, I wrote them requesting that they send the sword to me in Tennessee. I never received a reply.

At the conclusion of my leave, I reported to Fort Adams, Rhode Island, arriving on August,1, 1849. I was assigned to temporary command of Company B of the Third Artillery. My stay at Fort Adams was brief, however. Some of the remaining Seminoles in Florida were again causing trouble and, in September, I was given command of four companies of artillery and ordered to Florida by sea. It was anticipated that we would again fight as infantry, as we had done during the Second Seminole War.

On October 12th we disembarked at Palatka Florida. I saw no combat against the Seminoles on this tour of duty. Because the Seminole uprising consisted of a series of raids on white settlements followed by white reprisals, the War Department concluded that the construction of a series of forts stretching across Florida was the best way to protect the white settlers.

I was assigned to work with an army engineer, George Gordon Meade, to establish these forts. Meade, who would later command the Union army at Gettysburg, was a skilled civil engineer, well-known in the army for having constructed a number of lighthouses on the New Jersey and Florida coasts. I found him to be generally affable but with a terrible temper if his instructions to subordinates were not carried out to the letter.

Meade generally travelled ahead of me, located the best sites on which to situate the forts and planned their design. I followed several weeks behind him and garrisoned and supplied each site selected by Meade. I spent nine months on this assignment, crossing Florida from Fort Pierce on the Atlantic Ocean to Tampa Bay on the Gulf of Mexico. Once the forts were laid out, I was given command of one of them, Fort Myers, on the Caloosahatchee River near the Gulf.

In September, 1850, I received a most unexpected and welcomed letter from the War Department, advising me that I had been appointed as the new instructor of artillery and cavalry at West Point. This appointment came as a complete surprise, as I had not applied for the position. I learned later that my friend and former company commander, Braxton Bragg, had put my name forward.

I was delighted with my new posting and looked forward to returning to West Point from which I had graduated ten years before. It wasn't until Mid-November that my replacement as commander of Fort Myers relieved me of my command and I headed to Boston on the steamer *Thomas Leonard*.

The trip proved to be something of an adventure. Off the coast of North Carolina, a storm came up and the ship appeared to be foundering. I was approached by the First Mate who told me that the Captain was drunk and that he suspected the Captain intended to wreck the ship to collect on the insurance. He could take no action, he explained, without risking a charge of mutiny.

I visited the Captain in the wheelhouse and it took only a short conversation to confirm that he had been drinking heavily. I suggested that he go below and temporarily relinquish command of the vessel to the First Mate. He initially demurred but changed his mind when I returned to the wheelhouse with a complement of armed soldiers and threatened to have him put in irons. The First Mate then navigated us out of danger and the ship arrived in Boston without further incident.

I had expected to travel on to West Point immediately after landing in Boston but, after reporting at Fort Independence in Boston Harbor, I learned that my orders to report to the Academy had not yet come through. For two months I stewed at Fort Independence. Finally, in late March, I received my orders and arrived at West Point on April 3, 1851 to assume my duties as instructor of cavalry and artillery.

I was glad to be back at West Point. The youthful enthusiasm of the cadets was refreshing, the setting of the Academy high above the Hudson had lost none of its appeal for me and the New York climate was a welcome change from the heat of Florida and Mexico.

I was greatly disappointed, however, at the marked decline in conditions at the Academy since my student days, owing to severe budget cuts made by Congress. Long-outmoded texts taught tactics from the Napoleonic Wars. Cavalry horses were in short supply and the horses that were available were all candidates for the glue factory. The Academy lacked stables of its own, using old and decrepit public stables. Our saddles were out of date and in such poor condition that only six were actually usable.

In my artillery courses, I discarded the textbooks, teaching the cadets what I had learned in Mexico. Thus, in addition to the operation of heavy guns, which for many years had been the sole focus of training, I instructed the cadets in the use of artillery to support offensive and defensive infantry operations. The cadets seemed eager to learn from an instructor with practical experience in these tactics.

When I arrived at West Point, cavalry training consisted of little more than riding lessons and the cadets were not tested or graded. I successfully lobbied the Superintendent, Captain Harry Brewerton, to make cavalry training a formal part of the curriculum, with the cadets being graded on their performance. I taught the cadets the uses and tactics of cavalry, including reconnaissance and mounted and dismounted combat.

After seeing the sorry state of horses and saddles, I began requisitioning new mounts and riding equipment. Superintendent Brewerton lent no support to my requests, simply forwarding them on to the War Department without comment. Without the active support of the Superintendent, my requests stood no chance. I therefore appealed directly to the Army's Quartermaster General. This resulted, not in the procurement of new horses or equipment, but in a formal reprimand for not following proper procedures.

My frustrations ended in September,1852, when Colonel Robert E. Lee replaced Brewerton as Superintendent. Lee had a quiet air of self-confidence and gentility. He was reserved but cordial to everyone, no matter his rank or station. He usually kept his composure, rarely losing his temper or raising his voice. Yet he left no doubt when someone's performance fell short of his expectations, fixing the unfortunate individual with a steely stare of his blue-grey eyes and speaking to him with ice in his voice. Those subjected to his displeasure seldom committed the same transgression a second time.

As fellow Virginians, Lee and I felt an immediate kinship that grew into friendship as we worked toward our common goal of modernizing the Academy. I wasted no time and at our very first meeting, I advised Lee of our desperate need for new horses and saddles, and suggested that we should have our own stables rather than relying on the substandard civilian facilities we were leasing. After inspecting the horses, Lee remarked that they were not even fit for a travelling circus.

Lee was a hero of the Mexican War, having won accolades for his exploits while serving with General Scott. His reputation made it difficult for the War Department to turn down his recommendations to improve the Academy. In short order he succeeded in obtaining funds to procure thirty new horses and to construct new stables on the Academy grounds. Unlike his predecessor, he forwarded my requisition to the Quartermaster General for new saddles with a strong endorsement, as a result of which we obtained modern saddles for the cadets. Lee was instrumental in carrying out my suggestion that cavalry officers and dragoons be posted to the academy to aid in training the cadets, and in obtaining approval for the construction of a new riding hall to replace the decrepit and dangerous structure that had been in use for many years.

All of these measures contributed substantially to the improvement in the cadets' cavalry training that produced so many superb cavalry officers. J.E.B. Stuart, the commander of Lee's cavalry corps in the Army of Northern Virginia, was among my students, as was Philip Sheridan, his counterpart under Grant and Meade in the Army of the Potomac.

The most important event that occurred during my tenure as instructor at West Point was my courtship of and marriage to Frances Lucretia Kellogg, known to her friends and family as Fanny. The Kelloggs were residents of Troy, New York. I met Fanny at a tea one afternoon at the West Point Hotel where she was staying with her sister and widowed mother. I was immediately taken with her grace and manner. We began taking long walks on the Plain at West Point and I found her intelligent, cultured, practical, witty and charming.

I was certain after several months that I wanted to marry her and was fairly sure she felt the same about me. Before proposing however, I needed to make sure, for her sake, that she understood what marriage to a career army officer entailed. Therefore, one sunny afternoon on a bench overlooking the Hudson River, I explained to her that marriage to me would involve long separations and that, when we could be together, it would most likely be in uncomfortable and inhospitable surroundings. She assured me that her feelings for me were such that she would willingly endure such hardships.

Fanny and I were married in Troy on November 17, 1852. It was our mutual decision to have a small wedding and only Fanny's family was in attendance. Shortly after the wedding, I obtained leave and took my new wife to Virginia to meet my family. In just a short time, she overcame my family's uneasiness over the fact that she was a Yankee and she made a great hit.

After returning from Virginia, I again took up my duties as an instructor at West Point until the spring of 1854, when I received orders to report to New York City and take command of a battalion of the Third Artillery bound for San Francisco. My ultimate destination was Fort Yuma in the southeast corner of California, where I was to assume command.

My three years at West Point had been happy ones and I was sorry to leave and even sorrier that my new posting would mean a long separation from my wife. The California frontier, where I was headed, was no place for a woman in those days.

Colonel Lee was also unhappy about my transfer and petitioned the War Department to reconsider, but to no avail. I appreciated his efforts on my behalf and was gratified that he wanted me to stay on at West Point.

Chapter 6

Transporting troops from New York to California in the 1850's was not an easy affair. The army did not own any transport vessels and had to charter civilian steamboats, many of which were barely seaworthy. Two previous attempts by my new battalion to reach California had proven disastrous. The first voyage ended in a shipwreck off Cape Hatteras that claimed the lives of two hundred soldiers. On the second attempt, the ship became disabled off the Chesapeake Capes, forcing the battalion to disembark at Fort Monroe, Virginia.

The War Department was embarrassed by these debacles, and ordered me to take command of the battalion with the expectation that I would arrange for its safe transport to California. After reaching New York City, I procured what I deemed to be a seaworthy steamer, the *Illinois*, to take us to Panama and arranged for another ship, the *Sonora*, to rendezvous with us on the other side of the Isthmus to transport us to San Francisco.

The *Illinois* proved to be a fine vessel and, after ten days at sea, we landed in Panama. After marching across the Isthmus without incident, we boarded the *Sonora*, arriving in San Francisco at the end of May, 1854. We were billeted at a fort on the waterfront known as The Presidio, of which I was placed in command.

San Francisco in 1854 was a wild, lawless boomtown, in consequence of the gold strike in 1849. The municipal authorities were incapable of keeping order and vigilantes roamed the streets, supposedly to keep order and punish wrong-doers. Many of these vigilantes were nothing more than street toughs who enjoyed breaking bones and cracking skulls. The Chinese immigrants, who had come to dig gold or to work building the railroads, were often the target of their violence.

The notorious district known as the Barbary Coast was a particular hotbed of drinking, prostitution and gambling. I placed the Barbary Coast off-limits to my troops and posted provost guards at street corners near its borders to turn away any soldiers curious to sample its attractions. Only a few would-be miscreants had to be turned back.

In a much better section of San Francisco, I located my old West Point roommate, William T. Sherman, or "Cump" as he was known to his friends. Sherman had been posted in California during the Mexican War and had remained there after leaving the service. He was now married and had recently become involved in the banking business. He was happy, he told me, that he had left the army.

I saw Sherman and his wife several times during my short stay in San Francisco. He had changed very little since our West Point days. He was still full of nervous energy and was bursting with opinions about current affairs, including domestic politics, the Crimean War, the high cost of living in California and the Indian problem.

I would have enjoyed spending more time with the Shermans, but two weeks after arriving in San Francisco I was on my way to San Diego to pick up two companies of troops, and march them over two hundred miles to Fort Yuma.

The Pacific Command's decision to order this movement in the heat of the summer was not only foolish, but potentially catastrophic. The last six days of the march took us through the desert where the sun beat down relentlessly. The infrequent breezes served only to cover men, horses and equipment with fine, gritty sand. I could not accurately calculate the temperature because the highest my thermometer registered was 115 degrees. By ten am every day, the thermometer reached this mark. The mid-day temperatures must have been well over one hundred twenty degrees.

Recalling my similar march to Camargo during the war with Mexico, I had the troops rest during the day in the shade of the wagons and march only at night. Even so, the heat was barely tolerable. Water had to be rationed because there were no sources of fresh water along our route. The men were near the breaking point when I directed that the wagons be unloaded of all but essential supplies and loaded the soldiers aboard the wagons. We traveled by wagon for three days and reached the fort without the loss of a single soldier. But it was a near thing.

Fort Yuma had been constructed near the confluence of the Gila and Colorado Rivers to provide protection from the Yuma Indians to the many travelers to California and to the inhabitants of the nearby settlement of Yuma, situated across the Colorado River in New Mexico Territory. The fort overlooked a ferry across the Colorado River and, despite its remote location, the ferry was frequently used by emigrants, prospectors and cattlemen. In my time at Fort Yuma, we had no trouble with the Indians. The problem was protecting the whites from each other.

The most memorable thing about Fort Yuma was the heat. I considered it cool if the temperature during the day dipped below ninety degrees. I enjoyed telling newcomers who complained about the heat about one of my soldiers who died at the fort and whose ghost was seen in the guardroom several weeks later. Asked what he was doing there, he replied that he was looking for his blankets since it was too cold in hell for his comfort.

Despite the heat, I was able to resume my scientific explorations, sending many samples of animal and plant life to the Smithsonian Institution. Among my finds was a blunt-nosed bat not previously known to exist in the United States. I also learned the language of the local Indians and compiled a dictionary that I entitled *Vocabulary of the Kuchan Dialect of the Yuma Linguistic Family.*

Chapter 7

In May 1853, I was promoted to major and transferred to the newly-formed Second Cavalry Regiment. This regiment was the brainchild of Jefferson Davis, the Secretary of War in the administration of Franklin Pierce. I knew Davis as the officer who had led his Mississippi Volunteers to my rescue at the battle of Buena Vista.

Immediately after Pierce's inauguration as President in 1853, Davis began lobbying Congress to expand the army. In 1855, his efforts finally met with success when Congress voted to create two new infantry and two new cavalry regiments. Davis' pet project became the organization of the new Second Cavalry Regiment, which he envisioned as an elite unit that would serve as a model for the entire army. The Regiment's mission was the protection of the vast Texas frontier from Comanches and other hostile Indian tribes.

Davis, in consultation with General in Chief Scott, hand-picked the officer corps of the Second Regiment, selecting only West Point graduates who had distinguished themselves in the War with Mexico or in service on the frontier. The outstanding quality of these officers is reflected in the fact that sixteen of them became generals in the Civil War. Eleven served in the Confederate army. Indeed, four of the eight men who gained the highest rank of full general in the Rebel army, Albert

Sidney Johnston, Robert E. Lee, Kirby Smith and John Bell Hood served in the Second. Johnston, then a Colonel, was the regiment's first commander, and Lee, a Lieutenant Colonel, was his second in command.

I have read in a few accounts that Davis intentionally staffed the Second Regiment's officer corps with Southerners, to provide the South with experienced commanders in the event of civil war. I give no credit to this story. The Regiment's officers were appointed because they were the best officers the army had to offer and for no other reason. Moreover, Davis did not support secession in 1855 when the Second Regiment was organized.

In keeping with Davis' intention to make the Second the army's crack regiment, the War Department spared no expense in mounting and equipping its troopers. Unlike most cavalry horses, which were of very poor quality, the Second's mounts were all fine Kentucky horses. Each troop rode horses of matching colors, making a most impressive appearance. The saddles were also of the finest quality, as was all the other equipment. One of my squadrons was supplied with new breech-loading carbines, enabling me to observe, first-hand, the tremendous added firepower provided by these weapons.

One of the greatest mistakes made by the War Department before and during the Civil War was its decision to stick with muzzle-loading muskets, rather than arming the troops with breech-loading rifles. Late in the war when these firearms were finally made available on a limited basis, they proved far superior to the muzzle loading rifles, because they could be reloaded and fired so much faster. Arming our troops with breech loaders from the outset of the war would probably have significantly shortened the conflict, since it is doubtful that the Rebels had the means to manufacture them or acquire them abroad in large numbers.

On September 25th, 1855, I reported to Jefferson Barracks, Missouri, where the Regiment was forming up. Because I had been a cavalry instructor at West Point, I was assigned to train the junior officers and the enlisted men in cavalry tactics. We all knew that we would be confronting a formidable foe.

The Comanches were superior light cavalry fighters. Their war ponies were fleet and agile and their braves excelled at hit and run tactics, appearing out of nowhere to burn and kill and then disappearing into the trackless wilderness. They were extremely difficult to locate, subsisting for days on nothing but strips of raw meat they tied to their horses. They were also savage adversaries, brutally torturing male prisoners before killing them and carrying off most of the women and children.

When the Regiment broke camp in January, 1856, I did not immediately accompany it to Texas. Instead, I was posted to New York City to recruit musicians for the Regimental Band. This was a curious assignment since I have no particular musical aptitude. I remained in New York for five months, during which I managed to assemble a band, most of whose members could at least carry a tune.

My stay in New York was pleasant since I was reunited with my wife. It was at this time, however, that I received word from my family that my mother had died after a short illness. I was deeply saddened by her death, remembering how she had kept the family together after my father's premature demise. I had seldom been back to Virginia since my days as a cadet, and my mother's death represented another weakening of my ties to the Old Dominion.

In May, my recruitment duties were completed and I finally joined the regiment in Texas. I assumed command of Fort Moultrie and its six cavalry troops south of the confluence of the Colorado and Concho Rivers. Lieutenant Colonel Lee was in command of Fort Cooper about two hundred miles to the north adjacent to the Comanche Reserve, home to five hundred to six hundred Indians at any one time.

Once again my combat duties were deferred, this time by my assignment to sit as one of the judges on a series of court martials throughout Texas. The court martial sessions were generally tedious, the travel arduous and the accommodations barely tolerable. The only bright spots were a visit from my wife, who arrived in November, and the company of Robert E. Lee, who served on most of the same court martials and with whom I immediately resumed the friendship we had formed at

West Point. Whenever possible we traveled together and shared living quarters. Lee was an excellent travelling companion, always courteous and gracious no matter how trying the circumstances. His conversation was informed and thoughtful and he was an attentive listener. He was charming to the ladies and my wife was quite taken with him. Still, there was always a reserve about Lee that prevented anyone from getting too intimate. But I suppose that many people say the same thing about me.

In the spring of 1857, Colonel Johnston, who served as Commander of the Department of Texas as well as commander of the Second Regiment, was assigned to lead an expedition against the Mormons in Utah, who were refusing to recognize the authority of the territorial governor appointed by President Buchanan. David E Twiggs replaced him as commander of the Second Regiment. Twigs was close to seventy and had served in the army since the War of 1812. In his prime he may have been a competent officer, but when I had encountered him in Mexico I found him to be a stiff and pompous martinet. As I was to learn, he also knew how to hold a grudge.

I had a run in with Twigs after the Battle of Monterrey when my artillery company was moving through difficult country on our way to the battle of Buena Vista. Both my men and animals were having a difficult go of it.

While engaged on this march, Colonel Twigs sent for me and ordered me to provide him with one of my mule teams for use by his staff. I was only a lieutenant at the time, but declined to comply, explaining that I could not move my guns over the rough terrain without the use of all of my teams. Twigs became livid and ordered me to ride back to my company and return immediately with a mule team. I rode instead to General Taylor's headquarters and explained the situation to one of the General's aides. General Taylor was consulted and Twiggs' order was promptly overridden. I kept all of my mule teams but earned Twiggs lasting resentment.

By the summer of 1858, it had become apparent that the continued depredations of the Comanches, near the Texas border with the

Indian Territory, required the army to take action. At this time, I was in command at Fort Belknap, about one hundred miles northwest of Fort Worth. As the senior major of the Second Regiment, I assumed I would lead the expedition against the Comanches.

Colonel Twigs, however, in an obvious slight to me, gave the command to Major Earl Van Dorn, who was junior to me. He also stripped Fort Belknap of all but a token garrison, assigning most of my troopers to Van Dorn. My chagrin only increased when the news arrived in October that Van Dorn had apparently won a significant victory over the Indians, killing over forty warriors. Later it emerged that the Comanches Van Dorn had attacked were not hostile and were on their way to a peace conference. Van Dorn's attack served to inflame the Comanches and greatly complicated the efforts to bring them onto the reserve.

Twiggs continued to harass me, twice denying my requests for leave and forbidding me from taking the field. My days at Fort Belknap were dull and dreary and my pride was injured. I could not abide Twiggs' treatment of me in silence.

On several occasions, I went over Twiggs' head directly to the Secretary of War, John B. Floyd, to complain about Twiggs' conduct. It gave me at least a small measure of satisfaction that Floyd backed me on each of these occasions. Of course, this only increased Twiggs' antagonism towards me.

I finally got out from under Twiggs' thumb in the early summer of 1859, when Robert E. Lee returned from an extended leave and assumed command of the Second Regiment. Lee quickly restored me to active command in the field.

Future events were to prove Twiggs a traitor to the army and to his country. In February, 1861, after Texas had seceded, Twigs, then in command of all United States forces in Texas, surrendered the entire Texas command to the secessionists, without a shot being fired. All of the army's forts, armaments and equipment were turned over to the Rebels, and all Federal troops were disarmed and ordered to leave the State.

Twigs was made a general in the Confederate Army but died soon after the firing on Fort Sumter.

Upon his return to command, Colonel Lee found that the Texas settlers had become increasingly angry over continued Comanche raids. At least some of these raids were being made by Comanches living on reservations and many settlers blamed the government for not dealing harshly enough with the reservation Indians. On a number of occasions, armed groups of white civilians had entered onto the reservations and murdered Indian men, women and children.

In the summer of 1859, the Superintendent for Indian Affairs in Texas, Robert S. Neighbors, requested the army's assistance in removing about five hundred Comanches from reservations in Texas to the Indian Territory. Colonel Lee assigned me to this mission and in early August, I led four troops of cavalry and a regiment of infantry on a four hundred mile, three week march through hostile territory crossing the Red River into Indian Territory just below the mouth of the Big Wichita River. Eight hired ox teams hauled the Indians' goods and those too sick or elderly to walk. Even though they were savage adversaries, it was a sorry sight to see these once proud people reduced to such a state of misery.

The removal of these Indians failed to satisfy many of the settlers. Upon our return from the Red River, Superintendent Neighbors informed me that threats had been made on his life. Neighbors, a brave and good man, declined my offer of an armed escort and, in September, he was assassinated. His murderers were never caught.

After my return from Indian Territory, I led frequent expeditions deep into the Texas wilderness in search of hostile Comanches. These expeditions covered hundreds of miles and lasted for weeks, but we mainly encountered only heat and dust rather than Comanche warriors. The Comanches seemed to always be aware of our presence, and we would often see small bands of them watching us from distant hills. When we did come across Comanche camp sites, they had usually been abandoned days before our arrival.

On a few occasions we did manage to track down a war party and killed or captured a few warriors. My most notable encounter with the Comanches occurred in August, 1860. My command was making its way back to Fort Cooper after thirty-nine days in the saddle, when we came across fresh tracks of Indians leading a large herd of what were certainly stolen horses. In order to more rapidly pursue these hostiles, I sent most of the troopers back to Fort Cooper, keeping with me only one lieutenant, two sergeants and twenty-two enlisted men. With this reduced force, we made rapid progress following the Indians' tracks and soon overtook them.

On seeing us, the Indian band scattered, abandoning the stolen horses. One brave, however, remained behind to cover his fellows' retreat. He dismounted his horse and kicked off his moccasins, a sign that he intended to make a stand to his death.

He was armed only with a bow and arrow, but the rapidity and accuracy of his shooting was quite remarkable. He managed to wound eight of the troopers, fortunately none seriously, until he was felled by multiple gunshots. During the fight, as I charged toward the Indian, one of his arrows lodged in my chest. Fortunately, the arrow did not penetrate too deeply and I pulled it out as we made our way back to the fort leading the recovered horses. For a time, the wound caused me some pain, but did no permanent damage.

In November, my request for leave was finally granted. I intended to spend the first part of my leave in Southampton County and wrote to my wife asking that she meet my train in transit.

Chapter 8

Before leaving for Virginia, I rode to San Antonio to visit Colonel Lee. In addition to saying goodbye, I wanted to solicit his views on the perilous political situation facing the country.

On November 6th, 1860, Abraham Lincoln, the candidate of the Republican Party, had been elected as the sixteenth President of the United States. The Republicans were committed to preventing the expansion of slavery into the Territories. Lincoln won the election without carrying a single Southern State.

During the campaign, politicians in the Deep South had threatened to secede from the Union in the event of Lincoln's election. Now that his election was a reality, talk of secession intensified.

I had frequently discussed the deepening political crisis with Lee. In these conversations, Lee was equally critical of the Northern Abolitionists, whom he blamed for inflaming sectional tensions, and the Southern proponents of secession, the so-called fire eaters, for threatening to tear the country apart.

Lee's views began to change after John Brown's raid on the Federal Arsenal at Harper's Ferry, Virginia on October 17, 1859. Lee had been home on leave at Arlington at the time of Brown's raid and was given command of the detachment of United States Marines sent to Harper's Ferry to deal with Brown and his followers who had barricaded themselves in the Arsenal's engine house. After Brown refused Lee's order to surrender, the Marines stormed the engine house killing several of Brown's men and capturing Brown.

It was not Brown's raid that changed Lee' views, but the Northern reaction to it. Southerners saw Brown as a fanatic who intended to spark a bloody slave uprising, their worst fear. While some in the North condemned Brown for his unlawful and violent actions many, if not most, hailed Brown as a hero and, after his hanging, as a martyr.

When we spoke at San Antonio in November, Lee explained to me that the North's reaction to Brown's raid had convinced him that Lincoln and the Republicans intended to eliminate slavery in the South, not just to prevent its expansion into the Territories. "Lincoln's election may spell the end of the Union," he told me. "It reinforces my belief that the majority of Northerners are eager to free our slaves."

"But," I pointed out, "Lincoln has stated that he has no intention of interfering with slavery where it currently exists."

"He has also said that the nation cannot survive half slave and half free. There is no doubt about which alternative he intends. Lincoln and the Republicans intend to destroy our way of life. How can we control the millions of black people who live among us without slavery? If the Republicans persist with their policies, they will bring on a civil war. Secession by at least some of the Southern States will be inevitable."

"In such a case, what do you suppose Virginia will do?"

"Most Virginians have a strong attachment to the nation," he replied, "and will not lightly leave the Union. However, should Lincoln attempt to keep the nation together by force, I believe Virginia will secede rather than participate in any Northern aggression against any of its fellow Southern States."

"And what about you, Colonel? Where will you stand if Virginia secedes?"

"I have agonized over this question, as I assume you have. This nation is dear to me. I believe George Washington to be among the greatest men who ever lived, and I have always tried to emulate his example. Washington devoted his life to creating and strengthening the Union. My own father was a staunch Federalist. I cannot lightly forget these facts and I abhor the idea of secession. However, Virginia is my home and I cannot raise my hand against my own people."

He paused for a moment and then asked, "What about you, Major? Where do your sympathies lie?"

"I love Virginia also, Colonel Lee. But since joining the army, I have traveled all over the country, North and South. I suppose, like Washington, I have come to appreciate the greatness and strength of a united country, and I fear the consequences should it break apart. I must see how events unfold, but I am inclined to stick with the Union."

Shortly after my conversation with Lee, I boarded the train bound for Norfolk, my career as an Indian fighter at an end. I was never to see Lee again.

As planned, Frances joined me on the train in Charlotte, North Carolina. At Lynchburg, Virginia, during a watering stop, I told her that I wanted to stretch my legs and asked if she wanted to take a walk on the platform with me. Being tired from the journey, she decided to remain on board.

In the dim moonlight, I failed to detect a sharp drop from the platform and tumbled about twelve feet down, landing flat on my back. Pain such as I had never experienced radiated from my back down my legs. I tried to stand but could not.

My shouts for help finally brought several railroad workers. At my request, they sent for my wife, who peered down at me with the use of a lantern. I must have looked as poorly as I felt, for on seeing me the blood drained from her face. She kept her presence of mind, however, and directed the railroad workers to lift me from the ditch and put me back aboard the train. I declined the conductor's offer to take me to a doctor in Lynchburg, and was placed on cushions on the floor of our carriage.

The train proceeded to Norfolk and, although the trip took only a few hours, it seemed an eternity. Every jolt and bounce of the train sent waves of excruciating pain shooting through me.

Frances had already arranged for a suite of rooms in a Norfolk hotel and before having me removed from the train she located a doctor to accompany us to the hotel. After examining me, he concluded that nothing was broken, but that I had suffered a severe back strain.

In the hotel, I was confined to my bed. The least movement caused me extreme pain. Several old friends, hearing that I was in Norfolk, came to visit, but I had Frances explain that I was not well enough to entertain visitors. The only visitor I permitted was my brother, John, who lived in Norfolk at the time. Even his visits were short. After a time, I could sit up in bed, propped on pillows, and at least read books and newspapers.

The news reports on December 21st, though not unexpected, were sobering. The previous day, South Carolina had voted to secede from the Union. It was only a matter of time before other states in the Deep South followed suit.

In early January, I felt well enough to visit my sisters on the Southampton farm. We stayed with them for three weeks, with my sisters fussing over me and making me feel like a little boy again.

But my sisters were also intent on discussing the current political situation. During our visit, six more states voted to leave the Union. All three of my sisters expressed nothing but hostility toward President-Elect Lincoln, and believed that Virginia should secede, even if it meant civil war. They simply assumed, as did my brother John when he joined us, that if Virginia left the Union, I would resign my commission and fight for Virginia.

I did not share my family's views, believing that secession was wrong. Not wanting to provoke an argument, I kept this opinion to myself. I did tell them, however, that they should not speak so casually about war, since, from personal experience, I could tell them of its horrors.

At the end of our visit, Frances and I traveled to New York City, arriving in early February. My back, though improved, continued to cause me considerable pain. I could only walk with difficulty and mounting a horse was out of the question. As the weeks passed, I was forced to consider the possibility that my days of active army service were over.

I had never pursued any career other than the military, and the question of how I would earn a living became a pressing concern. At this point, Frances noticed an advertisement in the *National Intelligencer* newspaper, announcing that the Virginia Military Institute was looking for a Commandant of Cadets. This seemed to be a tailor-made opportunity to use my military training without having to undergo the rigors of active service. Virginia was still in the Union and I hoped that it would remain so. I promptly wrote to the Superintendent of VMI advising him of my interest in the position.

As Lincoln's inauguration date approached, a total of seven states had seceded. Jefferson Davis had been appointed as the provisional president of the so-called Confederate States of America. In late February, the newspapers reported that my old nemesis General Twiggs had surrendered his entire Texas command to the Rebels. I told my wife that if I had still been on duty, the Texans would not have captured a single man, weapon or flag. I would have taken command of the men, and marched them north until we reached the loyal states.

I was now feeling well enough to see visitors and a steady stream of friends, including fellow officers came to see me. Those from Virginia, almost to a man, informed me of their intention to join the Confederacy in the event Virginia voted to leave the Union. Most spoke optimistically about the South's chances of winning a war with the North.

I was also receiving daily correspondence from family members and old Virginia friends and neighbors urging me to accept a commission in the Confederate Army as soon as Virginia voted to secede. The feeling of my fellow Virginians was so uniform that, for a time, I began to question whether I was mistaken in my resolve to remain with the Union.

In my darker moments, I feared that, whatever decision I made, my days as a combat soldier were over. With this is mind, on March 1st, I wrote to the Adjutant General of the Army. "I have the honor respectfully to ask to be detailed as Superintendent of the mounted recruiting service for the next two years. My reason for making this application is: I am still quite lame from an injury which I received last November in Lynchburg, Va., and although I could attend all my ordinary duties I fear that I shall not have sufficient strength to perform every duty which might be required of me if with my regiment."

I did not receive an immediate reply to this letter, but did receive a response from the Virginia Military Institute in the form of a letter from a Major Gilham, informing me that another candidate had been selected to serve as Superintendent of Cadets. He added, however, that Virginia Governor John Letcher had asked him to inquire whether I would consider resigning from the army and accepting an appointment as Virginia's Chief of Ordnance.

My troubled state of mind is reflected in my reply to the Governor:

"I received yesterday a letter from Major Gilham of the Virginia Military Institute, dated the 9th instant, in reference to the position of Chief of Ordnance of the State, in which he informs me that you requested him to ask me if I would resign from the service, and, if so, whether that post would be acceptable to me. As he requested me to make my reply to you direct, I have the honor to state, after expressing my most sincere thanks for your kind offer, that it is not my wish to leave the service of the United States as long as it is honorable for me to remain in it, and, therefore, as long as my native state remains in the union, it is my purpose to remain in the army, unless required to perform duties alike repulsive to honor and humanity."

Two events now occurred that dispelled all my doubts about my future course. On April 6th, about a month after President Lincoln's inauguration, General in Chief Scott visited me to personally order me to take command of the Second Regiment, which was returning to New York City from Texas. From New York, the Regiment was to entrain for the barracks at Carlisle, Pennsylvania to be re-equipped and brought up to strength with new recruits.

Dismissing my protestations that I was not physically capable of performing this task, General Scott insisted that I could refit the Regiment and make it ready for combat, even if I could not mount a horse myself. The idea of returning to service was irresistible and, despite my doubts, I told General Scott that, bad back or no, I would do my duty to the best of my ability.

After reviewing the bedraggled remnants of the once-proud Second Regiment in New York, I said goodbye to Frances and boarded the train to Carlisle. Frances was to join me there once I had settled in. In Harrisburg, newsboys entered the train crying out the news that South Carolina had fired on Fort Sumter, and that after two days of shelling, Major Robert Anderson, the Fort's commander, had surrendered.

The attack on Sumter clarified my thinking as no other event could have. I realized that my loyalty to the Union was first and foremost. Whichever way I turned the matter over in my mind, my oath of allegiance to the Federal government always came uppermost.

I advised Frances not to join me in Carlisle, as we were now on the brink of civil war. That same day, I wrote my sisters, informing them of my decision to remain with the Union. They never responded to my letter, but friends have advised me that they turned my picture, which hung in the front parlor, towards the wall, and that they have refused to even mention my name since that day. I have not seen any of my sisters since the war and have never returned to Southampton County.

Chapter 9

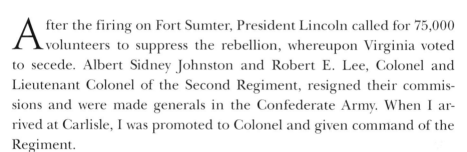

After the firing on Fort Sumter, President Lincoln called for 75,000 volunteers to suppress the rebellion, whereupon Virginia voted to secede. Albert Sidney Johnston and Robert E. Lee, Colonel and Lieutenant Colonel of the Second Regiment, resigned their commissions and were made generals in the Confederate Army. When I arrived at Carlisle, I was promoted to Colonel and given command of the Regiment.

In late May, I was ordered to take four companies of the Second, along with the volunteer First City Troop of Philadelphia, to join Major General Robert Patterson's army at Chambersburg Maryland and to take command of his army's first brigade. Patterson, a native Pennsylvanian, had been appointed as a Major General and put in command of an army because Pennsylvania had raised sixteen regiments in response to Lincoln's call for volunteers. His selection was ill advised. In Mexico, Patterson had been careless with the lives of his soldiers and I did not have a high opinion of him. As was to happen frequently during the war, political expediency took precedence over military considerations.

Across the Potomac River, in the Shenandoah Valley, waited a Confederate Army commanded by General Joseph E. Johnston. On July 2nd, our army crossed the Potomac River into Virginia. At Falling

Waters, our vanguard's advance was halted by the lead elements of Johnston's army, commanded by Thomas Jackson, who would earn his famous nickname "Stonewall" three weeks later at the First Battle of Bull Run. Marching to the sound of gunfire, my brigade attacked Jackson's left flank, forcing Jackson's withdrawal.

Falling Waters was a small action by any standard. It was important to me, however, because, although my back still caused me considerable pain, it had not impeded my ability to command my brigade in battle. I thereby regained confidence in my physical ability to lead troops in the field.

Patterson's main mission was to maintain contact with Johnston to keep him from slipping out of the Shenandoah Valley and joining his forces with those of General P.G.T. Beauregard near Manassas Junction. On July 27th, one of my junior cavalry officers reported to me that he had caught sight of a Rebel column marching from Winchester to the fords of the Shenandoah River.

With this officer in tow, I rode to Patterson's headquarters to notify him that the Rebels were on the move and recommended that we pursue and attack them before they could leave the Valley. Patterson disregarded my advice, telling me that the inexperience of his volunteer troops, most of whom had only enlisted for ninety days, would render such pursuit impossible.

Because of Patterson's unwillingness to engage the enemy, Johnston arrived on the battlefield in time to assist Beauregard in routing Irvin McDowell's Federal Army at the Battle of First Bull Run. A large share of the blame for the defeat properly fell on Patterson, and he was replaced in command by Nathaniel Banks. Unfortunately, Banks' appointment was also politically motivated and he proved almost as inept as Patterson.

The Union's loss at First Bull Run was a shock to the North. Most of the Northern population believed that the Federal Army would win a great victory that would crush the rebellion and restore the Union. As a Virginian, I knew enough about Southern pride, determination and courage to recognized that a single Union victory would not convince the South to abandon the fight.

Despite the fact that the Rebel States lacked the manpower and industrial might of the North, winning the war would not be easy. The Rebels were in control of a huge territory and had the advantage of interior lines, allowing for rapid movement of troops and supplies. They would be fighting a defensive war for what they viewed as the protection of hearth and home. The North would be the aggressor. To win the war, it would be required to capture and hold a huge, hostile territory.

While the attack on Fort Sumter had inspired a groundswell of patriotic fervor in the North, the Southern leadership could hope that, by keeping Rebel armies in the field, the Northern population would eventually grow tired of the war and allow the South to go its own way. Southerners also truly believed that their heritage made them better fighters than any troops the North could send against them.

Although in 1861, I expected a long and bloody war, I did not foresee the extent of the carnage the war would actually bring. Nor did I foresee that before the conflict was concluded, the destruction of Southern homes, cities, plantations and farms would become Union strategy.

Chapter 10

From the outset of hostilities, it was clear to political leaders on both sides that control of Kentucky was one of the keys to victory. Determined to hold Kentucky in the Union, President Lincoln asked newly-promoted Brigadier General Robert Anderson, the hero of Fort Sumter, to take command in Kentucky and Tennessee, now constituted as the Department of Kentucky. Lincoln also hoped that Anderson would drive the Rebels out of East Tennessee, whose citizens were generally Union sympathizers.

Anderson agreed, on condition that he could name his three principal subordinates, each of whom would hold the rank of Brigadier General of Volunteers. Anderson selected William T. Sherman, as his second in command, and Don Carlos Buell and me as the other two brigadiers. I received my new commission on August 17, 1861.

In early September, I arrived at Anderson's headquarters in Louisville. I found Anderson a changed man from the artillery instructor I had known at West Point. He was obviously in ill-health. He had lost weight, his hair had turned grey and his face was pale and drawn. I believe that the strain Anderson endured during the siege of Fort Sumter had a permanent effect on his health. Buell had not arrived when I met with Anderson and Sherman to discuss the military situation.

I was surprised to hear Anderson express doubts about our ability to hold Kentucky, let alone capture East Tennessee. Sherman was even more pessimistic. Pacing about Anderson's office with his usual nervous energy, Sherman voiced his concern that the Rebels were massing in large numbers in Tennessee, and were in position to sweep through Kentucky all the way to the Ohio River and beyond.

I did not share Anderson's and Sherman's dire outlook. I expressed my view that our existing troops, together with the additional volunteers daily swelling our ranks, when properly equipped and trained, could repel any Rebel attack on Kentucky and successfully drive the Rebel's out of East Tennessee.

Because of my optimistic assessment, General Anderson assigned me to the command of a brigade of new volunteers gathered at Camp Dick Robinson in Central Kentucky. These troops, when joined by others being assembled throughout Kentucky, were intended to form the army that would invade East Tennessee.

Arriving at Camp Dick Robinson, I found little to justify the confidence I had expressed to General Anderson. The six thousand raw recruits assembled there lacked uniforms, weapons and supplies of all types. Rations were in short supply, and the men were hungry and discontented. Up to that point, they had received virtually no training and discipline was lax. Compounding these problems, I did not find a single staff officer at the camp whom I considered competent.

My mission was to turn this disorganized mob into an army and I immediately set to work. Because I lacked capable staff officers, I was forced to divide my time between training the troops and attending to the massive quantity of paperwork required to obtain necessary food, clothing and supplies. Sleep became a luxury. I seldom got to bed earlier than one o'clock in the morning and was usually awake by five.

Despite conditions at the camp, I was greatly encouraged by my discussions with the men. I discovered that, although dispirited by the lack of food and clothing, they were anxious to fight and were looking for leaders to train them and lead them into battle. Although discipline required a somewhat lighter touch than was the case with Regulars, the men generally responded well. I concluded that these volunteers were fine raw material from which to form an effective brigade.

It has always been my observation that an army's health and morale is as important to victory as strategy or tactics. I therefore began besieging Quartermaster General Montgomery C. Meigs with requisitions for adequate supplies of food, uniforms and other material and equipment. I also scoured Kentucky for competent staff officers, eventually assembling a team on which I could rely.

The men under my command were mainly from Kentucky and East Tennessee. I formed four regiments of Kentucky Volunteers and two regiments of Tennessee Volunteers into the First Kentucky Brigade. I directed the men to clear miles of land around the camp to serve as drill fields and instructed each company's officers on the type of drills I wanted them to conduct.

Although General Meigs was extremely efficient in providing us with supplies, as winter approached the men had still not been issued overcoats. In order to insure that the men received their coats, I contacted the supplier and pledged my personal assets to guaranty payment. With this one gesture, I earned my men's loyalty. They soon began referring to me as "Old Pap", which I took as an indication that they understood and appreciated my concern for their welfare.

Because it was an open secret that my intention was to drive the Rebels out of East Tennessee, pro-Union politicians from this region made frequent visits to Camp Dick Robinson and requested permission to address the troops. These visits were a waste of the limited time I had to train and organize my brigade and, if I had not been ordered by General Anderson to permit them to visit, I would have banned politicians from the camp. After haranguing the troops with patriotic platitudes, the speakers would often ask me to say a few words. I always declined.

One of the political visitors to the Camp was Andrew Johnson, then a United States Senator from Tennessee. Johnson was the only member of the Senate who had not resigned his seat when his state seceded. He was direct, blunt and humorless and made no attempt to curry favor with small talk or friendly chatter. He had just conferred with Anderson and Sherman in Louisville, and was pleased that I did not share their pessimistic assessment of the military situation.

Albert Sidney Johnston, the former commander of the Second Cavalry Regiment, now a Lieutenant General in the Confederate Army, had overall command of all Southern troops in the vast area stretching from the Appalachian Mountains to the Mississippi River. Establishing his headquarters in Bowling Green, Kentucky, Johnston established a thin defensive cordon covering the entire border area of his command. This line extended over four hundred miles from the Cumberland Gap in East Tennessee to Columbus, Kentucky on the Mississippi River.

Strategically, Johnston's plan was a mistake. He had only about 45,000 troops under his command, not nearly enough to effectively defend the entire border area. Johnston could have mounted a much more effective defense by consolidating most of his troops in two or three strategic locations and using his interior lines to move units as needed. His deployment played into my plan to attack through the Cumberland Gap at the extreme eastern end of his line.

Johnston initially overcame the weakness of his position by bluffing attacks of his own at both ends of his line. Leonidas Polk, a West Point graduate, who had become an Episcopal Bishop, commanded the troops at Columbus and Felix Zollicoffer, a former newspaper editor, commanded at the Cumberland Gap. Johnston ordered both of them to advance, but directed them to pull back as soon as they met any resistance. Sherman checked Polk's move near Columbus and I drove off Zollicoffer from a defensive position I had established south of Camp Dick Robinson.

Despite the ease with which we repelled these movements, they had their desired effect of causing Anderson to hesitate in ordering an offensive of his own. Anderson's ill-health also contributed to his caution and forced him to resign his command on October 8, 1861. Sherman replaced him as the Commander of the Department of Kentucky.

Sherman correctly believed that control of the Tennessee River Valley was crucial to Union success. He was convinced, however, that Johnston greatly outnumbered him and that the Lincoln Administration was so focused on the war in Virginia that it was not providing him with sufficient manpower to prevent his being overwhelmed by the Rebels. He communicated his concerns to Washington in a series of increasingly frantic telegrams, causing Washington to begin questioning his mental stability.

Not sharing Sherman's concerns, I continued to plan an invasion of East Tennessee. My plan included a daring proposal made by Reverend William Blount Carter, a resident of East Tennessee, who had made his way through the lines to my headquarters shortly after I arrived at Camp Dicky Robinson.

Carter proposed that he organize a large force of guerilla fighters in East Tennessee to blow up nine bridges on the East Tennessee and Virginia Railroad that served as Zollicoffer's principal communication and supply line. The destruction of these bridges would be coordinated with my attack south through the Cumberland Gap. The Rebels, off-balance and confused by the destruction of the railroad bridges, would be ripe for destruction.

I greeted Carter's proposal with enthusiasm and recommended it to Sherman and to the new General in Chief, General George McClellan, advising them that the destruction of the railroad by Carter's guerillas "would be one of the most important services that could be done for the country".

McClellan approved the plan but Sherman was skeptical. He feared that by moving south, I would be risking annihilation and opening the door to a Rebel invasion of Kentucky. McClellan took my plan to President Lincoln who approved it, and McClellan ordered me to proceed, notwithstanding Sherman's reservations.

I began my advance toward the Cumberland Gap in late October with about 9,000 troops, keeping Carter, who was back in Tennessee, apprised of my movements. Carter got word to me that he had raised about a thousand Union supporters for his planned destruction of the railroad bridges. To me, the way seemed clear to drive the Rebels out of East Tennessee and capture Knoxville. Had I been allowed to proceed, I have no doubt that I would have accomplished this.

Sherman, however, in a series of dispatches, communicated his misgivings. His wires included the following, as I continued my movement toward the Cumberland Gap:

"Don't push too far. Your line is already long and weak."

"If you can hold in check the enemy to your south, that is all that can be attempted."

"If you find yourself outnumbered you are not bound to sacrifice the lives of your command, but should fall back in the direction of Lexington."

Finally, in mid-November, Sherman ordered me to call off my campaign. I remonstrated with him that by cancelling my offensive, we were placing Carter's guerilla's in grave danger. Sherman was not moved. With deep regret, I pulled my troops back.

Immediately after receiving Sherman's order to abandon the campaign, I attempted to get word to Carter that I would not be coming. I was never able to ascertain whether he failed to get my messages and thought I was on my way, or whether he simply decided to proceed on his own. On the evening of November 7th, he and his guerillas damaged or destroyed five of the nine railroad bridges.

The Rebels naturally thought that the destruction of the bridges was part of a Union invasion and were thrown into confusion. When they eventually realized that no Union attack was forthcoming, they declared martial law and rounded up large numbers of Union loyalists, regardless of whether they had been among Carter's guerillas. Many, including Reverend Carter, were hanged and more were imprisoned.

I was furious with Sherman for calling off my attack and leaving Carter and his men to the reprisals of the Rebels. There was nothing I could do, however, but to obey Sherman's order to withdraw into a defensive position.

Even after cancelling my invasion of East Tennessee, Sherman continued to worry that we were greatly outnumbered and were in imminent danger of destruction. In his almost daily telegrams to Secretary of War Cameron, Sherman gave impossibly high estimates of the number of Rebel troops in Tennessee and Kentucky and requested two hundred thousand reinforcements.

The frantic nature of Sherman's dispatches to Washington convinced the Administration that Sherman was mentally and emotionally unstable. On November 16th, Secretary of War Cameron removed him from command of the Department of Kentucky and named Don Carlos Buell as his replacement.

Buell was a West Point graduate, who had served with distinction against the Seminoles and in the war with Mexico. Anderson had selected him as one of his three chief subordinates, but before he could take up these duties he was selected by General McClellan to assist in the organization of the Army of the Potomac, in which he briefly commanded a division.

I knew Buell to be brave and industrious. As an army commander, he demonstrated a marked talent for logistics and organization. However, I found him to be overly cautious in the face of the enemy. By far his greatest failing though was his concern with his personal advancement.

From the forces in his Department, Buell organized the Army of the Ohio. The troops under my command were designated as the First Division in this new army.

Chapter 11

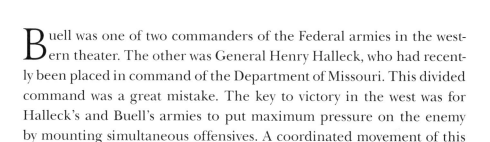

Buell was one of two commanders of the Federal armies in the western theater. The other was General Henry Halleck, who had recently been placed in command of the Department of Missouri. This divided command was a great mistake. The key to victory in the west was for Halleck's and Buell's armies to put maximum pressure on the enemy by mounting simultaneous offensives. A coordinated movement of this type required a single overall commander.

The problem of having the two armies acting independently was exacerbated by the personal ambitions of Buell and Halleck. Each wanted to be put in overall command and actively refused to cooperate with the other, believing that the surest road to promotion was to obtain his own victory.

President Lincoln's desire to capture East Tennessee had, if anything, grown stronger as a result of the fate meted out to Carter's men. General McClellan pressed Buell to mount such an attack. Buell, however, did not agree that invading East Tennessee was a priority. To him, the capture of Nashville was of paramount importance. He therefore ignored Lincoln and McClellan and ordered me to join him in Central Tennessee for an offensive against Nashville.

General Zollicoffer, however, saw my withdrawal from East Kentucky as an opportunity and, as soon as I marched west to join Buell, he moved into the territory I had vacated, overrunning several isolated outposts. By late December, Buell could no longer ignore Zollicoffer and, on Christmas Day 1861, he ordered me to retrace my steps and force Zollicoffer back into Tennessee. Buell would have been satisfied if I could accomplish this result through maneuver without forcing a battle. I was still smarting from Sherman's refusal to allow me to advance into Tennessee in November, and this time I was determined to strike a blow.

Zollicoffer was reported north of the Cumberland River at Beech Grove, Kentucky, about seventy miles southeast of my position. I began my march to confront him on New Year's day. The weather was cold and heavy rain had turned the roads to quagmires. In places, the mud was two feet deep. Wagons and artillery had to be drawn with double teams, slowing our progress to little more than four miles a day. Nevertheless, we pushed on.

On January 17th, after covering sixty-five miles, we reached Logan's Crossroads, about eight miles from Zollicoffer's army. Before attacking Zollicoffer, I intended to join my division with the brigade of Brigadier General Albin Schoepf. Schoepf's brigade was to have been part of the invasion of East Tennessee and had remained in an advanced position after Sherman called off the attack. My men were tired, muddy and soaked to the skin from their difficult march, but their spirits were high and they were ready for a fight.

Major General George Crittenden had taken over command from Zollicoffer while I was on the march. He found that, contrary to his orders, Zollicoffer had advanced his forces north of the Cumberland River. With the river swollen from the recent rains, the Rebels were unable to recross the river, meaning that in the event of a battle, they would be forced to fight with their backs to the river. Rather than waiting to be attacked while in this precarious position, Crittenden decided to take the offensive and to attack my division while it was still separated from General Schoepf's forces by Fishing Creek.

I had foreseen the possibility of a Rebel attack and had thrown out a strong picket line about a mile in front of my encampment with cavalry vedettes patrolling about three-quarters of a mile ahead of the pickets. I calculated that this would provide me with about an hour's notice of a Rebel advance.

In the early morning hours of January 19th, Zollicoffer, whom Crittenden had left in field command, drove in my picket line. As soon as the sound of gunfire reached the camp, I ordered my officers to muster the men and I rode toward the fighting.

When I arrived on the field, I found that only one of two regiments of my forward brigade was deployed. The young colonel in command of the other regiment still had his troops in line awaiting orders from his brigade commander. His face was ashen and he looked like he was on the point of fainting. I put my arm on his shoulder and pointed toward the sound of gunfire. "The enemy is there, son." I told him. "That is where I need you to deploy your men." This was all the encouragement he needed. In an instant, he pulled himself together and led his men forward toward the oncoming enemy.

As additional regiments arrived on the battlefield I deployed them to the enemy's front and flank. I kept the plan simple, this being my men's first battle. I also ordered up my artillery, which arrived in time to stop an attempt to turn my flank. As more and more troops arrived on the field, including units of Schoepf's brigade, we halted the enemy's attack and began advancing down the Mills Springs Road, forcing the Rebels back. After almost three hours of fighting, the enemy line collapsed and the Rebels fled headlong back to Beach Grove.

I was anxious to pursue the enemy and, as soon as I could reform the regiments and resupply them with fresh ammunition, we set off in pursuit. By the time we reached Beach Grove, the Rebels were well entrenched. Because nightfall was approaching and my men were weary, I determined to wait until early the next morning to storm the rebel defenses.

That evening, a stern-wheel riverboat arrived at the Rebel camp and Crittenden used it to ferry his army across the Cumberland River. After their last troops were safely across, the Rebels burned the steamboat and all other boats on the river preventing us from further pursuit.

My failure to trap and destroy the Rebel army was a great disappointment. That I was as inexperienced in commanding a battle as my troops were in fighting one was brought home to me as I stood in the middle of the now-empty Rebel camp, venting my frustration at the enemy's escape to Colonel Speed M. Fry, one of my regimental commanders.

"General," he asked, "why didn't you send in a demand for surrender last night?"

His question caught me up short. I considered for a moment before responding. "Hang it all, Fry. I never once thought about it."

I had about 4,000 effective troops at the Battle of Mill Springs, roughly the same number as the enemy. My losses of killed, wounded, captured or missing were 262. The enemy's losses were twice as great and included General Zollicoffer, who was killed when he blundered into our lines during the initial Rebel attack. In their haste to get away, the enemy left behind virtually all of their equipment and supplies including twelve pieces of artillery and over one thousand horses and mules.

Our victory at Mill Springs was the first significant Federal success of the war and provided a much-needed boost to Northern morale after the Union's disastrous defeat at the Battle of First Bull Run. From a military standpoint, the retreat of Johnston's right flank opened the way for the long-planned advance into East Tennessee.

The winter weather and the poor conditions of the roads that had impeded my advance toward Mill Springs would have made such an advance difficult, but I believed that, if properly supplied, my little army could have successfully made this movement. Buell, however, like Sherman before him, resisted the idea of an invasion of East Tennessee.

Buell had his mind set on the capture of Nashville and ordered me to join him at Louisville. From there, he intended to move directly on Nashville. When Andrew Johnson learned that Buell had again rejected the invasion of East Tennessee, he was furious. He began a campaign against Buell that ultimately led to Buell's loss of his command and his resignation from the army.

Ulysses Grant, under Halleck's command, had no hesitation about attacking into Central Tennessee. Acting in concert with Flag Officer Andrew Foote's gunboats, Grant captured Fort Henry on the Tennessee River on February 6th and Fort Donelson on the Cumberland River on February 16th.

These victories, coupled with the victory at Mill Springs, collapsed General Johnston's defensive line. He abandoned Bowling Green and Nashville and retreated into Mississippi. General Beauregard, in command on the western end of the Confederate line at Columbus, Kentucky, likewise retreated, joining forces with Johnston at Corinth, Mississippi.

Neither Halleck nor Buell took immediate advantage of the Rebel retreat. Buell did not credit the reports that Nashville had been evacuated and proceeded cautiously southward. Halleck essentially refused to allow Grant to move further up the Tennessee River until he was given sole command of the western theater. Lincoln acquiesced, and on March 13th promoted Halleck to overall command in the west. Buell was now to operate under Halleck's orders.

Halleck was a pompous, fussy man. He had a reputation as a brilliant tactician based upon his authorship of several tactical manuals used at West Point. In fact, his books were largely translations of French texts written shortly after the Napoleonic Wars. His greatest talent was in self-promotion, and he eagerly took credit for Grant's successes at Forts Henry and Donelson, even though Grant had acted on his own initiative. When in actual command of troops, his excessive caution resulted in the loss of a major opportunity to deal the rebels a crushing blow at Corinth.

Once Halleck was given sole command in the west, all impediments to further offensive movements disappeared. He ordered Grant to proceed south along the Tennessee River toward Corinth. Buell was to move to meet him at the small river town of Savannah.

By the beginning of April, Grant was at Pittsburg Landing on the Tennessee River, about nine miles upstream from Savannah. The head of Buell's army was on the march to Savannah to join him. My division was still at Nashville, preparing to begin the march to Savannah. On April 7th, I received a wire from Halleck advising me that Grant was under attack and ordering me to make forced march to Pittsburg Landing.

I immediately put my division on the road south. We arrived at Pittsburg Landing on April 9th, too late to participate in the Battle of Pittsburg Landing, or Shiloh, that had ended the previous day. I found Grant and Buell's forces in control of the field, with the Rebels in retreat. I readied my troops to pursue the enemy but Halleck ordered me to stay where I was.

In the days following the Battle of Shiloh, I toured the battlefield and spoke to many of the officers who had been engaged there. I learned that, prior to the battle, Grant had been careless, to the point of negligence. His camp was laid out in a haphazard manner. He did not order his men to entrench and was completely unprepared for an enemy attack.

Nor had Grant made any attempt to locate the enemy. He believed they remained at Corinth, too dispirited to take the offensive, at the very time when General Johnston, with his entire army, was marching toward Pittsburg Landing to attack him. Grant ignored persistent reports that Johnston was on the move, making no effort to ascertain the Rebel position. When the Rebels struck, Grant was not even on the field, but at Savannah visiting Flag Officer Foote.

General Sherman, who had been named as one of Grant's division commanders, was in charge of the campsite in Grant's absence. Sherman discounted reports that the Rebels were approaching and failed to take any steps to establish a defensive position. As a result, when Johnston's army struck, the Federal forces were completely surprised and driven back throughout the day on April 7th. To Grant's credit, once he arrived on the field, he acted with calm determination to mount a last-ditch defense, eventually forming a new line on high ground near the river, supported by almost all his artillery.

Buell's leading elements arrived in the late afternoon to reinforce Grant. The Rebels called off their attack toward evening. General Johnston had been mortally wounded during the battle and General Beauregard, his second-in command, unaware of Buell's arrival on the field, undoubtedly believed he would finish off the Federals the next morning. Instead, Grant, with the fresh troops provided by Buell, attacked on April 8th and drove the battle-weary Rebels from the field.

The outcome of the battle was a near thing. Had Buell's advance elements not arrived in time to reinforce Grant, or if Beauregard had not called off his attack on the evening of April 7th, it is likely that Grant would have suffered a devastating defeat. As it was, although Grant claimed a victory, its cost shocked the nation.

Grant's army suffered over 13,000 casualties, including 1,750 killed. By contrast, at the First Battle of Bull Run, up to that time the largest battle fought on the North American Continent, Union casualties were less than 3,000, of which 460 were killed. The staggering Federal casualties at Pittsburg Landing were directly attributable to Grant and Sherman's lack of vigilance and preparation.

Shortly after the battle, Halleck arrived at Pittsburg Landing. He was furious with Grant for having allowed himself to be caught by surprise on the first day of the battle, although, consistent with his nature, he said nothing about this directly to Grant. Halleck was also taken aback by the conditions he found in Grant's camp. The stench of refuse and rotting flesh pervaded the campsite and sanitation efforts were non-existent. As a result, sickness was rampant among the troops.

Halleck had come to Pittsburg Landing to personally assume field command of all the troops assembled there. These numbered over 100,000 men, consisting of Grant's Army of the Tennessee, Buell's Army of the Ohio and John Pope's Army of the Mississippi.

On April 20th, Halleck ordered a reorganization of his forces. Grant was removed from command of the Army of the Tennessee and named as Second-in Command to Halleck. This was Halleck's way of sidelining Grant, for, as Second-in-Command, Grant was given nothing to do.

Halleck formed the armies into three wings. Pope's Army of the Mississippi formed the left wing and Buell's Army of the Ohio the center. I was given command of the right wing, consisting of my Mills Springs division and four divisions of Grant's former command, the Army of the Tennessee.

Halleck was able to give me this command by pushing through my promotion as Major General of Volunteers that had been languishing in Congress for several months. Halleck did not expedite my promotion so much to reward me as to punish Grant, since, in my new rank it was appropriate for me to command an army. This enabled Halleck to remove Grant from command of the Army of the Tennessee.

Grant never seemed upset or angry with Halleck. Instead, although the situation was not of my making, Grant appeared to resent me for taking command of his army. Throughout the war, Grant and I did not get along well for a number of reasons. I believe, however, that Grant's ill-feeling towards me dated from my assumption of his former command.

Chapter 12

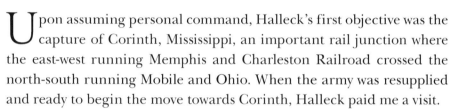

Upon assuming personal command, Halleck's first objective was the capture of Corinth, Mississippi, an important rail junction where the east-west running Memphis and Charleston Railroad crossed the north-south running Mobile and Ohio. When the army was resupplied and ready to begin the move towards Corinth, Halleck paid me a visit.

"I intend to set the army in motion three days from today, on the 29th," Halleck told me. "We will try to take Corinth without a fight, if at all possible."

I was astonished by Halleck's declaration. "Our army is fit and ready for battle," I responded. "I assumed your intention was to attack the Rebels at Corinth."

"No, no. Secretary Stanton has advised me that the Administration is extremely upset over the casualties sustained at Shiloh. They do not want a repeat of that experience. I feel it best if we capture the rail junction without bringing on a general engagement."

"General, the only way to win this war is to destroy the rebel armies. Capturing territory, even if strategically important, will not compel the South to submit. Our army is well-equipped and well-armed. The men are in good spirits and ready to fight. The Rebels are probably dispirited after their defeat at Shiloh. We should press them. Send the cavalry to develop Beauregard's position, get in his rear and crush him."

"Eventually of course, you are right. We will have to fight Beauregard. But not now. With the memory of Shiloh so fresh, we will try to force the Rebels out of Corinth without bringing them to battle. We will achieve a great strategic victory, without sustaining casualties."

On April 29th, we broke camp and were on the road to Corinth. The army did not so much march toward Corinth as crawl. It took a month to cover the twenty-two miles between Pittsburg Landing and Corinth. The cause of this glacial pace was Halleck's determination not to be surprised by the enemy, as Grant had been at Shiloh. After a short march each day, he ordered the army to stop and entrench.

On May 30th, we were at last on the outskirts of Corinth. About five o'clock that morning, I heard the sound of explosions coming from the direction of the enemy works. I sent a cavalry regiment to investigate and they confirmed that the Rebels were pulling out and heading south. I sent an aide to advise General Halleck and began readying my troops for pursuit. Halleck never gave such an order. He was delighted to have captured Corinth without a fight, and promptly wired Washington boasting of his great strategic success.

Several weeks later, Halleck advised me that he was considering restoring Grant to his former command and wanted to gauge my reaction. I made no objection, having always viewed my command as temporary, and returned to the command of my old division.

Halleck's assumption that the Administration would applaud his bloodless capture of Corinth proved correct. On July 1st, he was named the new General in Chief and headed to Washington. Halleck was given this position despite never having participated in a battle, let alone commanded troops in one.

As General in Chief, Halleck was largely ineffective, being unwilling or unable to plan and coordinate an overall strategy for Union victory. Whether he failed to appreciate the logistical, tactical and supply problems faced by the Federal armies or, as I think more likely, chose to ignore these problem in order to curry favor with Secretary of War Stanton, he used his position to attempt to bully his generals to take the offensive, regardless of the condition of their armies or logistical and supply problems. As far as I can determine, though he certainly knew better, he never advised Stanton and Lincoln of the difficulties faced by commanders in the field.

Chapter 13

Halleck's promotion to General in Chief ended unified command in the west. Grant, with his Army of the Tennessee, headed toward the Mississippi Valley and his eventual capture of Vicksburg. Halleck ordered Buell to advance toward Chattanooga on a route of Halleck's own devising.

Halleck's order to Buell to capture Chattanooga, rather than to invade East Tennessee, was another blow to Andrew Johnson. Johnson wrote to me, inquiring whether he could put my name forward to command an independent army charged with capturing Knoxville.

While a movement into East Tennessee and the capture of Knoxville continued to present significant strategic and political advantages, I quickly concluded that if I were beholden to Senator Johnson for my promotion, the campaign would be mired in politics and I would lack the independence of action I believed was necessary. I therefore wrote to Johnson as follows: "I most earnestly hope I may not be placed in that position [commanding an offensive into East Tennessee] for several reasons. One particular reason is that we have never yet had a commander of any expedition who has been allowed to work out his own policy, and it is utterly impossible for the most able General in the world to conduct a campaign with success when his hands are tied." Not surprisingly, I heard nothing further from Johnson on this subject.

Our march to Chattanooga would cover about two hundred twenty miles, following the route of the Memphis and Charleston Railroad west from Corinth to Stevenson, Alabama, and then northeast along the route of the Nashville and Chattanooga Railroad. Rebel cavalry raiders had torn up great stretches of these railroads and it was impossible to keep the army supplied on its march to Chattanooga except by train. Halleck put me in charge of making the repairs.

At this time, the quickest way we knew to repair the damage done by the Rebel cavalry raids was by employing massive amounts of manpower. I was therefore assigned about one-fifth of the entire Army of the Ohio to put the tracks in working order. Even so, it took almost six weeks to repair the seventy-five miles of track from Iuka, Mississippi to Decatur, Alabama, the first leg of the route to Chattanooga.

The railroads were the only effective way to move men and material across the vast distances of the military theater west of the Appalachian Mountains. If the Rebel cavalry raiders could destroy the railroads faster than we could repair them, our offensive capabilities would be crippled.

Therefore, as the work on the tracks from Iuka to Decatur progressed, I assembled a group of officers skilled in logistics, engineering and construction. Together, we formulated a system that enabled us to repair the rail lines faster and with less manpower. The pace of repairs quickened noticeably as we moved west, and in future campaigns, as we perfected our methods, we were able to repair tracks, rebuild bridges and open collapsed tunnels so rapidly that our offensive movements suffered no significant delays, despite the best efforts of the enemy cavalry raiders.

While I was engaged in the repair of the line from Iuka to Decatur, my old friend Braxton Bragg replaced Beauregard as commander of the army soon to be designated as the Army of Tennessee. Bragg had been my company commander before and during the Mexican War, and we had fought shoulder to shoulder when our artillery batteries held off the

Mexican attacks at Buena Vista. Later, he had put my name forward for a teaching position at West Point and had recommended me to Jefferson Davis for appointment as an officer in the Second Cavalry Regiment. The fact that I would now be facing him in combat was emblematic of the particularly tragic nature of the war.

Buell, knowing of my friendship with Bragg, asked me what we could expect from him. "Bragg will not stay on the defensive," I told him. "He is aggressive and will be looking to strike a blow. I think we must attack him before he is able to do so."

Buell agreed, but our movement toward Chattanooga got no further than Decatur. Here we learned that Bragg and General Kirby Smith were leading their armies north into Kentucky, Smith from Knoxville and Bragg from Chattanooga.

Smith's offensive was initially successful. He entered Kentucky on August 16th, won a small victory over William Nelson's raw recruits at Richmond, Kentucky on August 30th, and captured Lexington the following day. Bragg followed Smith into Kentucky, capturing a Union brigade at Munfordville on September 17th.

As soon as Buell learned that Bragg and Smith were heading toward Kentucky, he put our army on the march north to meet them. When we passed through Nashville, he left my division there as his rear guard.

Bragg's victory at Munfordville put him between Buell and our supply base at Louisville. The Rebel's capture of our main supply base would obviously be a major setback. More than this, however, the capture of Louisville would open the way for Bragg to cross the Ohio River and invade Ohio.

Bragg and Smith's offensives were occurring at the same time that Robert E. Lee was marching into Maryland, threatening Pennsylvania and even New York. Successful Rebel invasions of both Pennsylvania and Ohio would create tremendous public pressure on the Lincoln Administration to sue for a negotiated peace. It was therefore imperative that we reach Louisville before Bragg and blunt an invasion of Ohio.

Beating Bragg to Louisville would not be easy since he had a significant head start. Fortunately, a spirited defense by John T. Walker at the

Green River Bridge had delayed Bragg for four days before he finally captured Munfordville, affording Buell time to catch up with the Rebel army. I now received orders to rendezvous with the remainder of the Army of the Ohio about fifty miles south of Louisville, where they were confronting Bragg.

I set my division in motion for the one hundred mile march from Nashville to Prewitt's Knob, where Buell was waiting. The march was exceedingly difficult. Clothing, shoes and food were in short supply. More importantly, water was practically unobtainable owing to a summer-long drought. The few watering holes we encountered had been poisoned by the Rebels or polluted by horses, mules and cattle. When we eventually met up with Buell, my men were so hungry that when they deployed in front of the enemy, they battled the Rebel pickets for possession of an apple orchard located between the lines.

Bragg, now confronted by an enemy force larger than his own, elected not to bring on an engagement. Instead, he turned east to concentrate his army with Kirby Smith's near Lexington. The road to Louisville was now open. Wasting no time, I arrived there with the forward elements of my division on August 27th. The remainder of the army followed soon after.

Bragg had lost his opportunity to cross into Ohio. In Maryland, Lee had been stalemated by McClellan at the Battle of Antietam on September 17th and forced to withdraw back into Virginia. The twin threats of invasion had been blunted and a major crisis averted.

Two days after we entered Louisville, orders arrived from General Halleck directing Buell to turn over command of the Army of the Ohio to me. The Administration in Washington was unhappy that Smith and Bragg had been allowed to move into Kentucky and threaten Louisville, but the dissatisfaction with Buell went beyond that.

Andrew Johnson had been stirring up anti-Buell feeling ever since Buell's refusal to invade East Tennessee. In addition, Buell had incurred the wrath of the Radical Republicans in Congress because of his standing order not to disturb Southern civilians. Buell ordered his troops to return runaway slaves who made their way into Union lines, and refused to confiscate supplies from disloyal farmers. In one well-publicized incident, Buell brought charges against the commander of a Union regiment for failing to prevent his troops from pillaging Athens, Alabama. Added to this was Halleck's implacable enmity toward Buell, dating from their competition for overall command of the western armies.

Buell was gracious when he received the order placing me in command, offering to cooperate with me in whatever way he could. I informed Buell that I intended to refuse command of the army and showed him the telegram I intended to send informing Halleck that Buell's preparations to move against the enemy had been completed and respectfully asking that he be retained in command to carry out his planned offensive.

Halleck replied the next day, stating, "You may consider the order suspended until I can lay your dispatch before the Government and get instructions." A few days later, both Buell and I received wires from Halleck advising that the change in command was, "by the authority of the President suspended."

It was quite true that I was reluctant to relieve Buell just as he was readying his army to move against the enemy. He, not I, had developed routes of march and a plan of battle based upon a detailed knowledge of the location of his infantry, cavalry and artillery units. Had this been the only impediment to my assuming command, however, I probably would have done so. After all, later in the war, George Meade assumed command of the Army of the Potomac on its march to Gettysburg and managed quite well.

The main reason for my reluctance to replace Buell was my belief that the effort to remove him from command was not based on military considerations but represented the maneuvering of his political enemies. I refused to be a party to these machinations much less their beneficiary.

I knew that my declining to relieve Buell would not be well-received in Washington. I heard later that there were those who questioned my loyalty and others who assumed that I did not regard myself as capable of assuming an independent command. This could not be helped. Quite simply, I would not permit myself to be made use of to do an injury to a brave and honorable soldier.

Chapter 14

B uell had divided his army into three corps. Alexander McCook and Thomas L. Crittenden commanded the First and Second Corps. William "Bull" Nelson commanded the Third. I was named as second in command of the army, although my duties were not well defined. During the Perryville campaign, I travelled with Crittenden and essentially exercised command of the Second Corps.

Days before the army was ready to leave Louisville, I met with General Nelson at the Galt House Hotel. When the conference ended, General Nelson preceded me down the stairs. The unfortunately-named Union General Jefferson C. Davis was waiting for him in the lobby.

Nelson had recently reprimanded Davis over his performance in front of numerous witnesses and now Davis demanded an apology. The large and burly Nelson was not about to oblige. "Go away you damned puppy," he shouted. "I don't want anything to do with you."

Davis then tossed a wadded paper ball at Nelson and Nelson responded by slapping Davis across the face. I watched in horror as Davis drew a pistol and fired point blank at Nelson's heart. Nelson crumpled to the ground, his wound obviously fatal.

Pandemonium broke loose in the lobby. A group of officers surrounded Davis, who surrendered without protest, and I ordered him placed under arrest. I directed that Nelson be moved to a room off the lobby and placed on a couch. Only his great strength prolonged his life for a few hours. Two days later, Davis was indicted for manslaughter. Because of his political connections, Davis' case never came to trial and he continued to serve in the army throughout the war.

On October 1st, we moved out of Louisville in three columns in pursuit of Bragg. General C.C. Granger was named to replace Nelson as commander of the Third Corps. Kentucky was still suffering through a severe drought, and scouts were sent ahead to find water. Our route of march had to be frequently altered to bring the army to the few available fresh water sources. Despite our best efforts, the men were soon reduced to drinking brackish or muddy water, and stomach ailments debilitated a significant portion of the army.

Nevertheless, Buell pressed ahead and by October 8th, the army had advanced close to Perryville, a small town about sixty miles southeast of Louisville. Outside the town, a regiment of McCook's First Corps found an unsullied pool of fresh water and began filling their canteens.

Unbeknown to McCook's men, General Hardee, in command of Bragg's rear guard, had stopped in Perryville and his troops began to fire on the Federal water-gatherers. This initiated the battle of Perryville, as McCook quickly brought up the remainder of his corps. The Federals endured ferocious attacks from the Rebels and were eventually forced back to a new defensive position where they stood firm.

Several days prior to the battle, Buell had suffered a fall from his horse and established his headquarters about two and one-half miles from the scene of the fighting. Due to a peculiar atmospheric condition, known as an acoustic shadow, the sounds of the battle, which normally could have been easily heard at that distance, did not reach Buell. He was therefore unaware, until the battle was well underway, that McCook was engaged. I was with Crittenden's corps, about three miles south of the battlefield, and similarly did not hear the sounds of the fighting.

Late in the afternoon, a messenger from McCook reached Buell and reported that McCook was being hard-pressed by the enemy. Buell sent one of his staff officers, a Lieutenant Fitzhugh, to find me. He arrived at my headquarters about seven o'clock pm, after darkness had already fallen.

Fitzhugh advised me that McCook's corps had been battling the enemy all day and that General Buell wanted me to move Crittenden's corps to McCook's support. I questioned Fitzhugh closely but he was unable to provide me with any details about the day's fighting or to tell me whether Buell expected me to make a night march or to bring up my troops at first light.

I mounted my horse and set out for Buell's headquarters to get his orders first hand. He informed me that McCook's corps had been engaged in hard fighting, but appeared to be holding its own. Buell told me he intended to attack the Rebels the next morning and ordered me to bring up Crittenden's corps at dawn. He also ordered Granger to move to McCook's support at dawn.

By nightfall, Bragg had figured out that he had only been engaging one third of the Federal army. Realizing that he was likely to be attacked the following day by two fresh Federal corps, he elected to retreat. The next morning, when I brought up the lead elements of the Second Corps, Bragg's army was gone.

Because Buell was still immobilized by his fall, I led the army's pursuit of Bragg the following day. My goal was to catch up to Bragg before he reached the Cumberland Gap and retreated into Tennessee. But, as was so often the case with the Union armies at this stage in the war, my pursuit was hampered by the lack of effective cavalry.

During Bragg's march north from Chattanooga, John Hunt Morgan's cavalry had routed the Union cavalry at Hartsville, Tennessee. The Federal cavalry commander, General R.W. Wilson, was taken prisoner and his command effectively ceased to exist. During my pursuit of Bragg, the Rebel cavalry, ably led by General Joseph Wheeler, was therefore able to delay my pursuit by harassing my columns without interference by Federal horsemen. After two weeks and sixty-five miles,

I gave up the chase and returned to Bowling Green, where Buell had encamped after the Battle of Perryville.

Buell had been unlucky. The scarcity of water altered his route and resulted in a general engagement before he could unite his three corps. His fall from his horse prevented him from being up with McCook's troops when the fighting commenced, and the acoustic shadow kept him from realizing that McCook was under attack until it was too late in the day to bring up his remaining corps.

The fighting at Perryville had been heavy. Union casualties totaled over 4,200. Despite these losses, the Rebel army had escaped. Buell's political enemies among the Radical Republicans not only challenged his competence, but questioned his loyalty. They pressured the Administration into removing him from command and convening a special commission to review his conduct at Perryville.

The commission's proceedings, which took place at Nashville in December, were a farce. As I learned when I was called as a witness, there was never any intention of giving Buell a fair hearing. The leading questions posed to me by the hearing officers were clearly designed to elicit answers that would cast doubt on Buell's loyalty. I refused to criticize Buell, making clear that nothing I had observed, or that had been reported to me, suggested he had acted dishonorably or with some ulterior motive.

The hearing officers were hoping that I would discredit Buell, and my testimony was not what they wanted to hear. As a result, they attempted to impugn my conduct through the testimony of Lieutenant Fitzhugh, the messenger who had brought me Buell's verbal order on the evening of October 8th to bring up Crittenden's corps to support McCook.

Fitzhugh, who must have been promised some reward for his testimony, stated that Buell had clearly intended that I go to McCook's aid immediately upon receipt of his order. He also stated that a night march could have been easily accomplished since there was a full moon that night making the landscape "as bright as day."

Much to his credit, Buell did not attempt to exonerate himself by placing any blame on me. Instead, he testified that he did not expect me to move until dawn, thinking that a night march posed too great a risk, and anticipating that Bragg's army would remain on the field overnight.

The political motivation behind Buell's hearing was confirmed by the fact that the special commission never made a decision concerning Buell's conduct at Perryville or even rendered a report. Instead, Buell was simply shunted aside, waiting over sixteen months for a new assignment. Finally, in May, 1864, he resigned his commission. When General Grant became General in Chief, he offered to reinstate Buell and give him a new command, but Buell, now thoroughly disillusioned, declined.

With the close of the Perryville Campaign, I had time to consider the significance of the Preliminary Emancipation Proclamation issued by President Lincoln on September 22, 1862. The Proclamation declared that on January 1, 1863, all slaves in those States or parts of States still in rebellion against the United States "shall be then, thenceforward and forever free." In essence, Lincoln was giving the South three months to lay down their arms and return to the Union or face the prospect that a Federal victory would result in the end of slavery.

I was not greatly surprised at the issuance of the Preliminary Emancipation Proclamation. The heavy casualties sustained by the Federal armies in battles such as Shiloh, Antietam and the Seven Days made it highly unlikely that the war would end with "the Union as it was" to use a well-known phrase of the day. The North's huge expenditure of men and treasure in subduing the rebellion made it impossible for me to believe that the North would accept the return of the Southern States with slavery intact

Congress had already passed legislation prohibiting the army from returning escaped slaves and declaring that all slaves escaping into Union lines, or in Rebel territory occupied by the Union army, were to be deemed captives of war and be "forever free of their servitude and not again held as slaves." The war was inexorably leading to the end of slavery, and I viewed the Preliminary Emancipation Proclamation as the logical next step in this process. Of course, the North would have to win the war to accomplish emancipation, but I harbored no doubts about an ultimate Union victory.

I was far less concerned than some of my fellow generals about whether the Northern soldiers would continue to fight now that the end of slavery was an explicit war aim. I had spent enough time getting to know the men in the ranks to feel confident they would fight, and fight hard, until the rebellion was subdued, whether or not emancipation was a consequence of victory. President Lincoln very wisely framed emancipation as a war measure, aimed at depriving the Rebels of the slave labor on farms, plantations and factories that allowed a very high percentage of white men to serve in the Confederate army.

As to my personal views, I had come to believe that slavery was a moral injustice. Prior to the war, I could see no way to free the slaves without catastrophic consequences for both races. The rebellion of the Southern States, and the North's resolve to prevent the disintegration of the Union, cut the Gordian Knot of the slavery question. A Union victory would now bring about the end of slavery, although the cost in lives and treasure far exceeded anyone's prediction at the beginning of the war.

Chapter 15

With Buell's removal from command on October 24th, I assumed temporary command of the Army of the Ohio. I was in Lebanon, Kentucky when I read in a newspaper that General William Rosecrans had been named as Buell's successor. Only two days later did I receive a dispatch from Halleck formally notifying me of Rosecrans' appointment.

I am by nature an even-tempered man. Moreover, I have actively cultivated this attribute ever since my first experiences in combat showed me that remaining composed and cool-headed in the face of a crisis generated trust and respect among my men and strengthened their resolve. Over the years, remaining imperturbable became a habit. This is not to say that I lack strong emotions about situations and events that are important to me, only that I have learned to control my temper on most occasions.

My self-possession deserted me, however, when I learned of Rosecrans' selection to replace Buell. I felt both infuriated and humiliated. I made my feelings known in a letter to General Halleck the same day I was officially notified of Rosecrans' promotion.

"Soon after coming to Kentucky in 1861, I urged the government to give me 20,000 men properly equipped to take the field that I might at least make the attempt to take Knoxville and East Tennessee. My suggestions were not listened to but were passed by in silence. Yet, without boasting, I believe I have exhibited at least sufficient energy to show that if I had been entrusted with the command of that expedition at that time, I might have conducted it successfully. Before Corinth I was entrusted with the command of the right wing of the Army of the Tennessee. I feel confident that I performed my duty patriotically and faithfully and with a reasonable amount of credit to myself. As soon as the emergency was over I was relieved and returned to the command of my old division. I went to my duties without a murmur, as I am neither ambitious nor have I any political aspirations."

"On the 29th of last September I received an order through your aide, Colonel McKibbon, placing me in command of the Department of Tennessee and directing General Buell to turn over his troops to me. This order reached me just as General Buell had by most extraordinary exertions prepared his army to pursue and drive the Rebels from Kentucky. Feeling convinced that great injustice would be done him if not permitted to carry out his plans, I requested that he might be retained in command. The order relieving him was suspended but today I am officially informed that he is relieved by General Rosecrans, my junior. I feel deeply mortified and aggrieved at the action taken in this matter. I do not desire the command of the Department of Tennessee, but that an officer senior to me in rank should be sent here if I am retained on duty in it."

Halleck attempted to mollify me by expressing his confidence in my abilities and pointing to the efforts he had made on my behalf. "I cannot better state my appreciation of you as a general than by referring you to the fact that, at Pittsburg Landing, I urged upon the Secretary of War to secure your appointment as major-general, in order that I might place you in command of the right wing of the army over your then superiors. It was through my urgent solicitations that you were commissioned."

"When it was determined to relieve General Buell another person was spoken of as his successor and it was through my repeated solicitations that you were appointed. You, having virtually declined the command at that time, it was necessary to appoint another, and General Rosecrans was selected."

His letter next advised me that I was mistaken about General Rosecrans being junior to me, informing me that Rosecrans' commission dated prior to mine. He also reminded me that it was the prerogative of the Commander in Chief to select commanders regardless of seniority and that President Lincoln had done so in many cases. He closed with the following: "Rest assured, General, that I fully appreciate your military capacity, and will do everything in my power to give you an independent command when an opportunity offers. It was not possible to give you the command in Tennessee after you had once declined it."

I recognized that my prior refusal to replace Buell had played a role in the decision not to give me command of the Army of the Ohio. I wanted Halleck to know that it was solely the fact that I believed Rosecrans my junior that had disturbed me. I responded to his letter thanking him for the kind words he had expressed, and added: "I should not have addressed you in the first place if I had known that General Rosecrans' commission dated prior to mine. The letter was written not because I desired a command but for being superseded, as I supposed, by a junior in rank when I felt there was no cause for so treating me. I have no objection to serving under General Rosecrans now that I know his commission dates prior to mine, but I must confess that I should feel deeply mortified should the President place a junior over me without just cause although the law authorizes him to do so should he see fit."

Later, after the Battle of Chickamauga, when I had replaced Rosecrans as the Commander of the Army of the Cumberland, General Sherman advised me that, although it was technically true that Rosecrans was senior to me, this was only because his commission had been backdated, jumping him thirty-nine places in seniority. I was not surprised that General Halleck had been less than candid with me.

I also learned from Charles Dana, Secretary of War Stanton's assistant, who was with the army at Chattanooga, that the selection of Buell's successor after the Battle of Perryville had provoked a disagreement between Stanton and Secretary of the Treasury Salmon Chase. According to Dana, Stanton favored naming me to the command while Chase backed Rosecrans. Lincoln, Dana reported, sided with Chase, commenting "Let the Virginian wait." According to Dana, as the meeting broke up, Stanton turned to Chase and stated, "Well, you have made your choice of idiots. Now look out for the disaster."

I knew General Rosecrans well. He was two years behind me at West Point, where he was known as a brilliant student and a very likeable and genial companion. During his time at the Military Academy, he converted to Catholicism and was a devout practitioner of his religion. Notwithstanding this, Rosecrans' frequent and creative use of profanity was legendary. Also legendary was his short temper and impulsiveness.

Rosecrans had left the peacetime army to work as an engineer extracting coal from the mines in West Virginia. There, he began experimenting with coal oil lamps to replace the whale oil lamps generally in use. An explosion of one of his prototypes left his face permanently scarred.

With the outbreak of the war, Rosecrans re-entered the service, initially serving under McClellan in West Virginia where he won several small engagements, the credit for which went to McClellan, helping to propel McClellan to the command of the Army of the Potomac. Rosecrans later served under Grant in Mississippi, but a falling out between them had left him without a command.

On November 1st, Rosecrans arrived at Bowling Green to take command of the army, which he renamed the Army of the Cumberland. Upon his arrival, he asked to see me, obviously aware of my protests to Halleck.

"You are my senior in years, in the service and in merit," he told me. "We have been friends for years and I shall especially need your support and advice."

"You shall have it, General," I replied. "My protest to the War Department did not relate in any way to a belief that you were not capable of commanding this army. I shall do all in my power to aid and support you and to bring this army victories."

"I did not doubt it for a moment. I will give you any command you want in this army, whether one of its three corps or the place of second in command. You have but to name it."

"I believe I can be of greatest use to you as a corps commander," I replied without hesitation. Rosecrans immediately issued orders placing me in command of the XIV Corps. Probably recognizing that my even-temper would be a useful counterpoint to his own impulsiveness, Rosecrans came to rely on me as his closest adviser, a role I was happy to play.

Perhaps with a premonition of what was to come, after my initial meeting with Rosecrans I sent another wire to Halleck. "I have made my last protest while this war lasts. You may hereafter put a stick over me if you choose to do so. I will take care, however, so to manage my command, whatever it may be, as not to be involved in the mistakes of the stick." I recalled these words a year later when Rosecrans abandoned the battlefield at Chickamauga and my wing of the army was fending off repeated Rebel attacks, saving the Army of the Cumberland from total destruction.

I was personally fond of Rosecrans and he had many strengths as an army commander. He was a first-rate strategist and a master of logistics. He was also a tireless worker who drove himself and his staff unmercifully. He rose early and worked practically to midnight every day. His staff officers could not keep up with his pace and were forced to work in shifts.

Rosecrans' method of relaxation was unique. An incessant talker, he would gather his aides to his tent when he had finished work for the night and engage them in discussions on whatever topics happened to be on his mind. Whether it was history, literature, philosophy, art, politics, or theology, Rosecrans was well-informed and his observations were always interesting.

I learned of Rosecrans' peculiar habit shortly after he assumed command. A meeting with him ran past midnight and, when it ended, I prepared to return to my headquarters. Rosecrans stopped me and asked if I would like to join in a discussion with him and his staff. Not wishing to appear uncivil, I accepted his invitation and found myself listening to a two-hour conversation about the spread of Christianity in the Roman Empire.

On almost all future occasions, when I was invited to join in one of his late night discussion groups, I made my excuses, preferring to get a good night's sleep. Although I never broached the subject with any of Rosecrans' staff officers, I have no doubt that, if given the choice, most of them would have preferred to skip the late night sessions and get to bed early after a long day's work.

Although usually pleasant and friendly, General Rosecrans had a terrible temper and would loudly and profanely castigate subordinates, over even unimportant matters, if he believed they had failed to carry out his orders properly or in a timely fashion. I witnessed this behavior for the first time when Rosecrans summoned Brigadier General John Beatty to his headquarters and began to berate him over Beatty's failure to acknowledge receipt of an order. General Beatty explained that he had thought the order was intended for another Brigadier General by the name of Samuel Beatty and had passed the order on to him.

Rosecrans was not satisfied with this explanation, and continued to pour forth a string of obscenities at poor General Beatty. I noted with concern that Rosecrans made no attempt to shield Beatty from public humiliation, venting his anger in the presence of Rosecrans' staff. I saw or heard reports of similar conduct on frequent occasions and I began to question whether a man who could not exercise control over his own temper could exercise control over an army in the heat of battle.

William S. Rosecrans (Library of Congress)

Chapter 16

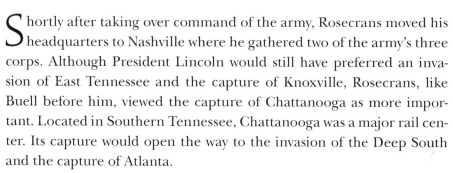

S hortly after taking over command of the army, Rosecrans moved his
headquarters to Nashville where he gathered two of the army's three
corps. Although President Lincoln would still have preferred an invasion of East Tennessee and the capture of Knoxville, Rosecrans, like
Buell before him, viewed the capture of Chattanooga as more important. Located in Southern Tennessee, Chattanooga was a major rail center. Its capture would open the way to the invasion of the Deep South
and the capture of Atlanta.

Rosecrans determined to fully re-supply and re-equip the army
before heading toward Chattanooga. He faced a problem however, because the Louisville and Nashville Railroad, connecting Nashville with
the army's main supply base at Louisville, was in near-total disrepair.
This rail line had not been constructed for military purposes and had
begun to collapse under the heavy weight of the military supplies being
constantly shipped over its tracks. This situation was made worse by the
frequent cavalry raids of Nathan Bedford Forrest, John Hunt Morgan
and Joseph Wheeler, who ripped up tracks and destroyed bridges and
tunnels. Thus, supplies for the army were arriving slowly, if at all.

Because of my experience in repairing the Memphis and Charleston
railroad after the capture of Corinth, General Rosecrans assigned me

the task of putting the Louisville and Nashville line back in service. I welcomed this assignment because it allowed me to reassemble my special railroad staff and to expand on the methods we had previously developed when repairing the Memphis and Charleston line.

I established and continuously enlarged and improved extensive repair shops in Nashville and in Chattanooga, once that city was in our hands. I recruited surveyors, engineers, construction, operation and maintenance men and detailed them for special service to keep the roads open and running. I also stockpiled material in safe and accessible places to insure that my crews always had the means required to perform necessary repairs. Special construction trains were outfitted and held in readiness at strategic locations so that crews could be dispatched where needed at a moment's notice. A rolling mill was constructed to straighten bent and twisted rails.

My first task was to open two tunnels near Gallatin Tennessee, thirty miles north of Nashville, that had been blocked by Morgan's raiders. I assigned this job to five hundred men from my old Mills Springs division. On November 13th, less than two weeks after beginning work, they had cleared the first tunnel, and two weeks later the second tunnel was open. Additional units were assigned to repair other damaged portions of the Louisville and Nashville line, and by mid-December supplies began to pour into Nashville.

Organizing the special railroad repair units brought into focus an idea that had been on my mind for quite some time. It had occurred to me that the striking force of an army could be greatly increased if that army were virtually self-sufficient, containing specialized units capable of rapidly responding to any contingency. As I was organizing my special railroad units, I began to implement this idea in my XIV Corps. Later, after I assumed command of the Army of the Cumberland, I extended this concept to the entire army.

To assist me in this endeavor, I disregarded the common practice of appointing friends or prominent politicians as staff officers. Instead, I sought out experts to take responsibility for specialized tasks, such as artillery, topography, signals, medicine, and intelligence. At camp and in battle, each staff officer was given clearly defined duties related to his expertise.

I applied this same principle to the corps itself, organizing units skilled in particular specialties, such as engineers and pioneers to design, build and repair roads and bridges, mobile hospital units to treat the sick and wounded as close to the battlefield as possible and telegraphers, who were often civilians, to construct and operate mobile telegraph stations to move with the army.

I placed great emphasis on maintaining an effective capability to gather and analyze information about the enemy's strength, location and morale. I used scouts, spies, cavalry patrols, loyal citizens and deserters, although the information provided by this latter source was inherently suspect. The members of my staff assigned to deal exclusively with intelligence about the enemy soon developed an expertise that usually provided me with an accurate picture of the enemy's size, disposition and probable movements.

On all too many occasions during the war, Union campaigns had come to grief because of faulty or outdated maps. Since the start of the war, I had kept a journal in which I created my own maps, showing the key topographical features of the areas in which my troops were operating. Now, I expanded this effort, creating a unit of cartographers to scout and prepare maps of the terrain over which we were to march and fight. My goal was to become at least as familiar as the Rebels with the local roads and topographical features of their territory. I wanted always to be sure, not only of our best lines of march, but the lines of march and defensive positions the enemy would likely employ.

Most importantly, I used whatever resources were necessary to insure that a logistical and supply system was in place to guarantee that my troops were well-fed, well-clothed and well-supplied, wherever our campaigns might take us.

I dislike making speeches and did not frequently address the troops on a formal basis. I did, however, continue my regular practice of walking or riding through the camp to speak with individuals or small groups of soldiers. This allowed me to measure their morale and reassure them that I was committed to their welfare. I also made it a point to routinely visit the field hospitals to make sure that the wounded were not suffering unnecessarily and had all the care and comfort we had the ability to provide.

Chapter 17

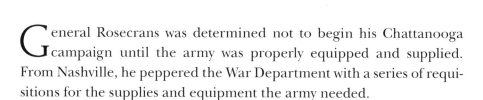

General Rosecrans was determined not to begin his Chattanooga campaign until the army was properly equipped and supplied. From Nashville, he peppered the War Department with a series of requisitions for the supplies and equipment the army needed.

Of particular concern to Rosecrans, as well as to me, was the state of our cavalry, which was lacking in both adequate mounts and trained horsemen. Our cavalry was clearly no match for Bragg's, which was his most effective arm. The Southern horsemen raided behind our lines with impunity, having no concern that we could prevent their attacks or effectively pursue them. Our inability to contend with the Rebel cavalry was brought home to me in a particularly painful way when John Hunt Morgan forced the surrender of an entire brigade that I had assigned to protect the area around Hartsville, Tennessee. Despite the obvious shortcomings of our cavalry, Rosecrans' frequent requests for more cavalrymen and mounts were ignored by Halleck and the War Department.

Typical of Halleck's refusal to improve our cavalry was his decision regarding the Spencer repeating rifle. Shortly after Rosecrans assumed command, he and I met with Christopher Spencer, a gun manufacturer who had come to Rosecrans' headquarters to demonstrate his new invention, a seven shot, breech-loading repeating rifle. It was apparent to us that if we could arm our cavalry with Spencer's new rifle, the massive increase in firepower could more than offset the Rebel's superior horsemanship.

Rosecrans immediately wired Washington, requesting that the government purchase enough Spencer Rifles to arm our entire cavalry force. The War Department denied this requisition without explanation. This was a tremendous mistake and cost the Federal army dearly in terms of missed opportunities and unnecessary casualties.

Fortunately, a young infantry officer, Colonel John T. Wilder, also met with Spencer and witnessed a demonstration of his new weapon. Wilder conceived the idea of mounting his infantry brigade and arming it with the seven-shot repeaters. When he learned that the War Department had refused Rosecrans' requisition, he and his men purchased rifles from Spencer with their own funds. With Rosecrans' consent, Wilder and his men raided the countryside to obtain horses. Thus was born Wilder's Lightning Brigade that was to provide such excellent service in the upcoming campaigns.

Having refused to assist Rosecrans in strengthening his army, in early November, even before the Louisville and Nashville Railroad had been fully reopened, Halleck wired Rosecrans threatening him with removal if he did not immediately move against the enemy. To his credit, Rosecrans would not be bullied. In his response, Rosecrans explained that he would leave Nashville as soon as the railroad was repaired and sufficient ammunition and rations were on hand to mount a successful campaign, but not before. "To threats of removal," Rosecrans advised Halleck, "I am insensible". When Rosecrans showed me his exchange with Halleck, I applauded him and promised him my full support.

In insisting that Rosecrans immediately take the offensive, Halleck was no doubt passing along the wishes of President Lincoln and Secretary of War Stanton. Lincoln and Stanton had been so frustrated by their inability to get General McClellan to move against Lee that they viewed any delay in taking the offensive in Tennessee as a repeat of their unsatisfactory experience with McClellan in Virginia and Maryland. In pressing Rosecrans to immediately commence his campaign, the President and the Secretary of War failed to appreciate the logistical problems posed by the vast scale of the western theater, its mountainous terrain, lack of adequate roads and the ever-present threat of enemy cavalry raids on our supply lines. Halleck did nothing to educate them.

As the repairs to the railroad progressed, I began to move elements of my XIV Corps into Nashville and was able to move my own head-quarters to that city on December 21st. The army was now well supplied and, although our cavalry was still woefully inadequate, we were ready to advance. Bragg' army of about 37,000 was at Murfreesboro, a small town on Stones River, about thirty-five miles from Nashville, blocking our route to Chattanooga.

In preparation for the campaign, Rosecrans had reorganized the Army of the Cumberland into three wings. The left wing, consisting of about 14,500 men was commanded by Major General Thomas L. Crittenden, a native Kentuckian. whose brother was a general in the Confederate Army. The right wing, of about 16,000 men, was under the command of Major General Alexander McCook. McCook had com-manded the First Corps of the Army of the Ohio, the only corps that had seen action at the Battle of Perryville, where it had received rough treatment at the hands of the Rebels. I commanded the center wing of about 13,500 men consisting of four divisions led by Major General Lovell H. Rousseau and Brigadier Generals James S. Negley, Speed S. Fry and Robert B. Mitchell.

On Christmas night, Rosecrans convened a meeting of his corps and division commanders and laid out his plan of campaign. The army would advance on Murfreesboro the next morning. Crittenden was to move southeast down the Nashville Turnpike, the major road between Nashville and Murfreesboro. McCook was to proceed south via the Nolensville Turnpike to the town of Triune where it would turn east toward Murfreesboro. Between these two columns, I would move almost due south from Nashville.

Our cavalry, consisting of a single division under Brigadier David S. Stanley, was divided among the three columns, one brigade being assigned to proceed ahead of each wing. As a result of Washington's failure to heed Rosecrans' pleas to improve the cavalry, our horsemen proved useless in the campaign, failing to properly screen our advance or to gather accurate information about the location and disposition of the Rebel army. In contrast, the Rebel Cavalry was highly effective, repeatedly striking well-behind our lines and disrupting our communications and supplies.

Rosecrans had at his disposal at Nashville about 80,000 troops equipped and ready for battle. Because of the threat posed by the Confederate cavalry raiders, we were required to reduce the size of our attacking columns by about 30,000 men, who were needed to garrison Nashville, to protect the Nashville and Chattanooga Railroad and to guard the army's wagon train. In my case, I was required to deploy nine of my fourteen brigades for these purposes, leaving only five brigades in the army's center wing. Thus, the superiority of the Rebel Cavalry substantially reduced our numerical advantage over Bragg's army.

After laying out his plan, Rosecrans ordered glasses of toddy to be distributed to toast the season. He closed the conference with the following admonition: "We move tomorrow, gentlemen. Press them hard, drive them out of their nests. Make them fight or run. Strike hard and fast. Give them no rest. Fight them, fight them, fight them, I say."

Early on December 26th, we began our advance toward Murfreesboro. It was cold and rainy and we were hindered by the constant raiding of Joseph Wheeler's cavalry. Morgan and Hunt carried out raids deep behind our lines, cutting railroad lines and capturing or destroying supplies. Nevertheless, we pressed forward.

December 29th dawned chilly and damp. As we marched toward Murfreesboro, heavy fire erupted on Crittenden's front to my left. I halted the column briefly and rode to the top of a nearby hill to try to ascertain what was happening. Crittenden's column was hidden by the dense cedar forest which covered the ground between the two columns, but I hoped that I could determine what was happening from the sound of the gunfire. After a few minutes, one of my aides, who sat his horse next to mine, asked me the meaning of the gunfire we were hearing. "It means a fight tomorrow at Stones River," I replied.

On December 30th, as we drew closer to Murfreesboro, I became increasingly concerned with the terrain. We were in the midst of a cedar forest so thick that artillery and supply wagons could not get through, and even the infantry was finding it difficult to make progress. It was for just such a contingency that I had formed a pioneer brigade and I set them to work early that day cutting roads through the forest so that men and artillery could freely move as circumstances might dictate. The next day, when the battle commenced, the pioneers equipped themselves with muskets and fought beside the rest of my troops. At Stones River and thereafter, my pioneers were among the unsung heroes of the war.

By the evening of December 30th, the Army of the Cumberland had moved into position about two miles northwest of Murfreesboro. Our line was about four miles long, running southwest to northeast. The Army of the Tennessee was in line opposite us, astride the major roads into Murfreesboro.

Late that afternoon, Rosecrans convened a council of war with his senior commanders. With his unrivaled flair for profanity, Rosecrans began by cursing the War Department for refusing his repeated requests to strengthen our cavalry, thereby enabling the Rebel cavalry to roam at will and preventing us from accurately gauging the disposition of Bragg's forces.

With that off his chest, Rosecrans gave his orders for the next day. At dawn, Crittenden, on the left, was to cross the river and get around the enemy's right flank into his rear, cutting Bragg off from Murfreesboro and Chattanooga. I was to demonstrate against the enemy center, holding it in place until Crittenden had gotten around Bragg's right, at which time my center wing and McCook's right wing were to advance, pinning the Rebels between our wings and Crittenden's and destroying Bragg's army.

The soldiers in both armies, only about 700 yards apart, knew that a battle would be fought the following day. After dinner, several of our regimental bands struck up "Yankee Doodle", "Hail Columbia" and other patriotic songs. Not to be outdone, the Rebel musicians responded with "Dixie" and "The Bonnie Blue Flag". After a few minutes of silence, one of our bands began playing "Home Sweet Home" which was immediately taken up by all the Federal musicians. Soon, the Rebel bands joined in, and many men in both armies began to sing along.

Aside from the music, the camps became unusually silent and still. I was deeply moved by the realization that the song expressed the deep longing of the men in both armies to put down their rifles and return home, and that so many of them would never do so. After a time, the music died away and the men bedded down to whatever sleep they could get.

The next morning, Crittenden's wing crossed Stones River in preparation for its enveloping movement around the Rebel right. As it turned out, Bragg had formed the same battle plan as Rosecrans, sending his left to outflank the Federal right, get in our rear and cut us off from our base at Nashville. Bragg's left, consisting of 10,000 troops under the command of General William Hardee, struck at dawn, before Crittenden's planned attack got underway. General McCook, in command of the Federal right, was caught completely off guard by Hardee's attack and by ten o'clock his troops were pushed back almost three miles to the Nashville Pike.

Complete disaster was averted by General Philip Sheridan, commanding the division on the left of McCook's line. Alerted by one of his brigade commanders that pickets had spotted large numbers of Rebels moving toward the far right of the Federal line, Sheridan had his men up early, ready to meet an attack. When the Rebels swept away the Federal units to his right, Sheridan's division stubbornly hung on, repulsing repeated attacks.

When General Rosecrans' realized that his right wing had caved-in, he called off Crittenden's attack and began to construct a new line across the Nashville Pike. Loss of the Pike would cut off our route of retreat to Nashville and spell disaster. Rosecrans sent me word that the fate of the army depended on my holding off the Rebels for at least an hour, the time he needed to establish his new line.

It was now shortly after ten am. Negley's division was holding the line on Sheridan's left. I ordered Rousseau to reinforce Sheridan and Negley and rode with his division to the front. An hour of very hard fighting ensued with Confederate General Polk adding the weight of his corps to the assaults upon the center of our line.

Shortly after 11 am, Sheridan rode up and advised me that his men were out of ammunition and that he would be forced to retire. This opened a gap in our line that Hardee's men were quick to exploit, making it impossible to hold our position.

It had been a hard fight, but we had given Rosecrans his hour. I ordered a withdrawal of about half a mile to reunite my forces with the remainder of McCook's right wing, now occupying the new line formed by General Rosecrans astride the Nashville Pike. An orderly withdrawal in the face of an enemy attack is one of the most difficult maneuvers in battle. Even the smallest misstep can turn the withdrawal into a rout. In this instance, my officers and men performed superbly.

Our withdrawal was assisted in no small measure by the elite regiment of regulars I had formed several months prior to the battle. These regulars fended off the combined weight of attacks by two Rebel corps, giving time for the remainder of my wing to take up its new position adjacent to McCook.

My new line faced roughly southwest until, on my extreme left, the line curved to join with the right of General Crittenden's wing that had been recalled from its abortive attack and faced east. This curve ran through a section of rocky ground covered by cedar trees known to the locals as Round Forest. By the end of the day, it would be known to our troops as Hell's Half Acre. Round Forest was defended by Colonel William B. Hazen's brigade, dug in on a railroad embankment. The Rebels continued to attack all along the new line, and were repulsed again and again with heavy losses. Hazen's position, being the most exposed, was the focus of the heaviest attacks.

I did my best to strengthen Hazen's position, massing over fifty big guns in the rear of his brigade. As I supervised the placement of the artillery, I could not help but recall the battle of Buena Vista where Captain Bragg and I had manned our guns side by side and fought off Santa Anna's attacks against the salient in General Taylor's line. Now Bragg was my adversary and I would attempt to do to him what he had done to Santa Anna.

In the early afternoon, the force of Hardee's and Polk's attacks was spent and there was a lull in the fighting. Then, at about two pm, a new rebel force appeared in front of Round Forest. These troops were two brigades of General Breckenridge's division that had been posted on Bragg's right and had not yet seen action. This changed in an instant as Breckenridge's men, with a great shout, charged Hazen's position. Hazen's men staggered the attackers with a round of musket fire and then our massed artillery opened fire with a tremendous roar. Almost instantaneously, the Rebel line simply ceased to exist, as the guns blew the attackers away.

With this repulse, I believed that Bragg was probably through for the day, but I was mistaken. At about four pm, the remaining two brigades of Breckenridge's division, reinforced by elements of Polk's corps, formed up in front of Round Forest and the scene of Breckenridge's first charge was repeated. Once again the Rebels surged forward only to be slowed by Hazen's infantry and obliterated by the artillery massed in its rear. Bragg's decision to order this second attack resulted in one of the most useless waste of lives I witnessed during the war.

After Breckenridge was again repulsed, I ordered a limited counterattack to clear the enemy from my immediate front. With this accomplished, the day's fighting came to an end.

The men rested on their guns, cooked a well-earned meal and engaged in the relieved chatter typical of soldiers who have survived sustained combat. The fighting had indeed been intense. The Rebels had fought bravely, mounting attack after attack against withering musket and artillery fire. My men had performed extremely well. Though forced from their original position when Sheridan withdrew his division, they did not panic. Instead, after withdrawing in good order to a new line, they exhibited a rock-steady determination to hold their position against a series of fierce attacks.

The battle had been fought on ground so rocky that in many places the blood of the wounded and dead was prevented from seeping into the soil. Bloody pools had formed and now, as evening fell, the blood was reflected by the flames of the men's campfires, giving the battlefield an eerie quality. After seeing that the wounded were being properly tended to, I rode among the men to give them my thanks and to listen to their conversations. Despite the hard fighting they had endured, I found that their morale was good and they appeared ready to take on the enemy again the following day.

About ten pm, Rosecrans summoned his senior commanders to his headquarters for another council of war. After a day in the saddle, my back was causing me great pain and after seating myself at the table, I closed my eyes and tried to relax my back muscles. I must have dozed off because the next thing I remember is General Rosecrans asking me whether I could protect the army's rear if he were to order a retreat the next morning

General Rosecrans' question startled me. After an early setback, owing to McCook's lack of preparation, the army had fought well. The infantry occupied a strong position, supported by a large force of artillery. Without hesitation, I replied to Rosecrans, "This army does not retreat."

This put an end to any discussion of a withdrawal. Rosecrans decided that the Army of the Cumberland would remain in place the next day and see what General Bragg intended to do.

All through that New Year's Eve a cold rain fell. The discomfort of the troops was exacerbated by Rosecrans' order that all campfires be extinguished to prevent the enemy from ascertaining the position of our troops.

New Year's day 1863 was generally quiet with only sporadic firing up and down the lines. I spent most of the day riding among my troops, giving them words of encouragement.

General Bragg, perhaps having expected us to retreat after the first day's fighting, took no action that day beyond ordering Wheeler's cavalry to harass our lines of communication, including the wagons carrying the wounded back to Nashville. The movement of our wagons reinforced Bragg's conclusion that he had won the battle and that we were in the process of retreating. Instead, Rosecrans ordered Crittenden to send Van Cleve's division, now commanded by Colonel Samuel Beatty, following Van Cleve's wounding the previous day, to cross the river and extend our left.

Sleet and snow fell that night but ceased toward morning. We awoke at dawn to a cold, gray day. Throughout the morning and early afternoon, sporadic musket fire again played up and down the line, and Rosecrans ordered that Beatty's position east of the river be strengthened by additional artillery. On high ground directly across the river from Beatty, Captain John Mendenhall, Crittenden's chief of artillery, positioned 45 guns. Another 12 guns were deployed about a mile to the southwest, on Beatty's right, in perfect position to provide enfilading fire against any Rebel attempt to ford the river.

Late in the afternoon, around four pm, Bragg ordered Breckenridge to capture the high ground on his right, occupied by Beatty's division, despite the fact that Breckenridge's division had been mauled on the first day of fighting. Breckenridge threw his men into the attack and, once again, the results were disastrous for the Rebels. After some initial success in driving Beatty's line, Breckenridge's division was hit with the full force of the artillery massed behind and to the right of Beatty. The artillery fire devastated the enemy troops, halting their attack. I ordered General Negley to counterattack with his division and the Rebels were driven back to their original line. Breckenridge lost at least one-third of his division in this attack.

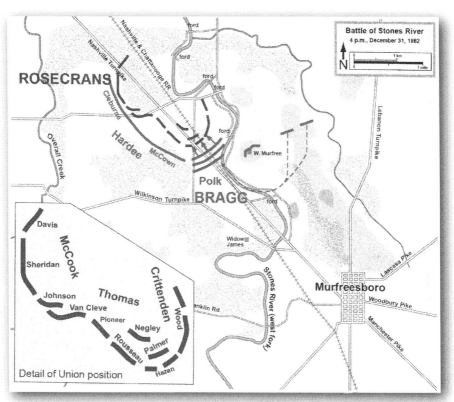

Battle of Stones River (Map by Hal Jespersen, www.cwmaps.com)

The following day, January 3rd, I attacked the center of the Rebel line with two regiments of Rousseau's division to end the enemy sharpshooting that was harassing my troops. The attack drove the Rebels from their entrenchments and captured about 30 prisoners. This sally brought an end to the battle of Stones River. Bragg retreated that night, withdrawing about thirty-five miles south to Tullahoma, Tennessee. Rosecrans occupied Murfreesboro on January 5th. After convening a council of war, he elected not to pursue the retreating Rebels.

I fully concurred in General Rosecrans' decision. The battle of Stones River had seen some of the hardest and bloodiest fighting of the entire war. We suffered almost 13,000 casualties. Rebel losses must have been substantially higher. The casualties on both sides probably exceeded thirty percent of the total forces engaged.

Our heavy losses, coupled with the problems caused by the winter weather, made it virtually impossible for us to advance with any hope of catching the Rebels and bringing them to a successful battle. The Army of the Cumberland would need reinforcements and resupply before it was ready for another fight.

Our success in driving the Rebels from Middle Tennessee provided a much-needed boost to Northern morale. Just two weeks before Stones River, the Army of the Potomac, commanded by General Burnside, had sustained a disastrous defeat at Fredericksburg, Virginia. On January 1st, the same day the Battle of Stones River commenced, President Lincoln had signed the Final Emancipation Proclamation.

Defeat of the Army of the Cumberland at Stones River, on the heels of the debacle at Fredericksburg, may well have fatally sapped Northern support for emancipation and for the continuation of the war. President Lincoln acknowledged the importance of our victory at Stones River in a letter to Rosecrans, composed after the General's removal as commander of the Army of the Cumberland: "I can never forget, whilst I remember anything, that about the end of last year and the beginning of this, you gave us a hard-earned victory, which, had there been a defeat instead, the nation could hardly have lived over."

In my visits with the men after Stones River, I questioned them about their views concerning the Final Emancipation Proclamation, as I had done after the issuance of the Preliminary Proclamation the previous April. Most of the men viewed the measure favorably. Some expressed strong anti-slavery views but most, having battled the Rebels for almost two years, supported emancipation because they believed it would shorten the war. Very few believed that black men would fight effectively, but they calculated that negro soldiers could serve as garrison troops and laborers, freeing-up more white soldiers for combat.

Up until early 1863, the Administration's policy had been to conciliate white Southerners in an attempt to convince them to abandon support for secession. I had become increasingly frustrated by this policy, as the civilian population continued to be openly hostile and to provide aid and support for the Rebel cavalry raiding behind our lines. Shortly after issuance of the Emancipation Proclamation, I made my views known to General Halleck, writing him: "The conciliatory policy has failed and however much we regret the necessity, we shall be compelled to send disloyal people of all ages and sexes to the South or beyond our lines. Secession has so degraded their sense of honor that it is impossible to find one tinctured with it who can be trusted. Removal of hostile civilians would free our troops to penetrate and occupy the insurgent territory with more certainty as we would not then be under the necessity of keeping up with such strong guards in our rear to secure our lines of communication."

Halleck approved my proposal and we soon began to round up Rebel sympathizers, removing them to locations where they could no longer cause us trouble. Fearing that the new policy would encourage pillaging and other depredations, I served notice that such conduct would not be tolerated, and unnecessary destruction of civilian property was a relatively rare occurrence.

Chapter 18

Our victory at Stones River had not opened the way to Chattanooga since Bragg had only retreated to Tullahoma, about seventy-five miles northwest of Chattanooga. Chattanooga remained our objective, being one of the key transportation centers of the Confederacy. The Nashville and Chattanooga Railroad ran north-south between the two cities and served as our army's supply line. The East Tennessee and Virginia, running northeast through Knoxville and into Virginia was the sole railroad connecting Virginia and the western theater. Lee's army in Virginia relied on it for food and supplies and for the rapid movement of troops between east and west. A third line ran south to Atlanta, making Chattanooga the gateway to the Deep South. A fourth connected Chattanooga to Memphis in Western Tennessee on the Mississippi River.

Rosecrans advised Halleck that he was confident he could capture Chattanooga but that the Army of the Cumberland needed to be resupplied and reinforced, especially with cavalry, before it could undertake another campaign. He also explained to Halleck that the winter weather had made the roads impassable and that he could not commence his campaign until spring.

Halleck, in an effort to convince Rosecrans to immediately move against Bragg and Chattanooga, employed a combination of threats of removal and promises of promotion, but Rosecrans proved impervious to Halleck's tactics. Rosecrans often complained to me about the pressure he was under to prematurely commence the campaign and on all of such occasions, I assured him of my support.

While in Murfreesboro, Rosecrans again reorganized the command structure of the army, creating four infantry corps and a corps of cavalry. I was again given command of the XIV Corps, now comprised of four divisions, commanded by Brigadier General Absalom Baird, Major General James S. Negley, Brigadier General Milton Brannan and Major General Joseph Reynolds. General McCook was given command of the newly-formed XX Corps, comprised of three divisions, and General Crittenden commanded the XXI Corps, also containing three divisions.

The Army of Kentucky consisting of two divisions commanded by Major General Gordon Granger was merged into the Army of the Cumberland and designated as the Reserve Corps. Granger was a West Point graduate and career army officer who had served with distinction in Mexico under Winfield Scott and on the frontier. He was to become one of the heroes at the Battle of Chickamauga.

General Stanley remained in command of our cavalry forces, now organized into a corps, comprised of two divisions. He was replaced by Brigadier General Robert B. Mitchell prior to the Battle of Chickamauga.

In the spring of 1863, when Grant began his siege of Vicksburg, Halleck increased his pressure on Rosecrans to move against Bragg, threatening to transfer troops from the Army of the Cumberland to Vicksburg to reinforce Grant. Rosecrans continued to resist Halleck's exhortations, believing the army was not quite ready to commence its campaign.

By mid-June, Rosecrans was satisfied with the condition of the army. On June 24th, we marched out of our camps around Murfreesboro, bound for Tullahoma and Bragg's army on our way to Chattanooga. The campaign from Murfreesboro to Chattanooga proved to be Rosecrans' finest hour. It consisted of a brilliant series of rapid and deceptive maneuvers that had no equal during the war and that resulted in the capture of Chattanooga with minimum casualties.

Bragg had his headquarters on the Duck River at Tullahoma, with his forces spread out along a chain of hills northwest of town, known as the Highland Rim. This position appeared strong because an attacking army could only advance by passing through several heavily defended mountain gaps.

Rosecrans divided his forces into several columns sending Stanley's cavalry and Granger's Reserve Corps swinging wide to the west to get around Bragg's left flank at Shelbyville, hoping to deceive Bragg into thinking this movement was the main Federal attack. Crittenden's XXI Corps marched east to get around Bragg's right flank. The main thrust of our attack was aimed at two mountain gaps in the center of Bragg's line. McCook's XX Corps and my XIV Corps advanced toward these gaps.

While encamped at Murfreesboro, I had implemented new training methods, having concluded that most of the maneuvers in the training manual were designed for the parade ground and were as useless on the battlefield as dancing lessons. In place of these maneuvers, I employed simplified drills designed to simulate actual battlefield conditions.

I knew, however, that all training, no matter how necessary, is nothing to the training which is done in the face of death. I determined that my men would learn the art of war in the field, the only school of practical instruction.

I explained my thinking to my staff one night at dinner. "Put a plank six inches wide five feet above the ground and a thousand men will walk it easily. Raise it five hundred feet and one man out of a thousand will walk it safely. It is a question of nerve we have to solve not dexterity. It is not to touch elbows and fire a gun but to have to do them under fire. We are all cowards in the presence of immediate death. We can overcome that fear through familiarity. Southerners are more accustomed to violence and therefore more familiar with death. What we have to do is to make veterans."

"McLellan's great error was in his avoidance of fighting. His congratulatory report was 'All quiet on the Potomac.' The result was a loss of morale. His troops came to have a mysterious fear of the enemy."

As we approached the enemy at Tullahoma, I instituted a constant series of reconnaissance patrols to accustom the men to being in the presence of the enemy. I maintained this practice for the remainder of the war and, in this way, I took the raw material provided me and shaped it into an army of veterans.

Throughout our march to Tullahoma, heavy rain fell, turning the roads to mud and drenching the men as we advanced. Nevertheless, we moved as rapidly as possible toward our objective, Hoover's Gap, which was heavily defended by Rebel cavalry. In the front of my column was Colonel Wilder's Lightning Brigade of mounted infantry, armed with their Spencer repeating rifles. Wilder's men, in the aggressive and efficient manner that was to become their hallmark, scattered the enemy cavalry and poured through Hoover's Gap before the Rebels could bring up infantry support. When the Rebel infantry did arrive, Wilder's men easily repulsed them.

Only the incessant rain kept us from reaching Bragg's rear and cutting him off from his base at Chattanooga. As it was, Bragg found himself with strong Federal forces on both of his flanks and in his front. He had no choice but to retreat across the Elk River and take up a defensive position at Chattanooga. We gave chase but the continued heavy rain and the lack of pontoons or boats to cross the Elk River forced us to give up the effort.

We paused at Tullahoma to plan the next phase of the campaign. The advance to Chattanooga was fraught with logistical difficulties. To reach the city, we would have to cross both the Cumberland Mountains and the Tennessee River. There were few roads through the mountains and these were little more than rutted wagon trails, totally inadequate for the movement of an army. Once across the mountains, the route to the Tennessee River was heavily wooded, dotted with a few poor farms, meaning we would find no forage for our animals. Our reconnaissance parties reported that the Rebels had destroyed all the bridges across the Tennessee River and had moved all of the available boats to the far shore. Once we managed to cross the river, we would have to traverse massive Lookout Mountain, which protected Chattanooga from the south.

My engineers and pioneers set about the task of improving the existing roads and cutting new ones through the mountain passes. We also made necessary repairs to the Nashville and Chattanooga Railroad, our only supply line, and constructed supply depots along our route to store forage, rations and other supplies for the army on its march. In addition, we fabricated the pontoon bridges we would need to ford the Tennessee River.

Once again Halleck either did not understand or, as is more likely, pretended not to understand the enormous logistical problems we had to overcome to reach Chattanooga. He sent dispatch after dispatch insisting that Rosecrans move immediately on Chattanooga to follow up the recent Northern victories at Gettysburg and Vicksburg. Rosecrans was infuriated by Halleck's refusal to defer to his judgment as the commander on the ground.

At a council of his senior commanders, Rosecrans shared with us the string of telegrams between him and Halleck and read to us his proposed response to Halleck's most recent dispatch, in which he pointed out that he was energetically engaged in overcoming the many logistical difficulties faced by the army and pointing out the dangers to the army if it moved before these difficulties were overcome. "That's right," I said, after he read his proposed reply. "Stand by that and we will stand by you to the last." Everyone in attendance loudly concurred in this sentiment.

Rosecrans also used this occasion to explain his plan for our movement against Chattanooga. Once again, he intended to rely on speed and deception, this time to force Bragg to either fight outside his defensive works or abandon Chattanooga.

Specifically, Crittenden's corps would advance in three columns to the north of Chattanooga to deceive Bragg into believing that this was the route of our main attack. Actually McCook's and my corps would constitute the major attacking force, crossing the mountains and fording the river south of the city, then making our way over and around Lookout Mountain, turning Bragg's position.

On August 6th, Crittenden began his march north. As we hoped, this movement distracted Bragg's attention from our approach from the south. Our diversion was augmented by Wilder's Lightning Brigade that arrived on the north bank of the Tennessee River opposite Chattanooga on August 21st and briefly shelled the city.

On August 29th, I began crossing the Cumberland Mountains with McCook crossing to my south. I arrived at the Tennessee River unobserved by the enemy on September 4th, and we began our crossing that night.

The crossing of the Tennessee was one of the most dramatic scenes I witnessed during the war. All the bridges over the river had been destroyed by the enemy. I selected two locations for my corps to cross. Large rafts we had constructed were dragged to the riverbank and launched into the water. My men had been practicing in secret for two weeks, and troops, horses and wagons were crowded onto the rafts and ferried across the water by specially trained oarsmen. Other men, who had been singled out for their swimming prowess, jumped into the water and hung onto the rafts, helping to guide them to shore.

I rode back and forth between the two crossing points assuring myself that all was proceeding according to plan. I was never prouder of my men then I was that dark and moonless night. The tread of boots as they boarded the rafts by the flicker of torchlight, the whinnies of reluctant horses and the creaking and groaning of the wagons and caissons as they were loaded aboard the rafts all mingled with the lapping of the oars and the splashing of the swimmers as the rafts made their way across the murky water. So many things could have gone wrong and I worried about them all. Yet the men carried it all off without a hitch. By the morning of September 5th, my entire corps was across the river.

The crossing of fourteen hundred foot Lookout Mountain still remained. My corps crossed over Stevens Gap, the first pass south of the Tennessee River, and on the evening of September 8th, I reported to Rosecrans that I had reached the top of the mountain and held Steven's Gap. On the same day, McCook reached Winston Gap, the next pass in

Lookout Mountain. Bragg's position was now turned and he elected to evacuate Chattanooga the next day, marching south on the road leading to Rome, Georgia.

Rosecrans' campaign from Murfreesboro to Chattanooga had been a brilliantly conceived and executed triumph. While incurring less than 600 casualties, we had captured one of the major strategic centers in the South and forced the Army of Tennessee out of the state for which it was named.

Chapter 19

After the capture of Chattanooga, Rosecrans began to lose his footing. Our forces were widely scattered and Bragg's intentions were unclear. Rosecrans' excitable temperament began to get the better of him and, euphoric over his recent successes, he convinced himself that the Rebels were in full retreat.

It is also possible that Halleck's ceaseless admonitions urging Rosecrans to display a more aggressive attitude clouded his judgment. In any event, Rosecrans reckoned that he could intercept the fleeing Rebels and destroy Bragg's army before it had the chance to establish a strong defensive line.

I urged Rosecrans to consolidate our widely scattered forces in Chattanooga and ascertain Bragg's true intentions before moving after him. "Don't risk the gains you have made by striking blindly at the enemy," I advised him. "We know that Bragg has been reinforced by troops from Mississippi and we have reliable information that Buckner is on his way with additional troops from Knoxville and that Longstreet is bringing his corps from Virginia. Unite our army here in Chattanooga, determine as best we can Bragg's strength and his dispositions, and then move against him in strength."

For one of the few times in our relationship, Rosecrans disregarded my advice. "No, no," he told me. "We have Bragg on the run. He is fleeing toward Dalton. I will overtake him, cut off his retreat and crush him. We will win a victory that will make Grant's capture of Vicksburg seem like a skirmish and silence Halleck once and for all." From Rosecrans' tone, I recognized that his mind was made up and took my leave.

Rosecrans' new Chief of Staff, Brigadier General James Garfield, walked with me to my horse. Garfield was a particularly affable and self-confident young man who favorably impressed almost everyone. Rosecrans' mercurial temperament and non-stop work habits made Garfield's role as Chief of Staff quite challenging, but he handled his duties superbly.

I knew that Rosecrans valued Garfield's judgment and so, before mounting my horse, I ventured the following: "Garfield, I believe very strongly that General Rosecrans is misinterpreting the enemy's movements. If I am correct, he is placing our army in serious jeopardy. I have failed to persuade him to my view. I believe you would be doing him and our army a great service if you could convince him to consolidate our forces at Chattanooga before pursuing Bragg. I would not normally make such a request to you, but I believe the situation demands that I do so."

Garfield paused, weighing his words carefully. He was obviously reluctant to say or do anything that might be construed as critical of Rosecrans. Finally, he said, "I think the case you have presented is a strong one, General Thomas. It seems to me that it has much to recommend it. I will speak to the General and see if he will reconsider his decision."

Unfortunately, Garfield had no more success than I in changing Rosecrans' mind. He told me later that Rosecrans had come close to losing his volcanic temper when Garfield had raised the subject, ending the discussion with a curt, "You are dismissed, Garfield."

Garfield had a bright future as either a line or staff officer. He chose, however, to leave the army in 1864 to successfully run for a seat in

Congress from Ohio. In 1864, when I assumed command of the army in Nashville, I wrote to him asking him to resign his House seat and serve under my command in whatever capacity he wished. In reply, Garfield expressed his thanks for my confidence in him, but declined my offer, stating his belief that he could best serve the cause of the Union by remaining in Congress.

As we were to learn to our regret, I had been correct in concluding that Bragg was not in full-scale retreat. Heavily reinforced to a strength that would soon reach 70,000, he had withdrawn to Lafayette, Georgia, about thirty miles due south of Chattanooga, with the intention of assuming the offensive.

Rosecrans sent three of his corps down the east side of Lookout Mountain in pursuit. Once again, I occupied the center, with Crittenden and McCook on my right and left. My corps began its descent on the morning of September 9th through a little valley called McLemore's Cove. From there, I was to advance east through Dug Gap over Pigeon Roost Mountain. I sent Negley's division into McLemore' Cove with orders to halt and await the arrival of General Brannan's division before advancing through Dug Gap. The next day, I rode into McLemore's Cove with General Brannan's troops and deployed them next to Negley's division.

I was extremely uneasy about our position. Once the three corps had descended from Lookout Mountain, we were widely scattered over a forty mile front with nothing but wilderness between us. When we reached McLemore's Cove, Bragg's forces were closer to me than I was to either McCook or Crittenden. If, as I suspected, Bragg was not retreating, but was reforming for an attack on the far side of Pigeon Roost Mountain, he might be able to defeat each of the three Federal corps in detail before we could unite.

I probed Dug Gap and found it heavily defended, confirming my concern that Bragg had not retreated, but was seeking an opening to attack us. Despite Rosecrans' orders, I directed Negley and Brennan to withdraw from McLemore's Cove and notified Rosecrans that the

Rebels were present in force on my front. I again urged Rosecrans to unite the army before proceeding south.

Bragg had indeed planned to attack Negley's and Brannan's divisions in McLemore Cove and to simultaneously attack Crittenden's corps. Fortunately for us, discord between Bragg and his subordinates delayed these attacks, affording Rosecrans, who had finally realized the danger he was in, time to reunite his army.

Rosecrans now ordered McCook, Crittenden and me to rendezvous at Lee and Gordon's Mill on the Lafayette Road on the east bank of Chickamauga Creek. On the morning of September 18th, the Army of Tennessee attempted to cross Chickamauga Creek at Alexander's Bridge and Reed's Bridge north of Lee and Gordon's Mill in an attempt to turn our left flank. These bridges were defended by Union cavalry that were able to delay Bragg's advance. Wilder's Lightning Brigade particularly distinguished itself, holding off an entire Rebel corps at Reed's Bridge for over five hours.

Late in the afternoon of September 18th, Bragg finally secured the two crossings, putting him in position to outflank us the following morning. At about four o'clock, I met with General Rosecrans at his headquarters at the Gordon-Lee Mansion. It was now obvious that Bragg's plan was to get behind us, block our route back to Chattanooga and trap and destroy us.

The only way to prevent being outflanked on the left was to extend our line to the north, beyond the position on our far left occupied by Crittenden's corps. We agreed that I would march my corps north, past Crittenden's corps, to a point near the junction of Reed's Bridge and the Lafayette Road, the main north-south artery leading back to Chattanooga. We originally considered delaying the march until dawn, but soon abandoned this idea, recognizing that the threat to the army was too great.

On the night of September 18th, I put my entire corps in motion to take up its new position on the left of the Federal line. Night marches are always difficult, none more so than this one. The night was dark and moonless, the dirt roads over which we traveled rocky and rutted. The men and horses struggled to make their way in the pitch dark often stumbling over unseen obstacles in their path. Officers struggled to insure that no units lost their way, since it would be all too easy to take a wrong turn and wind up behind enemy lines.

We traveled over six miles that night and, for me, the march was agony. Not being able to see the road, my horse often stepped into ruts, sending shivers of pain down my back. Often I would detour from the road to allow troops or artillery to pass, travelling over even more uneven ground. As dawn approached, we reached Kelly's Field, our objective. Even then, I was reluctant to dismount, fearing that the pain and stiffness in my back would prevent me from remounting later.

I deployed one division north of Kelly's Field facing north and the remaining divisions facing east in a line running south through Kelly's Field, crossing the Lafayette Road and linking up with Crittenden's left. I was now confident that our line extended beyond the Rebel's right, making it difficult for Bragg to outflank us.

On the morning of September 19th, I received a report of an isolated group of Rebels between Kelly's Field and Chickamauga Creek. Not wanting to lose the opportunity of bagging this enemy force, I sent elements from my left to probe the area. They found Nathan Bedford Forrest's dismounted cavalry. I ordered General Palmer of Crittenden's corps to take his division and attack Forrest's men on the flank, while I met them head on. I was sure that Forest would send for reinforcements, and I intended to whip them in detail. I communicated my plan to Rosecrans and requested that he order the rest of Crittenden's corps to join my attack from the south.

General Rosecrans rejected my plan. Instead of ordering Crittenden to reinforce me, he ordered me to terminate my attack and to take up a strong defensive position. With this order, the initiative passed to the Rebels and we did not regain it for the remainder of the battle.

Chapter 20

It would be hard to imagine terrain less suitable for a battlefield than the ground between Lafayette Road and Chickamauga Creek, where the Battle of Chickamauga was fought over the next two days. The ground was heavily forested, and dense thickets grew between the trees, limiting visibility and impeding all attempts to move units in concert. The only break in the forest was provided by a few small farmsteads. The roads through the forest were little more than dirt tracks, totally useless for the movement of wagons and artillery.

After Rosecrans ordered me back to a defensive position, Forrest was reinforced by infantry units and fighting raged up and down the line from Kelly's Field south to Lee and Gordon's Mill. The heaviest Rebel attacks were aimed at my position on the north or left flank of our army. Bragg was intent on turning our flank and placing his army between us and Chattanooga.

When a Rebel attack drove us back, we would reform the lines, counterattack and drive back the Rebels in turn. The dense underbrush made it impossible to maintain the cohesion of our attacking units, since each man had to clear his own way through the thickets. Our attacks were also hindered by the lack of visibility in the dense undergrowth. Visibility was made even worse because sparks from the men's muskets set off countless fires in the dry brush, creating a dense pall of smoke over the battlefield. While our attacks met with initial success in pushing the enemy back, the officers were forced to halt the men to reform their units, preventing us from routing the Rebels.

I initially took up a position on a knoll slightly in the rear of Kelly's Field, from which I expected to have a good view from which to direct the progress of our arms. However, the dense smoke and thick foliage made it impossible for me to see the fighting. I therefore mounted my horse and rode closer to the action. While my view of the field was still poor, I was at least in position to more quickly receive reports from my division commanders and to dispatch orders to them.

The fighting continued back and forth throughout the day, reaching a fury of musket fire in the late afternoon unmatched in any other battle in which I ever participated. Darkness finally brought the day's fighting to a close. Despite heavy casualties, neither side had gained an advantage.

At about eight pm, I received word that General Rosecrans was convening a council of war. Before riding to his headquarters at the Widow Glenn's house, which stood southwest of my position, I ordered that my men construct breastworks.

I was bone tired and suffering from intense back pain as I rode to Rosecrans' headquarters. When the council got underway, I suggested to Rosecrans that if I was reinforced, I could launch a counterattack and break the Rebel line. I described for Rosecrans the manner in which the divisions of Generals Palmer and Johnson had broken a Rebel attack that day and launched a counterattack that gained initial success. "Whenever I touched their flanks," I told Rosecrans, "they broke, General, they broke."

But Rosecrans had no interest in taking the offensive, and I soon lost interest in the meandering discussion that ensued. On each occasion that Rosecrans asked for my opinion, I replied simply, "I would reinforce our left." I was impatient to get back to my command and continue my preparations and silently chafed as the discussion went on and on. Since

Rosecrans had decided to stay on the defensive and await the Rebel attack, what more was there to talk about?

When Rosecrans at last brought the conference to a close around midnight, I got up to leave only to have him request that McCook, who was reputed to be a fine singer, entertain us with a song. This was more than I could bear. "At the risk of being rude," I said, "I have a long night ahead of me and must not delay any longer." I saluted Rosecrans and left the room. Mounting my horse, I made my way back to my lines.

The night brought with it its own horrors. The brush fires continued to burn between the lines, and the cries of the wounded unable to move out of the fire's path filled the darkness. We did what we could to locate the wounded and bring them back into our lines, but heavy smoke, flames and enemy musket fire meant that many poor souls perished in a most terrible fashion that night.

I inspected the new breastworks thrown up in Kelly's Field and gave their defenders encouragement that we would whip the Rebels in the morning. Next, I visited our hastily constructed field hospital as the wounded, many of them suffering burns in addition to their battle wounds, were brought in. I gave them what little comfort I could, all the while thinking that my fellow corps commanders could make better use of their time by seeing to it that their wounded were being properly cared for rather than by listening to General McCook's serenade.

During the night, we also questioned the prisoners we had captured. Many were from Bruckner's Mississippi army demonstrating that Bruckner was indeed on the field. In addition, some of the captives were from Lee's Army of Northern Virginia, confirming the rumors that Longstreet had been sent to reinforce Bragg. Although it was clear that Bragg's army had been augmented, we were unable to determine the extent of his reinforcements.

At about two am, I received word from General Baird, manning the extreme left of my line, that he lacked sufficient manpower to extend his line north to Reed's Bridge Road as he had been ordered. I rode out to see for myself and discovered that Polk, who commanded the right wing of Bragg's army, had extended his right about a quarter mile past my left. I immediately sent a message to Rosecrans advising him of this development and requesting that he send me Negley's division, which had been detached from my command the previous day.

The night passed quickly as I readied my forces for what I anticipated would be a dawn attack. For the second straight night, I got no sleep. Rosecrans, wishing to be prepared for an attack anywhere along his line, pulled Crittenden's corps out of the front lines to serve as a reserve and shifted McCook's corps northward to link up with my right.

Chapter 21

Dawn on September 20th broke without the expected Rebel attack. General Rosecrans arrived at my headquarters at around six am, and together we toured my lines from north to south. Rosecrans noted for himself the danger we faced at Reed's Bridge Road and dispatched a messenger with orders for Negley to march north to reinforce me. We proceeded south through Kelly's Field. Here, Rosecrans left me, again promising to send Negley's division as quickly as possible. This was the last I saw of General Rosecrans for over forty-eight hours.

About an hour after Rosecrans left me, I heard sporadic musket fire coming from the left flank. Desultory firing continued for about an hour, when D.H. Hill's corps of Polk's wing commenced a series of heavy attacks all along my lines. Fighting behind their hastily constructed breastworks, my men repulsed these attacks at great cost to the Rebels.

At about eleven am, there was a lull in the fighting, and I feared that Polk and Hill were shifting to the north to get around my left flank. I had no troops with which to match such a movement, Negley not yet having arrived. I sent another message to Rosecrans asking where Negley was and suggesting that if he could not come quickly, Rosecrans send me whatever troops he had available.

At the same time, we were repulsing Hill's assaults, a series of missteps to my south were about to culminate in disaster. Word was brought to Rosecrans that General Brannan's division had moved north to reinforce me and that a gap therefore existed in the Federal line. In fact, there was no gap. Brannan had his troops deployed in thick woods somewhat back from the troops of Reynold's division on his left. A staff officer riding down the line mistakenly thought that Brannan had vacated his position and reported this to Rosecrans.

Rosecrans could easily have sent a staff officer to confirm whether Brannan had pulled his division out of the line, but he failed to do so. Instead, he simply assumed the accuracy of the report and dictated an order to General Thomas Wood, who occupied the position on Brannan's right, intended to plug the non-existent gap. The order read "The general commanding directs that you close upon Reynolds as fast as possible to support him."

Wood received this order shortly before eleven am just about the time my troops were repelling the last of D.H. Hill's attacks on our position in Kelly's Field. To Wood, who was aware that Brannan was still in position on his left, the order was ambiguous and confusing. Because Brannan was in line between his division and Reynolds, the only way he could support Reynolds was to take his troops out of line and march behind Brannan until he reached the rear of Reynold's division. Wood was an experienced division commander and surely must have questioned whether this was what Rosecrans actually intended.

Wood was less than two miles from Rosecrans' headquarters and could easily have ridden there to get a clarification of Rosecrans' order. But now, Rosecrans became a victim of his inability to control his temper. Earlier that morning, Rosecrans had ordered Wood to relieve Negley's division in preparation for sending Negley to my aid. Sometime after this order was given, Rosecrans discovered that Wood had not yet started his movement and flew into one of his infamous rages, loudly and profanely berating Wood in front of both of their staffs.

Wood had no taste for a repeat of this incident and therefore, without seeking clarification from Rosecrans, he moved with alacrity to comply with Rosecrans' order, pulling his division out of line and marching north to locate Reynolds. Rosecrans order, therefore, had the effect of creating a real gap in the line in an attempt to plug a purely imaginary one.

Wood's timing could not have been worse. By a stroke of ill-luck, General Longstreet, commanding Bragg's left wing, launched a massive attack directed at the precise spot just vacated by Wood. The Rebels, finding the position to their front undefended, poured through the gap and expanded it to the north and south, routing the entire right wing of the Union army and sending it fleeing over McFarland Gap all the way back to Chattanooga. Only the Lightning Brigade, on the extreme right of the Federal Line, maintained its position, even attempting a counter-attack.

I was unaware of the collapse of the army's right wing when the lull in the fighting on my front gave me the opportunity to ride south to try to scare up the reinforcements I had been requesting all morning. Reaching the top of a small rise, I received one of the great shocks of my life. Where I had expected to see Sheridan's division of McCook's corps, I saw instead only gray and butternut clad troops. Spurring my horse, I galloped back to my own lines.

Until that moment, I had assumed that Bragg was concentrating his strength against my position and that his remaining forces were sufficient only to keep up a demonstration against the Union right. It was now apparent that the enemy was present in far greater numbers than I had supposed, allowing Bragg to mount strong attacks against the entire Union line. The Rebels had obviously broken through to my right.

The situation was now critical. It was only a question of time before Longstreet faced his divisions in my direction and struck me in the flank. Although I was not yet aware of the full dimensions of the catastrophe that had befallen Rosecrans, it was apparent that I could not expect reinforcements any time soon.

I rode over my lines looking for some high ground where we would have a chance to hold off the Rebels. I found suitable ground on a series of hills and ridges near a cabin owned by a farmer named Snodgrass. A small number of Federal units, chased from their original positions, had already reformed here, and I rode among their officers, telling them that help was coming and that they must hold their position at all costs. I then rode back and forth between Kelly's Field to the east and Snodgrass Ridge moving troops into position to establish a new line.

I placed Brannan's division on a ridge on the right of my new line, facing south. I was very pleased when General Wood's division fought its way to me. Negley occupied the position to the left of Brannan but once Wood arrived, I pulled Negley's division out of line, replacing it with Wood's. The position occupied by Brannan and Wood became known as Horseshoe Ridge.

I directed Negley to round up all the artillery he could find and laid out positions for the placement of the guns when they arrived. Negley assembled forty-eight guns that would have immeasurably aided our cause. However, these guns never reached me. Negley concluded that our situation was hopeless and took his entire division and his forty-eight guns and marched them off the field to Rossville.

As they withdrew from Kelly's Field, I formed the remainder of my forces east of Horseshoe Ridge in a semicircle on Snodgrass Hill facing west and south. Reynolds, Baird, Johnson and Palmer occupied this line from north to south.

My men were still filing into the new lines when Longstreet launched his first attack. The Rebels came rushing up all along our front hollering and yipping in the eerie fashion that had become known as the rebel yell. We met them with a hail of musket fire that sent them tumbling back down the ridge. Time after time the Rebels charged, and time after time we sent them flying. I counted twenty-five separate attacks that afternoon, yet at times the space between attacks was so brief that it seemed like one continuous assault. Fortunately, we had dealt so harshly with Polk's right wing that morning that Polk was unable or unwilling to support Longstreet's attacks until much later in the day.

As the afternoon progressed, our position became ever more critical. We were running low on ammunition and water was scarce. Up until about two pm, Longstreet's attacks had been uncoordinated, but now he was extending his left further and further beyond my right in preparation for launching a massive attack against Wood and Brannan on Horseshoe Ridge. With a combined force of only 2,700 men, it seemed unlikely they could hold off another attack.

As I contemplated shifting troops to reinforce Horseshoe Ridge, I spied a cloud of dust to the north, indicating the approach of a large body of troops. If these were reinforcements, we still had a chance. If they were Rebels, all was lost.

I raised my field glasses to my eyes but it was impossible to see the colors of the advancing force through the dust. As I peered northward, my horse grew balky and his prancing prevented me from steadying my binoculars. I handed them to an aid and asked him if he could ascertain the identity of the advancing force. After about a minute, he shouted, "They are Federals, General."

Relief flooded over me but I was reluctant to accept the good news. "Do you think so? Do you think so?" I shouted. Taking back my field glasses I peered northward just as a breeze cleared away the dust. Now I could clearly see that the approaching troops were clad in blue and carried the American Flag. Despite myself, I gave a loud whoop. My staff, unaccustomed to such displays of emotion from me, were momentarily puzzled, but glancing in the direction of my gaze, they gave shouts of their own.

The advancing troops were Major General James Steedman's division of Granger's Reserve Corps. Granger had been posted about two miles to my northwest. He had been hearing the sounds of battle all day but had received no orders to advance. Finally, his patience at an end, he ordered his men to march toward the sound of the guns. Steedman's division arrived first.

"I am always happy to see you General," I said, when Steedman galloped up to me, "but never more so than right now. How many muskets have you brought with you?"

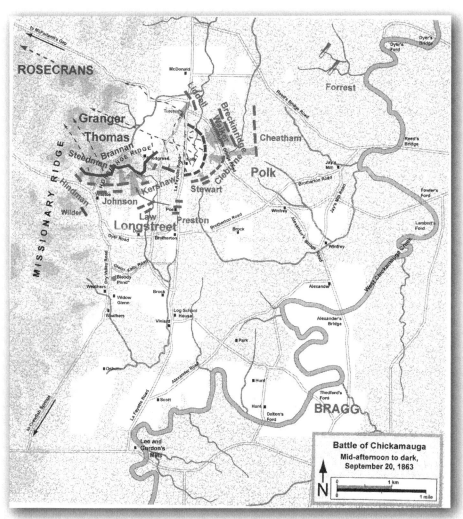

Thomas' stand at Snodgrass Hill and Horseshoe Ridge
(map by Hal Jespersen, www.cwmaps.com)

"About 7,500, he replied. "And they are all at your disposal. Where would you like us?"

"To your right, there," I said pointing to Horseshoe Ridge. "General Longstreet has begun charging that hill and I would be obliged if you would knock him off of it." Steedman saluted, formed his men into line and headed for the charging enemy. He struck them hard just as they had reached the crest of the hill and were poised to break through. The force of his charge sent the rebels careening down the far side of Horseshoe Ridge and Steedman's men followed close at their heels, sending them back into the woods. All along our lines, the men hollered and cheered. When he returned to our lines, I posted Steedman in the center of my position.

Granger soon came up with the remainder of his Reserve Corp. He brought with him 90,000 rounds of ammunition and several artillery pieces. I congratulated and thanked Granger for his initiative in bringing his corps to my aid. In doing so, he had saved the day. I had the ammunition distributed to the men and placed the guns where they could do the most damage. I put most of Granger's men into line but posted the brigade of Daniel McCook to the north and rear of our lines to keep open the road to Rossville and McFarland Gap in case we were required to retreat.

Shortly after three pm, a few minutes after Granger's arrival, General Garfield rode into my lines from the direction of Rossville, located about ten miles northwest of our position, on the road to McFarland's Gap and Chattanooga. He confirmed my suspicion that there were no longer any Federal troops to my south. Crittenden's and McCook's corps had been swept from the field by Longstreet's charge through the gap created by Wood's withdrawal from the line, and were in full flight over McFarland's Gap heading for Chattanooga.

"Where is General Rosecrans?" I asked.

"I left him at Rossville," Garfield replied. "He is on his way back to Chattanooga to organize the city's defenses. He directs that you retreat to Rossville and rejoin the army in Chattanooga as soon as you can."

I was astounded by this news. With almost half his army still engaged with the enemy, Rosecrans had taken himself out of the battle. I could imagine no circumstance that could account for such behavior. At the time, however, I had no time to question Garfield further. I did, however, recall the statement I had made to Halleck, when Rosecrans was named the Commander of the Army of the Cumberland, that I would manage my command so as to protect it from the mistakes of my superiors. Now, I would have to make good on that boast.

I had long since determined that an attempt to withdraw in daylight ran a great risk of destruction. "It will ruin the army to withdraw it now," I explained to Garfield. "This position must be held until night."

After Steedman's charge repelled the assault on Horseshoe Ridge, there was a brief lull in the fighting, but the enemy soon resumed its attacks. Late in the day, Polk's wing rejoined the fight, directing its assaults against Snodgrass Hill on my left. We were hard pressed from the front and both flanks, but continued to fight off the Rebels.

As I sat my horse in the rear of Steedman's division, Steedman approached me. "General Thomas," he said, "we have given the Rebels more than they can handle. I believe that if we counterattack them now, the field will be ours."

I appreciated his aggressive instincts and had myself given some thought to a counter-attack but had decided against it for reasons I now explained. "No, Steedman," I replied. "We are under orders to fall back to Rossville. What is more, the men are exhausted and short of ammunition. It has been a near thing today. I think our best course is to fall back to Rossville, as ordered. There we can regroup, get resupplied and hit Bragg on the march if he moves toward Chattanooga."

As the sky darkened, we began pulling out of our lines and heading toward Rossville. I made the withdrawal by division from east to west. Although the men were exhausted and the enemy poised for another attack, the withdrawal went smoothly. The men knew what they had accomplished and, though weary, were in good spirits. The enemy cavalry attempted to interfere with our retreat, but we brushed them aside with little trouble. My troops filed into Rossville during the night, entrenched and slept on their muskets.

On the march to Rossville, I rode beside General Garfield and at last had time to inquire of him the circumstances under which General Rosecrans had ridden from the battlefield. Garfield had obviously been going over the events of the day in his mind. He spoke slowly and carefully. "The collapse of our position occurred so suddenly that we were taken completely by surprise. Before we had time to react, the men of Sheridan's and Davis' divisions came pouring through our headquarters at the Widow Glenn's house, followed closely by massed columns of the enemy. General Rosecrans and I attempted to rally and reform the men, wading into the torrent with drawn sabers. But our efforts were unavailing. Nothing could stop the flood and it eventually swept us away with it. The Commanding General and I finally reached a fork in the Dry Valley Road a few miles short of McFarland Gap. One fork led over the mountains to Chattanooga and the other toward your lines."

"Here we paused. The General told me that he intended to ride towards your lines to determine your situation. He told me to ride to Chattanooga and began to give me a detailed set of orders concerning the deployment of forces to defend the city. These orders were spoken rapidly and contained intricate instructions for each division. I must admit that I had great difficulty following his instructions and this must have shown on my face."

"'General Garfield,' Rosecrans asked me, 'can you give these orders?'"

"'General, there are so many of them. I fear I might make some mistake; but I can go to General Thomas for you, see how things are, tell him what you will do, and report to you.'"

"The General thought for a moment and then said, 'Very well. I will take Major Bond and give the orders myself. I will be in Chattanooga as soon as possible. There is a telegraph office in Rossville and you can send me reports from there'. And so General Rosecrans proceeded on to Chattanooga and I rode to you."

I pondered Garfield's story in silence. Rosecrans had not just made a poor decision. He knew that I had almost half the army with me and he had no idea what was happening along my lines. As Commanding General, he also knew that his proper place was with the portion of his army still fighting. At the critical moment when he elected to return to Chattanooga, he was a beaten man. He had undoubtedly lost the respect of his soldiers and it was difficult to imagine his regaining their confidence.

In the early hours of September 21st, I completed my dispositions for a stand at Rossville. I waited all morning and afternoon to see if Bragg intended to attack me. His losses during the previous two days of fighting had been so heavy, however, that he did not order an attack. I sent a dispatch to Rosecrans asking for permission to launch an attack of my own. Late that afternoon, I received orders from Rosecrans to fall back to Chattanooga. The Battle of Chickamauga was over.

With the exception of Gettysburg, Chickamauga was the bloodiest battle of the Civil War. The Army of the Cumberland had approximately 58,000 effectives when the fighting began. Sixteen hundred of these men were killed on the battlefield. Another fifteen thousand five hundred men were wounded, captured or missing. I estimate that with the reinforcements he received, Bragg had about 70,000 effectives when the fighting began. His army sustained over eighteen thousand casualties of which about twenty- three hundred were killed.

The Battle of Chickamauga was the saddest chapter in the history of the Army of the Cumberland. However, although we had suffered a setback, we had avoided a disaster thanks to the brave men who were with me at Snodgrass Hill and Horseshoe Ridge.

After reaching my position at Snodgrass Hill, Garfield had managed to get a dispatch through to Rosecrans, alerting him that I was still on the field and describing me as standing "like a rock." The newspapers picked up this story and began writing about me as the "Rock of Chickamauga", a sobriquet that has stuck to me ever since. But I do not deserve this nickname. The brave fellows of that noblest military force the world ever saw made the Rock of Chickamauga, not I. On that sunny September afternoon as they stood in a half circle facing the enemy that again and again poured a superior force three lines deep upon our front, not a man of them but knew that our right had been shattered and our left disorganized, and yet the brave fellows plied their guns, cool, firm and determined. They made success possible under all circumstances.

Chapter 22

We began our withdrawal from Rossville after dark and by seven am the next day my men were manning Bragg's old entrenchments guarding Chattanooga. As soon as I was satisfied with their deployment, I rode in search of Rosecrans. I found him at his headquarters, a large house near the center of our defenses. I was startled by his appearance. In place of the jaunty, energetic and voluble man I knew, he was weary-looking and haggard.

"Ah, General Thomas," he said, looking up and attempting to put some of his former enthusiasm into his voice, "I am very happy to see you. I owe you a great debt of gratitude."

"You owe me nothing, General," I replied. "I did nothing more than my duty." I instantly regretted this comment, concerned that Rosecrans might find in it a tacit suggestion that he had failed to do his. I had meant no such thing, but indeed Rosecrans seemed to find this meaning in my words. He put his head in his hands and muttered more to himself than to me, "I should not have left the field. I should not have left the field. I let the circumstances overwhelm me. It was such a shock to watch my great army crumbling around me. And I could do nothing to prevent it."

I could think of no words of comfort to give Rosecrans and, in any event, he was so distraught that nothing I could say would have consoled him. Therefore, I changed the subject, inquiring about the dispositions he had made to defend the city. Much to my surprise, I learned that Rosecrans had failed to defend Lookout Mountain, south of the City, which Bragg's men occupied without a fight. With the Rebels atop Lookout Mountain, our supply route, which ran along the base of Lookout Mountain from the railroad terminus at Bridgeport, about twenty-five miles to the west, was blocked.

The only way to resupply the army from Bridgeport was via a circuitous route over rough mountain trails north of Chattanooga. Rosecrans' failure to defend Lookout Mountain showed that there was more than a little truth in Lincoln's famous comment that, following Chickamauga, Rosecrans appeared "dazed and confused, like a duck hit on the head."

The next morning Rosecrans and I rode along our lines to inspect our defenses. When the men recognized me, they gathered around, cheered and called my name. Rosecrans was ignored. I would normally have responded heartily to the cheers by doffing my hat, but to prevent further embarrassment to Rosecrans I merely nodded in recognition of the cheering troops. This same scene repeated itself again and again as we rode along the lines. Rosecrans barely spoke on the return ride to his headquarters.

Fortune continued to frown on Rosecrans over the next few weeks. Any prospect of bringing adequate supplies from Bridgeport over the mountains depended on dry weather. Shortly after I arrived in Chattanooga, however, it began to rain heavily. As the days passed and the rain did not abate, the roads, that were little more than rutted trails at the best of times, turned to mud and became virtually impassable for our supply wagons. The men were put on short rations, and while our situation was not yet critical, it was rapidly threatening to become so because we lacked the capability of feeding the horses and mules. More and more animals died every day, and our ability to haul rations over the long mountainous supply line quickly deteriorated. The men would begin to share the fate of the horses and mules unless we could find a way to reopen a direct supply route from Bridgeport.

The only good news to reach us was that General Joseph Hooker, with two corps from the Army of the Potomac, totaling about 23,000 men, was on his way by rail to reinforce us. In an impressive logistical feat, Hooker's men were transported over one thousand miles by railroad in just fourteen days. As there were insufficient rations in Chattanooga to feed Hooker's men, they halted at Bridgeport.

In late September, Charles Dana, the Assistant Secretary of War, who was with the army in Chattanooga, received a telegram from Secretary of War Stanton containing a direction to share its contents with me. The telegram read, "I wish you to go directly to see General Thomas personally; say to him his services, his abilities, his character, his unselfishness, have always been most cordially appreciated by me and that it is not my fault that he was not in chief command months ago."

Dana explained to me that the decision had been made in Washington to replace Rosecrans as commander of the Army of the Potomac and that Lincoln and Stanton had determined that I would be his replacement. I asked Dana to inform Stanton that I was deeply grateful for his kind words but that, rather than replacing Rosecrans, I would prefer to be given an independent command of a new force that I could recruit, organize and train myself. Dana's response to Stanton passed along my thanks but omitted any reference to my preference for a new command.

Before any change was made in the command of the Army of the Cumberland, Lincoln and Stanton determined that the strategic situation required the appointment of a single commander for the entire western theater. By virtue of his victory at Vicksburg, Grant was the obvious choice to command the newly created Department of Mississippi, encompassing virtually all the territory west of the Appalachian Mountains.

On October 18th, Grant assumed his new command while in Louisville meeting with Stanton. Stanton handed Grant two sets of orders. One set of orders kept Rosecrans in command of the Army of the

Cumberland and the other named me as its new commander. Stanton told Grant to choose between them.

My relations with Grant were cool, but actual animosity existed between Grant and Rosecrans. This ill-feeling stemmed from the Battle of Iuka, Mississippi, fought in September of 1862. Prior to this battle, Grant and Rosecrans had been good friends, making their falling out all the more bitter.

At Iuka, Grant, in command of the Army of the Tennessee, and Rosecrans, in command of the Army of the Mississippi, conceived a strategy to trap and crush a Rebel army under Sterling Price. Rosecrans was to attack from the southwest and, upon hearing the sound of Rosecrans' guns, Grant was to send General Ord, with three divisions of the Army of the Tennessee, to attack Price from the northwest, trapping the Rebels between the two Federal armies.

Rosecrans attacked as planned, but Ord's attack never materialized. Although Rosecrans won a limited victory, driving Price from Iuka, the bulk of the Rebel army escaped via a route that should have been blocked by Ord. The newspapers hailed Rosecrans as a hero and excoriated Grant for not launching his attack, some even alleging that Grant had failed to give the order to attack because he was drunk. Grant and Ord insisted that they had not heard the sound of Rosecrans' guns due to an acoustic shadow.

Rosecrans, in private conversations, criticized Grant, blaming him for the failure to destroy Price's army. Reports of these comments reached Grant and, from that time on, Grant and Rosecrans were no longer on speaking terms. There was no doubt that when given the choice between retaining Rosecrans or replacing him with me, Grant would choose the latter course.

On October 19th, the day after being placed in charge of the new Department of Mississippi, Grant sent me word that I was to replace Rosecrans. Since his demand for "unconditional surrender" at Fort Donelson had made him a household name, Grant took great pains to phrase his dispatches in a manner designed to capture favorable public attention. Grant's instructions to me were: "Hold Chattanooga at all hazards. I will be there as soon as possible." This admonition was quite unnecessary, as neither Rosecrans nor I was giving any consideration to abandoning Chattanooga. I read Grant's wire as being intended for the newspapers rather than for me.

Viewing Grant's dispatch in this light, I somewhat puckishly composed a reply calculated to gain even greater attention. I wired Grant, "I will hold the town till we starve." The newspapers reported my reply and the public loved it.

Simultaneously with my receipt of Grant's wire, Rosecrans received a telegram from Grant notifying him of the change in command. It was with some trepidation that I went to see Rosecrans to discuss with him the arrangements for the transfer of command, and to ascertain in detail his plans to reopen the supply line from Bridgeport.

I so hated the politics prevalent in the army, that I wanted Rosecrans to understand that I had not intrigued to oust him from command. I started to explain to him my reluctance to supersede him, when he interrupted me.

"George, we are in the face of the enemy. No one but you can safely take my place. Now, and for the country's sake, you must do it. Don't fear; no cloud of doubt will ever come into my mind as to your fidelity, friendship and honor."

Having set my mind at ease, Rosecrans sent for Brigadier General William E. "Baldy" Smith, who had recently joined the army as its chief engineer. Rosecrans explained to me that he had directed Smith to devise a plan to reopen the army's supply line directly from Bridgeport, and Smith assured me that he was hard at work on this task. The three of us closely examined maps of the area and traded ideas for a possible new supply route.

Shortly after I took over command of the Army of the Cumberland, I made the difficult circuitous ride to Bridgeport to meet with General Hooker, believing it important to inspect his troops to determine their fitness for combat. I knew Hooker slightly, having served with him in Florida during the Seminole War and in Mexico, where he was on General Taylor's staff.

"Fighting Joe" as the newspapers called him, was highly intelligent, with keen military instincts. He was also a braggart and a shameless self-promoter. As a corps commander in the Army of the Potomac, he had been openly contemptuous of both McClellan and Burnside, and had openly lobbied to replace Burnside as commander of the Army of the Potomac.

After Lincoln reluctantly put him in command of the Army of the Potomac, Hooker publicly bragged that he would easily whip Lee's Army of Northern Virginia and end the war. He did manage to outmaneuver Lee, near Chancellorsville, Virginia, putting his army in position to defeat Lee. On the eve of battle, he lost his nerve and pulled his army back, ceding the initiative to Lee and Stonewall Jackson, who promptly thrashed him. When Lee followed up his victory at Chancellorsville by invading Pennsylvania, Lincoln replaced Hooker with George Gordon Meade.

Hooker expressed to me his desire to redeem his reputation by performing well at Chattanooga. At least outwardly, however, he had not lost any of his bluster or braggadocio. I found it distasteful to spend time in his company and made my visit as short as possible. For much the same reasons, Grant detested Hooker.

I found conditions at Bridgeport to be highly unsatisfactory. Hooker's staff was undisciplined and conducted business in a slipshod, haphazard manner. Drinking and gambling occupied most of their spare time. I was unimpressed by most of the senior officers I met, but I found the troops adequately supplied and I was hopeful they would acquit themselves well in the fighting to come.

On October 22nd, back in Chattanooga, Smith presented me with his plan to reopen our supply line. Chattanooga lies on the south bank of the Tennessee River. After flowing west past the city, the river curves sharply south, then west, and then sharply north, creating a loop, before it continues its course north and west. The north bank of this loop is known as Moccasin Point. From Moccasin Point, it is about twenty miles downriver, that is north and west, to Bridgeport and the railroad terminus.

Lookout Mountain rises south of Moccasin Point and therefore the north face of the mountain overlooks the river as it curves west and then north. By occupying Lookout Mountain, Bragg had been able to block supplies from reaching us from Bridgeport via water or land.

Smith suggested the construction of a pontoon bridge crossing the river to Brown's Ferry, about three miles north of Moccasin Point, beyond the range of Bragg's guns on Lookout Mountain. Supplies could then be taken from Bridgeport by wagon along the south bank of the river to Brown's Ferry, across the river over the pontoon bridge and into the city. Supplies could also be sent from Bridgeport to Brown's Ferry by boat, where they could be loaded onto wagons that would cross the pontoon bridge and proceed into the city.

Smith proposed that, under cover of darkness, an elite force be floated downriver from Chattanooga on pontoons towed by assault boats, to seize Brown's Ferry by surprise and establish a bridgehead. Hooker would march upriver from Bridgeport with a sufficient force to hold Brown's Ferry against a counter-attack. The pontoons would be used to construct the bridge across the river that would enable us to bring supplies into Chattanooga.

I thought Smith's plan was brilliant and told him that I wanted him to personally command the operation. I issued orders for Hooker, at Bridgeport, to begin a movement toward Brown's Ferry. I also issued orders for the construction of the pontoon bridges and the assault boats needed to implement Smith's plan. I wired Halleck that I expected to have the supply line open in a few days but was delaying the operation pending approval by Grant, who was expected in Chattanooga momentarily. I had little doubt that Grant would endorse Smith's plan.

About two pm the next day, while I was working with my staff, General Grant arrived at the two story wooden house I was using as my headquarters. He had wired me the previous day from Bridgeport that he planned to arrive in the late afternoon and had requested that my senior officers be assembled to meet with him upon his arrival. Due to his early arrival, none of my senior officers were on hand, causing me a good deal of embarrassment. I immediately sent aides scurrying to round up my corps and division commanders and bade Grant to have a seat by the fire. I sat down on the other side of the fireplace. As usual, we found making conversation difficult.

To reach Chattanooga, Grant had endured a miserable ride through the rain over the same muddy, rutted mountain roads we were using to bring in supplies. HIs discomfort was intensified by the fact that he had recently fallen from his horse and was in pain. In my haste to assemble my senior commanders, I failed to notice that Grant's uniform was wet and muddy or to inquire about whether there was anything I could do to make him more comfortable. Grant, stoic and taciturn by nature, at least with me, said nothing about the difficulties he had endured on his ride from Bridgeport.

Some minutes after Grant's arrival, James Wilson, one of Grant's young aides, later to be the commander of my cavalry corps, entered the room and quickly sized up the situation. Though I hardly knew him, he addressed me in the self-assured manner I later came to know well. "General Thomas, General Grant has had a long ride. He is wet and muddy. Could not one of your staff find some dry clothes for him until his baggage arrives? I am certain a hot meal would also be appreciated."

As soon as Wilson spoke, I realized that I had been remiss. I apologized to Grant for not seeing to his needs earlier, and ordered that the table be immediately prepared for a meal and that clean dry clothes be furnished him. The uneasiness that always existed between Grant and me temporarily vanished during this meal but soon returned. We were simply not comfortable in each other's presence.

Chapter 23

Ulysses Grant had many admirable qualities as a commander. He was energetic and possessed of a bulldog determination. No matter how dire his situation, he always assumed that the enemy was worse off than he, and pressed his attacks unrelentingly. He was a quick thinker on the battlefield and, as he demonstrated at Vicksburg, if his original plan failed, he did not give up, but kept trying different approaches until he found one that worked. He had great self-confidence and strength of will. Quite simply, he would not accept defeat.

All successful commanders need to be lucky, and Grant was favored by fortune to an extraordinary degree. At Fort Donelson, the Rebels launched a successful attack from their fortifications and were on the verge of breaking out of Grant's envelopment, when the Rebel commanders inexplicably ordered their men back to the fort. At Shiloh, if not for the fatal wound suffered by General Johnston and the arrival of Buell's army on the afternoon of the first day's battle, Grant's command might well have been annihilated. Later in the war, at the Battle of the Wilderness in Virginia, General Lee's failure to exploit Grant's exposed right flank until late in the day probably saved the Army of the Potomac from destruction.

Despite Grant's positive qualities, I found much wanting in his abilities as a general. He was not a careful planner. He made little effort to ascertain the enemy's position by gathering intelligence, relying instead on his instincts about what his adversary was likely to do. He paid little attention to map-making and was often unaware of the terrain over which he would be fighting. His strategy usually consisted of locating the enemy and striking with massed force against what he perceived to be its weakest point. He was generally impatient, impulsive and not sufficiently concerned about incurring casualties.

To me, careful planning was essential. I insisted on accurate maps so that I knew the terrain at least as well as my enemy. I oversaw extensive intelligence gathering and analysis concerning all aspects of the enemy's situation, including his strength, location, intentions and even morale, using a network of spies, reconnaissance patrols and the questioning of deserters, prisoners and loyal civilians.

Two years of war had demonstrated to me that the odds in battle favored the defense. Therefore, if possible, I preferred to maneuver so that the enemy was forced to attack me on ground of my own choosing. If required to take the offensive, I avoided uncoordinated attacks, preferring to hurl simultaneous attacks against several points in the enemy's lines. The ability to improvise is a necessary quality in any successful commander, because the course of a battle never goes completely as planned. Nevertheless, it seemed to me only common sense that planning for the most likely contingencies multiplied my chances of success.

Although he liked to portray himself as a simple soldier, Grant was a master politician. Early on in the war, he realized the importance of cultivating political connections, and he used these connections to great advantage. Congressman Elihu Washburne, from Grant's hometown of Galena, Illinois, was his political champion and used every opportunity to advance Grant's career.

Grant was jealous of the success and fame of others and used every opportunity to tear down his enemies, real and imagined. Grant's dealings with John McClernand, an important Democratic politician from Illinois, serves as a good example of Grant's methods.

Before Grant commenced his Vicksburg campaign, President Lincoln, who needed the support of the War Democrats in Illinois, had made McClernand a general and toyed with the idea of giving him command of the Vicksburg campaign. This idea was scrapped when Grant objected and instead McClernand was given command of a corps in Grant's army. Grant feared McClernand as a rival and, although McClernand performed competently as a corps commander, Grant criticized his conduct at every opportunity. Finally, when McClernand issued a statement of congratulations to his corps, giving them the major credit for the success of the Vicksburg campaign, Grant, characterized it as a slight to the rest of his army and used it as a pretext to strip McClernand of his command. Although McClernand was the professional politician and Grant the soldier, McClernand proved no match for Grant's political machinations.

Grant gathered around him a small group of supporters on whom he could rely for unquestioned loyalty and support. As his career advanced, he made sure his friends advanced with him. Chief among these, of course, was William Tecumseh Sherman. Without Grant's support, little might have been heard from Sherman after his panicky exaggeration of enemy strength caused his removal from command of the Department of Kentucky. But Grant never forgot Sherman's loyalty after the near-disaster at Shiloh, and the two developed a deep friendship. Grant was also not unmindful that Sherman's brother, John, was a powerful Republican Senator from Ohio.

As will be related later in these pages, after the battles around Chattanooga, Grant gave Sherman command of the western armies, although Sherman had done little to justify this promotion. At Shiloh, Sherman's refusal to heed warnings of the enemy's approach contributed to the initial rout of the Union forces. His assault on Chickasaw Bluffs in the Vicksburg Campaign was an unmitigated failure and, at Chattanooga, with six divisions at his disposal, his attack on Missionary

Ridge was thwarted by a single Rebel division. His elevation to command the western armies was due solely to his loyalty to Grant and the fact that he did not pose any threat to Grant's continued ascension.

Philip Sheridan, a division commander in the Army of the Cumberland, made a favorable impression on Grant during the fighting at Chattanooga. When Grant went east, he took Sheridan with him, appointing him to command of the Army of the Potomac's cavalry corps, despite the fact that Sheridan had no prior experience commanding cavalry. Sheridan won promotion and lasting fame as a result of his connection with Grant.

At Chattanooga, Grant saw a decisive victory over the Rebels as his stepping stone to promotion as General in Chief. Whether because he viewed me as a potential rival, or because he was intent on enhancing Sherman's reputation, Grant shaped his strategy to minimize my role at Chattanooga, while giving Sherman the opportunity to strike the decisive blow.

In fact, I was not interested in vying with Grant for the position of General in Chief. I was experienced enough to know the importance of political connections in gaining advancement in the army. Being from Virginia, I lacked the support of any influential Republican politicians to advance my cause with the Administration.

More importantly, I lacked both the skill and inclination to curry political favor as Grant did. I saw that my best chance for advancement lay simply in winning battles. I achieved a measure of success in this manner, but Grant saw to it that, after himself, his supporters, principally Sherman and Sheridan, received the lion's share of credit for winning the war.

Chapter 24

On the evening of his arrival in Chattanooga, after Grant had changed into dry clothes and we had eaten dinner, I asked General Smith to explain his plan for reopening our supply line. Smith unfurled a map of Chattanooga and described his plan to Grant, who nodded his understanding and occasionally interjected a question. When Smith had completed his presentation, Grant expressed his preliminary approval but indicated that he wanted to see the ground for himself before giving the final go-ahead.

Before we adjourned for the evening, Grant handed me a letter from Stanton. "You stood like a rock, "the letter read, "and that stand gives you fame which will grow brighter as the ages go by. You will be rewarded by the country and by the Department."

Four days later, I received a note from Grant: "Allow me to congratulate you on your appointment as Brig. Gen. in the regular Army, for the battle of Chickamauga. I have just received a dispatch announcing the fact." While I was gratified by my promotion, it brought home to me the disadvantage of being a Virginian and not having a political sponsor. The promotion put me fifteenth on the list of brigadier generals in the regular army. Those senior to me included Hooker and Sherman.

Early the next morning, Grant, Smith and I rode as far towards Brown's Ferry as the Rebel pickets would allow, with Smith pointing out to Grant the features of the terrain he had shown him on the map the previous evening. Grant expressed himself completely satisfied and directed me to put Smith's plan into effect.

On the night of October 26th, William Hazen's brigade boarded assault boats, towing behind them the pontoons for the construction of the bridge and headed downstream from Chattanooga, floating past the unsuspecting Rebels on Lookout Mountain. The boats rounded the bend in the river at Moccasin Point and, by early morning, reached a point on the east bank of the river opposite Brown's Ferry. Smith had also sent General John B. Turchin's brigade across Moccasin Point to link up with Hazen's men on the east bank. Rebel pickets were scattered and Hazen's and Turchin's men began construction of the pontoon bridge at first light. Meanwhile, Hooker's men, after a late start, arrived at Brown's Ferry from Bridgeport and secured the west bank of the river. Hooker's men drove off a night attack by Longstreet's troops at Wauhatchie, south of Brown's Ferry, securing the bridgehead.

When the pontoon bridge at Brown's Ferry was completed, the supply line from Bridgeport to Brown's Ferry and on into Chattanooga was opened and supplies began to reach the troops. The men dubbed this makeshift route the "cracker line."

I personally oversaw the allocation of supplies to be carried over the cracker line. I determined that sixty carloads of freight a day could be unloaded at the Tennessee River. I directed that thirty-five of these be devoted to subsistence food supplies for men and animals. I divided the remaining carloads among fresh meat, ordnance and other necessities. The supplies we would bring in over the cracker line were not sufficient to allow us to provide the men with full rations until January. Nevertheless, the threat of starvation disappeared and even the partial rations the men began to receive had an immediate positive impact on their morale.

I had hoped that after his march to Brown's Ferry, Hooker would be able to drive the Rebels from Lookout Mountain, but in this he failed. Possession of Lookout Mountain would allow the reopening of the permanent railroad supply line from Bridgeport to Chattanooga, thereby greatly increasing the rate at which the men and animals could be fed. In addition, control of Lookout Mountain would provide our armies with interior lines of communication, allowing us to quickly move troops along our lines where needed.

For these reasons, when Hooker failed to capture Lookout Mountain as part of the operation to open the route from Brown's Ferry, I urged Grant to order Hooker to make a full-scale attack against the Rebel position and drive the enemy from Lookout Mountain. Grant refused my request, believing, as he told me, that the cracker line was sufficient to provide the troops with food and supplies for the remainder of the campaign.

My next step in restoring the morale of the army was to replace the incompetent officers who had failed the men at Chickamauga. McCook and Crittenden were removed from corps command and eventually faced a court of inquiry regarding their conduct at Chickamauga. Negley, who had left the field at Chickamauga with most of my artillery, was denied another field command. I did not stop there but reached down to the division and brigade levels, removing generals and colonels who had lost control of their troops on that field.

To replace these officers, I selected men who had stayed the course with me at Chickamauga. I named John Brannan, who had selected and defended a strong position on Horseshoe Ridge, my chief of artillery. J.J. Reynolds had bought the army valuable time by holding off an entire Rebel corps with a single regiment at Kelly's Field, and I named him my interim chief of staff. Granger, who had marched his men to the sound of the guns, was placed in command of the newly created IV Corps, which combined the former corps of McCook and Crittenden. I named John Palmer, who had kept his division intact despite sustaining heavy casualties during his retreat from Kelly's Field to Snodgrass Hill, as the new commander of my old XIV Corps.

I continued to strengthen our lines, which ran in a semicircle for a length of about three miles from a point on the River north of Chattanooga to a point on the river south of the city. Our lines faced southeast with Chattanooga behind us and Missionary Ridge in our front. Hooker's lines were to our southwest, facing east toward Lookout Mountain. I was confident that Bragg could not mount an attack that would break my lines.

I was also confident that we could break out of Bragg's semi-siege and deal him a stinging defeat as soon as General Sherman arrived with his 25,000 troops from the Army of the Tennessee. Sherman had started towards Chattanooga from Vicksburg in late September, but was still over one hundred sixty miles from us when Grant arrived in Chattanooga on October 23rd. Sherman informed Grant that his slow pace was the result of Halleck's order to repair the railroad along the route of his march, and Grant directed Sherman to leave off the repairs and proceed to Chattanooga as quickly as possible.

Even after receiving these instructions, Sherman continued to crawl toward Chattanooga. HIs vanguard did not arrive in Bridgeport until November 15th, having averaged less than six miles per day, even after Grant relieved him of the responsibility of repairing the rail line. During the Atlanta campaign, when I was informed that Sherman was deflecting criticism of his lack of progress by blaming me for being slow on the march, I recalled Sherman's glacial progress towards Chattanooga and was bitterly amused.

While we waited for Sherman, reports reached Washington that Bragg had detached Longstreet to attack General Burnside's command in Knoxville. Stanton began to press Grant to assist Burnside. Grant was always concerned with complying with the Administration's wishes, whatever the military necessities might dictate. He conceived a plan to attack the northern end of Missionary Ridge to compel Bragg to recall Longstreet to Chattanooga, thereby relieving Burnside.

When Grant informed me of his plan on November 6th, I was incredulous. I pointed out to him that if I took my army out of its lines to attack the Rebels before Sherman's arrival, there was nothing to prevent Bragg from simply moving forward and capturing the city. Moreover, without the support of strong flank attacks on Bragg's position, a frontal assault on the heavily defended north end of Missionary Ridge was likely to result in heavy casualties and had little chance of success.

I also told Grant that Washington was making too much of Longstreet's movement toward Knoxville. "Longstreet's move is little more than a raid upon our supplies." I explained. "Burnside at this moment has three men to Longstreet's one. Once Sherman reaches us, we will greatly outnumber Bragg's army and if in our attack we can bring the crushing weight of our full force to bear on him, we are sure to win." I reiterated my view that if any attack were to be made before Sherman's arrival, it should be directed against Lookout Mountain, the opposite end of the enemy line from the assault proposed by Grant.

Grant would not be dissuaded. On November 7th, he sent me an order directing me to attack the north end of Missionary Ridge no later than the following morning. I had no doubt that complying with this order would result in disaster. I therefore went to see Baldy Smith, who I understood, had consulted with Grant in devising the contemplated attack. I explained my concerns to Smith and requested that he ride with me to the north of our line to see for himself the strength of the enemy's position. Smith was soon convinced that an attack would be a mistake and rode to Grant's headquarters to so advise him. Later that day, I received a message from Grant calling off the attack.

This change in plan was embarrassing to Grant, who had already informed Halleck and Stanton that he would be relieving Burnside by an attack on Bragg's lines. Although I was certain that Grant would blame me for my unwillingness to carry out the attack, and that this would further strain our relationship, this could not be helped. I was not prepared to sacrifice my men on a foolhardy attack simply to placate Halleck or Grant. I reflected on these events in June, 1864, when I received the report of the useless carnage sustained by the Army of the Potomac in Grant's headlong attacks against Lee's entrenched position at Cold Harbor.

Finally, on November 15th, Sherman arrived in Chattanooga, ahead of his men. At a conference with Sherman and me the following day, Grant unveiled his plan of attack. Sherman and his Army of the Tennessee, reinforced by certain elements of my army, would launch the main attack against Bragg from the northern end of Missionary Ridge. From there, he would sweep south, rolling up the Rebels occupying the crest of the ridge. To keep Bragg from reinforcing his right against Sherman's assault, Hooker was to demonstrate against Lookout Mountain on our right and I was to do the same in front of Missionary Ridge.

Grant did not ask for comments but I offered mine anyway. I pointed out that the southern end of Bragg's line was his weakest point and that Hooker could attack Lookout Mountain and then sweep north. Sherman could attack the north end of Missionary Ridge, as Grant suggested, but with both of Bragg's flanks weakened in this manner, the Army of the Cumberland could then launch an attack against the enemy's center.

Grant quickly rejected this proposal. He explained that he had no confidence in Hooker's ability to conduct an offensive operation. He also expressed his view that the Army of the Cumberland was still demoralized from its loss at Chickamauga, and he doubted its ability to fight outside of its entrenchments. He then turned to Sherman and asked him when he would be in a position to launch his attack. Sherman responded that his army could be in position in five days, on November 21st. Grant fixed this date for the commencement of the offensive.

I thoroughly disagreed with Grant's assessment of my army. Far from being demoralized, my troops were in good spirits and anxious to avenge their defeat at Chickamauga. Nothing in their conduct, since supplies had begun to flow over the cracker line, justified Grant's conclusion that my men were unwilling to fight outside entrenchments. It was clear to me, however, that Grant's mind was made up and I said nothing further. It was also clear that Grant's intention was to give the major role in the offensive to Sherman to bolster his friend's reputation with Stanton and Halleck.

The next day, I convened a conference with my senior commanders to explain Grant's plan. To a man, they expressed disappointment, bordering on anger, over Grant's decision to relegate our army to a supporting role. Like the men in the ranks, they were anxious to prove that Chickamauga was an aberration and that the Army of the Cumberland was the finest in the Union. I reminded them that battles seldom went as planned and that they should be prepared to launch a full scale attack against Missionary Ridge if circumstances required. I explained that a frontal assault against the Rebels' entrenched position on the heights of Missionary Ridge might be possible if one or both of Bragg's flanks was rolled up first. "I want you all to be ready to attack if the order comes," I told them.

Chapter 25

Several days after the meeting with Grant, a young woman from Chattanooga requested to see me. She was very nervous but had obviously set her mind to the task at hand and spoke in a quiet but firm voice.

"General Thomas, I am told that you are a good and fair man. My husband is a lieutenant serving in General Bragg's army. Since your army has occupied Chattanooga, I have been unable to get a letter to him. When he was last at home, our son was ill and we despaired that he would recover. Through God's grace, he is well again. I know that my husband has been sick with worry and I have written to tell him of our son's recovery. If there is any way you could arrange for my letter to be carried through the lines to my husband, you will earn my undying gratitude."

She showed me the letter and its contents were as she described. Seeing the opportunity, in a small way, to alleviate some of the hardship caused by the war, I told her I would do my best to see that her letter was delivered. As soon as she was shown out, I composed a note to my old comrade-in arms, General Bragg:

Headquarters, Army of the Cumberland
Chattanooga, Tennessee

Dear General Bragg,

The enclosed letter was handed me by a young lady of Chattanooga whose husband is an officer in your army. She has been unable to send any communication to him for several months, and is anxious that he be made aware of his young son's recovery from a serious illness. She requested that I arrange to send her letter through the lines so that it might reach her husband. I am pleased to be able to comply with her request and forward her letter to you herewith so that it might be forwarded on to her husband.

If you would be so kind as to inform me when her letter has been delivered, I can so advise her, which I am sure will greatly ease her mind.

Your obedient servant,
George H. Thomas
Major General, Commanding.

I dispatched a member of my staff under a flag of truce to hand my letter to the first Rebel officer he encountered, with a request that it be delivered to Bragg. Later that day, a courier arrived at my headquarters with a reply from Bragg. Sherman was visiting me at the time and, before opening Bragg's letter, I explained the background to him. Instead of the note I expected, informing me that the woman's letter had reached her husband, I found the following written on the back of the envelope containing my letter: "Respectfully returned to Gen. Thomas. Gen. Bragg declines to have any intercourse or dealings with a man who has betrayed his state."

I was incensed. Passing the envelope to Sherman, I said, "I will make Bragg pay for this."

"So Thomas," Sherman said, with a chuckle, "I always knew you were not as imperturbable as you like to make out."

Shortly after this incident, another communication concerning my Virginia roots affected me in a very different manner. Charles Dana, who had come to my headquarters to dine with me and my staff, brought with him a copy of a wire Lincoln had sent to a New Yorker who had apparently questioned my loyalty shortly after the battle of Chickamauga. "The President wanted you to see this," he told me, handing me the wire. It read in part: "I hasten to say that in the state of information we have here, nothing could be more ungracious than to indulge any suspicion towards General Thomas. It is doubtful whether his heroism and skill exhibited late Sunday afternoon has ever been surpassed in the world." I received many accolades during the war and have received many since, but few touched me as deeply as these words from President Lincoln.

Chapter 26

On November 17th, Sherman's men left Bridgeport and crossed the Cumberland River at Brown's Ferry. Grant's plan called for Sherman to march along the north bank of the river and to recross it on a pontoon bridge at a point opposite the north end of Missionary Ridge. To accomplish this second crossing, my pioneers had constructed one hundred sixteen pontoons that were hauled to North Chickamauga Creek, about eight miles upstream from Chattanooga. The pontoons were transported in secrecy and hidden from view.

When Sherman gave the signal, the pontoons were to be floated down the river and assembled into a bridge at Sherman's planned crossing point. Brannan's artillery was moved to a position to support Sherman's crossing. Grant and Sherman planned that Sherman would be across the river on November 21st, in a position to strike the right flank of Bragg's army, before the Rebels knew he was there.

Sherman had to cover a distance of about forty miles from Bridgeport to his crossing point opposite the north end of Missionary Ridge. By mid-day it was clear that he was not moving fast enough to reach the river crossing by November 21st. The attack was postponed until the next day and then postponed day after day as Sherman struggled to get his men in position to cross the river.

On the evening of November 22nd, Grant received a report that Bragg was retreating to join Longstreet opposite Knoxville. Grant sent me instructions to conduct a reconnaissance-in-force the next day to determine whether Bragg had actually retreated.

About a mile and a half from our lines, halfway to the enemy's entrenchments on Missionary Ridge, the Rebels held a fortified position, anchored in the center on an elevation known as Orchard Knob. This was the logical objective for my reconnaissance-in force. However, I determined to do more than merely probe this position. I planned to use this opportunity to demonstrate to Grant, and the doubters on his staff, that the Army of the Cumberland, far from being unwilling to fight outside our entrenchments, was ready and able to leave our lines and strike the Rebels in theirs.

I ordered Wood, Johnson, Baird and Sheridan to assemble their divisions for an attack on Orchard Knob. I directed Howard to place his corps in their rear as a reserve. The route of march would be across Chattanooga Valley. At one thirty pm, the time fixed for the advance, the men marched out as if on parade in perfectly formed ranks, flags fluttering and sunlight glinting off their gun barrels. The attack was supported by the guns of Fort Wood, in the center of our lines.

General Grant and his staff, General Hooker, Quartermaster General Meigs and Assistant Secretary of War Dana, among others, gathered on the ramparts of Fort Wood to witness the attack. The remaining units of the Army of the Cumberland, who remained in their lines, also had a good view of the assault.

The attackers swept over the Rebel pickets and the advanced rifle pits, seemingly without pausing. At this point, it was evident that the Rebels had not withdrawn and the goal of the reconnaissance-in-force had been accomplished. But the four division commanders had orders to take Orchard Knob and they pressed the men forward. At the head of Wood's division, I had placed Willich's and Hazen's brigades that had performed so bravely at Snodgrass Hill.

Willich's brigade reached Orchard Knob first and drove the Rebels from the summit. Hazen's men, fighting hand to hand with bayonets, captured a lower hill to the right and Sheridan's division drove the Rebels on Hazen's right. At four pm, Wood signaled me that he had carried the line of enemy entrenchments. I received the signal on the parapet of Fort Wood where I stood watching with Grant. "Hold on; don't come back," I signaled Wood in reply. "You have gained too much; entrench your position."

Grant turned to me. "That was quite a show, Thomas. Much more than I bargained for. You and your men are to be congratulated. That hilltop will make an excellent observation point. I think I shall move my headquarters there."

I thought it a good time to renew my suggestion that Hooker be authorized to capture Lookout Mountain. "General," I replied, "I still believe that General Hooker should be instructed to attack Lookout Mountain tomorrow morning. He is strong enough to capture the heights, sweep east to Rossville and drive in the Rebels on their left flank. If Sherman can do the same on their right flank, I am confident that my men can capture Missionary Ridge."

"No, Thomas. My plans are firm. You and Hooker are to limit yourself to demonstrations. Sherman will drive the Rebels from Missionary Ridge." I was disappointed but not surprised. Grant was still determined that he and Sherman would be the only heroes at Chattanooga. The Rebels, however, refused to cooperate.

By the evening of the 23rd, Sherman still had not put any men across the river. Grant reluctantly gave me permission to authorize Hooker to move against Lookout Mountain the next morning. There was some ambiguity in Grant's orders as to whether Hooker was to make a demonstration only or was to make a full-scale assault. Hooker chose to interpret the order as permitting him to capture the summit if he thought it feasible.

At four am, Hooker moved out with 10,000 men, over two-thirds of whom were from the Army of the Cumberland. This was the start of the famous Battle Above the Clouds that resulted in Hooker's men driving the Rebels off of Lookout Mountain. When Hooker's men planted the American Flag on the summit, the troops below reacted with wild cheering.

Sherman had also begun his movement on the morning of the 24th. By daylight, the pontoons had been floated downriver and the pioneers had constructed the bridge. Sherman put 8,000 men across the river, but instead of marching them toward Missionary Ridge, he ordered them to entrench until his entire force had crossed the river. Only then did he head for his first objective, a section of the ridge known as Tunnel Hill on the north end of Missionary Ridge.

Shortly after four pm, Sherman, whose men, thus far, had encountered only skirmishers, signaled Grant that he had reached Tunnel Hill and was going into bivouac for the night. Unfortunately, due to his poor maps, Sherman failed to realize that the north end of Missionary Ridge is not continuous but is broken into several detached hills to the north of the main ridge line. Sherman's men were on one of these detached hills, not on the ridge itself, as Sherman believed.

When Sherman launched his attack the next morning, it soon became clear that he was not on Missionary Ridge and was still over a mile north of Tunnel Hill. His men would have to march down the south side of the hill they occupied and climb the north end of Missionary Ridge proper to reach Tunnel Hill.

Overnight, Bragg had sent General Cleburne's division to hold Tunnel Hill. Sherman had six divisions under his command, three of his own army and three from the Army of the Cumberland. Despite this advantage in manpower, Sherman made no progress against Cleburne's defenders. He failed to coordinate his attacks, throwing one brigade at a time against the enemy. All of these disjointed attacks were repulsed. Sherman's struggles were easily witnessed from our observation post on Orchard Knob. To complete Sherman's embarrassment, a portion of his forces were routed in the early afternoon by a counterattack launched by the heavily outnumbered Rebels.

When it became apparent that Sherman was making no progress, Grant finally ordered Hooker to proceed down the south side of Lookout Mountain to capture Rossville Gap on the far left of the Rebel lines. I continued to believe that if one or both of the Rebel flanks could be broken, I would be able to carry the center of the enemy's line on Missionary Ridge. I therefore waited expectantly for news of Hooker's progress, but no word from him reached us.

Hooker, it turned out, had been delayed because the Rebels had burned the bridge over Chattanooga Creek, about a mile from Rossville Gap. The pioneers rebuilt the bridge and Hooker left his guns and wagons behind to expedite his advance. Even so, he did not reach Rossville Gap until about three-thirty pm. We did not know that he had driven the Rebels from Rossville Gap until after our capture of Missionary Ridge.

At about two pm, while we watched Sherman struggle and waited for word from Hooker, Grant conferred with his chief of staff, General John A. Rawlins. Rawlins was a thin, prickly, tightly-wound young man. Before the war he had been an attorney in Grant's hometown of Galena, Illinois, and lacked any military experience. He proved to be an effective staff officer, although the rumor in camp was that his primary responsibility was to keep Grant sober.

Rawlins apparently suggested to Grant that I be ordered to launch a demonstration to assist Sherman. Grant approached me and said, "General Sherman seems to be having a hard time. Don't you think it's about time you ordered your troops to advance against the enemy's first line of rifle pits?"

I scanned the enemy's lines in my front through my field glasses. From what I had observed, I had no expectation that Sherman would be able to break through on Tunnel Hill, even if I created a diversion on the enemy center, which is what Grant had in mind. Even so, I continued to believe that if Hooker could break the Rebel's left flank, my troops could storm Missionary Ridge and send the Rebel's flying. "I still have hopes for Hooker," I replied. "There is still plenty of daylight. I would prefer to wait a while longer." Grant seemed satisfied with my response and walked away.

About a half hour later, after another conference with Rawlins, Grant approached me again. He had made up his mind that he would wait no longer for me to make a demonstration to aid Sherman. "General Thomas, order your troops to advance and take the enemy's first line of rifle pits."

Having received a direct order from Grant, I could wait no longer. I summoned Granger and Palmer, the commanders of the IV and XIV Corps, and told them to prepare their men for an assault on the first line of rifle pits at the base of Missionary Ridge. The signal for the advance was to be the firing of six guns in quick succession from Orchard Knob. At about three-forty pm, I gave the order for the signal guns to fire.

As the report of the final gun sounded, 18,000 men, along a three-mile front, stepped forward and advanced toward Missionary Ridge about one and one-half miles ahead. A good part of the ground between the two lines had been stripped bare of vegetation, allowing the enemy to pour musket and artillery fire into our ranks. My men pressed forward, scattering the Rebel pickets and reached the rifle pits at the base of the Ridge. These were quickly cleared. The men had achieved their objective.

But they did not stop. At first in isolated groups and then *en masse*, my soldiers began to climb the 600-foot face of Missionary Ridge. A second line of defenses halfway up the Ridge was overrun, and the men swarmed toward the Rebel line on the crest. At first the Rebels put up a stiff defense, rolling down improvised grenades made from artillery shells, raking the attackers with musket fire and pounding them with artillery. But my men were not to be deterred and continued their upward assault.

Grant could not believe what he was seeing. Here was the "demoralized" Army of the Cumberland storming the high ground occupied by an entrenched enemy. "Thomas," he growled, "who ordered those men up the ridge?"

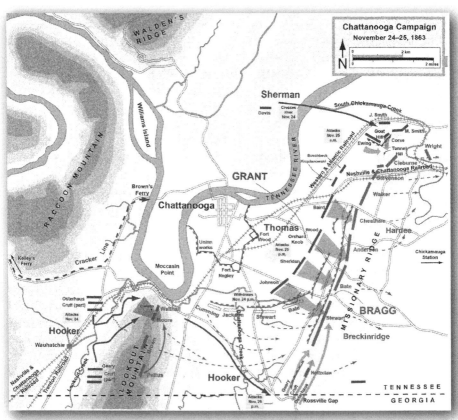

Battles around Chattanooga (map by Hal Jespersen(www.cwmaps.com)

"I don't know," I replied. "I did not."

Grant then turned to Granger. "Did you order them up, Granger?" he asked.

"No," Granger replied, "but once those fellows get started, all hell can't stop them." I could not repress my smile at Granger's response.

"Someone will suffer if this attack does not succeed," Grant muttered.

Nothing else was said. I watched through my field glasses as the blue-clad troops struggled up the hill. In all my years in military service, I never before or since witnessed an assault such as this. Though occasionally slowed by heavy musket and artillery fire, the assault did not stop until the men had reached the crest of the ridge. As they ascended, they roared and chanted "Chickamauga, Chickamauga," announcing their intent to avenge themselves for that defeat. Then, with a shout, they were up and over the enemy entrenchments. Most of the defenders fled. Others threw down their weapons and were captured in their trenches.

In the days following the battle, many regiments took credit for being first to reach the enemy lines. In fact, I counted no less than six regimental banners that reached the summit almost simultaneously. As soon as I saw this, I mounted by horse, Old Billy, and rode up the hill.

The men were jubilant. Seeing me, they shouted, "It's Old Pap" or "Pap Thomas is here" and clustered around my horse. They always took great liberties with me. I swung my hat in the air and called out, "Well done, boys. You gave them hell today." A private, close to me exclaimed, "Why general, we know that you have been training us for this race for the last three weeks." I laughed and replied, "Training you well, it appears." Then seeing a steamship on the river below, I said, "And as your reward, here come the rations." The men whooped and shouted again.

Pursuit of the fleeing rebels began in earnest early on the morning of November 27th. Bragg was retreating south toward Dalton, Georgia. Hooker, with 12,000 troops, was in the vanguard of the pursuit. His men ran into Cleburne's division near Ringgold Gap, Georgia. Hooker was taken by surprise and, although he outnumbered the Rebels almost three to one, was unable to break through Cleburne's blocking position. Cleburne's stand allowed the Rebels to escape with most of their wagons and artillery. Shortly after noon, Cleburne withdrew.

Grant decided to call off the pursuit at this point because of the pressure he was getting from Washington to relieve Burnside, who was believed to be running out of rations in Knoxville. He sent Sherman's Army of the Tennessee to Burnside's assistance. When they arrived in Knoxville, they found that Burnside was not besieged. Longstreet had marched away into winter quarters and Burnside's army was actually better fed than the men sent to relieve them. Burnside had simply not bothered to inform Grant or Halleck that he was in no danger.

Chapter 27

After the Rebel positions on Missionary Ridge had been overrun, I observed Sheridan's division returning to our lines over a gently rising meadow very close to my position on Orchard Knob. I must have startled my staff when I observed that the location traversed by Sheridan's men would make an excellent site for a cemetery. But for some time past, I had been giving thought to the idea that the nation owed it to those killed in battle to provide them with a final resting place worthy of their sacrifice. The dedication of the cemetery at Gettysburg, about a week before the battles around Chattanooga, had given my idea a fresh impetus. But the Gettysburg Cemetery was conceived and established by private citizens. In my mind, the army itself should play the primary role in honoring our fallen comrades.

I continued to contemplate the establishment of a cemetery and on Christmas day 1863, I mentioned my idea to the army's Chaplain, Thomas B. Van Horn. Together, we rode out to the location I had in mind. He agreed that the site I had selected was well-suited for its intended purpose, and gladly agreed to my request that he assume responsibility for overseeing the establishment of the cemetery. As soon as I arrived back at my headquarters, I issued orders for the creation of what became the first national military cemetery.

As work on the cemetery proceeded, I met regularly with Chaplain Van Horn to discuss his progress. At one of the early meetings, the Chaplain advised me that he contemplated laying the men to rest according to their home states. Reflecting on the events that had led up to the war, I replied, "No, no. Mix them up. Mix them up. I've had enough of states' rights."

In early January, I received a letter from Congressman Garfield in Washington congratulating me on the victory at Chattanooga. Garfield also informed me that he was spearheading a movement to have me placed in command of the Army of the Potomac, and that Secretary of War Stanton viewed this prospect favorably.

I wasted no time in composing a reply. As far removed as I was from the eastern theater, it was clear to me that the Army of the Potomac was a hotbed of political intrigue, both inside the officer corps and among the politicians in Washington, most of whom felt free to offer advice on strategy and none of whom hesitated to second-guess every decision made by the army's commander. I could imagine nothing worse than being thrust into the center of that perpetual hurricane.

Thanking Garfield for his complimentary words about the battles around Chattanooga, I then set forth, as clearly as I could, my aversion to taking command of the Army of the Potomac. "You have disturbed me greatly with the information that command of the Army of the Potomac may be offered to me. It is a position to which I am not in the least adapted. I would prefer not to be placed in a position where I would be utterly powerless to do good or contribute in the least toward suppression of the rebellion. The pressure always brought to bear against the commander of the Army of the Potomac would destroy me in a week, without having advanced the cause in the least." Whether it was as a result of my reply to Garfield, or for some other reason, nothing further was ever communicated to me on this subject.

After being driven from Missionary Ridge, Bragg retreated about twenty-five miles southeast to Dalton, Georgia. Jefferson Davis relieved him of command of the Army of Tennessee and replaced him with

Joseph E. Johnston. Johnston had previously commanded the army designated by his successor as the Army of Northern Virginia. He had been out of action since suffering a bullet wound at the Battle of Seven Pines on the Virginia Peninsula. It was an old joke in the Federal army that Jefferson Davis should have pinned a medal on the U.S. soldier who shot Johnston because Johnston's replacement was Robert E. Lee. By the time Johnston was well enough to return to the field, Lee was a hero, and there was no possibility that command of the Army of Northern Virginia would be given back to Johnston. When Davis decided to replace Bragg, Johnston was the logical choice.

A lull in the fighting ensued in the winter of 1863-64. I determined to use this opportunity to bring to bear, as never before, the huge industrial and agricultural resources of the Northern States to strengthen the Army of the Cumberland. For example, I ordered and supervised an extensive enlargement of the supply depots that had been established in Nashville and Chattanooga and stockpiled them with massive quantities of arms, ammunition, clothes, food and all other essential supplies.

Railroad yard at Nashville with locomotives (Library of Congress)

To insure that rations and other supplies in sufficient quantities could be transported the one hundred fifty miles from Nashville to Chattanooga, despite the efforts of the Rebel cavalry raiders, I supervised the construction of a huge locomotive repair facility in Nashville and hired a picked force of civilian mechanics to maintain and repair the engines. This facility was capable of servicing thirty-four locomotives at the same time. Three thousand additional freight and baggage cars were put into service, as well as additional hospital cars, armored cars and other specialized carriages.

I also organized mobile repair teams that quickly became skilled at rapidly repairing or replacing damaged tracks, bridges and tunnels. As an example of our new methods, we constructed standardized bridge trusses in sixty foot sections that were dropped into place by mobile railway cranes.

For some time, I had been constructing blockhouses at strategic points along the railroad to defend against cavalry raids. I now accelerated the pace of construction along the route from Nashville to Chattanooga, building blockhouses strong enough to withstand attack from the light artillery pieces carried by the Rebel cavalry.

As a result of these efforts, we were able to maintain an uninterrupted supply of rations and other supplies from Nashville to Chattanooga. By mid-January all three of the armies around Chattanooga were on full rations and we were also able to feed our prisoners of war and the civilian populations of Chattanooga and Nashville.

The capture of Chattanooga opened the route to Atlanta, our next objective. Because the Western and Atlantic Railroad connecting the two cities would serve as our only supply line, it was imperative that we keep the road open both behind and ahead of our advancing columns.

Up to this time, the pioneer battalions I had organized to perform railroad and bridge construction had largely consisted of volunteers commanded by officers with engineering experience. These battalions had performed very well, but my goal was to establish permanent pioneer units headed by trained engineers.

The need for such units became more evident as the Atlanta Campaign unfolded. In May, at my urging, Congress authorized me to raise ten additional regiments of pioneers and a permanent corps of trained engineering officers. Our pioneer regiments proved critical in keeping the railroad open and the armies supplied as they moved toward Atlanta. An example of the prowess of our pioneer battalions was their rebuilding of the seven hundred eighty-foot long, ninety feet high, bridge over the Chattahoochee River in less than five days.

To maximize the effectiveness of our pioneers and mobile repair teams, it was critical to ascertain the condition of the railroad we would encounter on our march so that we knew what repairs would be required as we advanced. I therefore organized a special network of spies and scouts for the specific purpose of providing us with intelligence about the condition of the railroad ahead of us. The intelligence gained in this manner enabled us to prefabricate bridges and pre-cut lumber using portable sawmills to make necessary repairs immediately upon reaching damaged sections of the railroad.

On our upcoming campaign we would have to cross many unfordable rivers and streams, requiring us to rely on pontoon bridges. I was dissatisfied with the pontoons then in use because they were heavy, cumbersome affairs, about twenty-two feet in length that could only be transported with special pontoon carriers, making them difficult to move. Moreover, once the pontoons reached their destination, it took considerable time to deploy them, requiring several men to lift each pontoon into position and fasten the sections together.

When General Rosecrans had commanded the Army of the Cumberland, he had toyed with the idea of a folded pontoon system, but had failed to develop it. I now asked my Chief Engineer, Captain William E. Merrill, to revisit the idea of folded pontoons. He soon developed hinged pontoons that could be folded up, rather than disassembled, and transported on ordinary supply wagons. The new pontoons were much easier to put together in the field and, though much lighter than the old version, were strong enough to support artillery and fully-loaded wagons. After inspecting the prototype, I was so pleased with Merrill's design that I ordered my workshops in Nashville to construct fifty of them. These devices became known as "Cumberland Pontoons."

The winter lull in the fighting also enabled me to further my goal of making the Army of the Cumberland a truly modern, self-sufficient army. We continued to train the men in a manner that prepared them for actual combat conditions, rather than for the parade ground. My map making teams and spy networks were enlarged and improved. Instead of the men cooking their own meals, we established a system of trained regimental cooks. This improved both the quality and nutritional value of the men's meals.

I also turned my attention to medical care. Up to this point in the war, many officers made it a practice to commandeer ambulances for their personal use during and after battles. I found this practice intolerable, believing that our wounded troops deserved the best care we could provide. I therefore reorganized the ambulance service, assigning each corps its own ambulance teams under the overall command of the army's medical director. Orders were given that ambulances were to be used only to transport the wounded and could not be requisitioned by officers for any other purpose.

I also improved our hospital trains to make them safer and more comfortable. I saw to it that the best locomotives and the best train crews were assigned to the hospital trains and had the smokestacks painted red and the words "Hospital Train" painted in red on each car. So that the hospital trains could be recognized at night by both friend and foe, three red lanterns were hung on the locomotives below the headlight. I ordered that hospital trains be given the right of way in all circumstances.

One day in early February, General Howard and I were chatting at my headquarters when, noting that both Grant and Sherman were on leave, he asked me why I didn't take leave before the upcoming spring campaign. "Oh, I cannot leave," I replied. "Something is sure to get out of order if I go away from my command." Thinking back to my days at Camp Dick Robinson, I added, "It has always been so, even when I commanded a post. I had to stick by and attend to everything or else affairs went wrong." Correctly or incorrectly, this remained my philosophy throughout the war.

In mid-February, Grant requested that I make a reconnaissance-in-force toward Dalton, Georgia and occupy it, if possible. In addition to gaining information about Johnston's dispositions, the purpose of my movement was to prevent Johnston from detaching troops to oppose Sherman, whom Grant had sent to raid Meridian, Georgia. I designated four infantry divisions, supported by cavalry on both flanks to carry out this operation.

On the day specified for the commencement of the movement toward Dalton, my back seized up and I was forced to remain in bed. I assigned General Palmer to lead the operation, instructing him to map the roads and mountain passes lying between Chattanooga and Dalton and to get as close to the enemy lines as possible. Palmer moved out and engaged in three days of heavy skirmishing. He found the Army of Tennessee entrenched in force on the heights of Rocky Face Ridge, a chain of steep hills running from north to south. The only way to reach Dalton from Chattanooga was through Buzzard Roost Gap, whose steep, narrow sides were strongly defended by the Rebels.

I was now sufficiently recovered to join up with Palmer and agreed with his conclusion that Dalton could not be taken by a frontal assault. Grant's desire that I capture Dalton was quite impossible. I withdrew my forces back to Chattanooga, reporting to Grant that a frontal assault against Dalton, even if made by the entire Army of the Cumberland, was not feasible.

I also reported that we had discovered an undefended route through Rocky Face Ridge through Snake Creek Gap, south of Buzzard Roost Gap. The road through Snake Creek Gap ran to Resaca, south of Dalton. The Western and Atlantic Railroad, Johnston's life line also ran through Resaca.

Johnston's failure to defend Snake Creek Gap presented me with a golden opportunity to march through the Gap, cut the rail line at

Resaca and get in Johnston's rear. Johnston would then be forced to fight me on open ground of my choosing. I had no doubt that in such a scenario, we would destroy the Army of Tennessee.

I expected Grant to quickly endorse my plan. I waited in vain, however, for a reply from him. Grant had other things on his mind.

Chapter 28

In March, 1864, Congress revived the rank of Lieutenant General, and President Lincoln promptly promoted Grant to this rank, making him General in Chief. Grant became the first man to hold the rank of Lieutenant General in the United States Army since George Washington. Halleck essentially became the army's chief of staff.

Although he gave some thought to returning to the western theater, Grant decided to remain in the east and make his headquarters with the Army of the Potomac. This necessitated the appointment of a new commander for the Department of Mississippi. Many of the high command in the west anticipated that, as the senior major general in the Department, I would be named to this command.

Knowing Grant, however, I did not hold out great hope that I would be named to command the western armies. I knew that Grant would put his own man in command and had no doubt that Sherman would be his choice. I was therefore not surprised when Sherman was promoted to replace Grant as commander of the Department of Mississippi.

Shortly after Grant named Sherman as his replacement, General Howard came to see me, complaining of Sherman's promotion. "It is an outrage that Sherman has been promoted over you," Howard told me. "He has done nothing to deserve it. He failed at Chattanooga and

Chickasaw Bluffs. Compare this to what you have accomplished. You saved the Army of the Cumberland from destruction at Chickamauga, and it was your army that carried the heights at Missionary Ridge. You should protest to Stanton."

"No, Howard," I replied. "I have made my last protest against serving under juniors. I have made up my mind to go on with this work without a word and do my best to help get through with this business as soon as possible."

In mid-March, Sherman returned to Chattanooga from a meeting with Grant in Nashville, full of swagger and high spirits. This was very much in his character. When things were going well, Sherman was boastful and confident, sure that his military genius would carry all before him. When matters did not go as planned, he became despondent, and was quick to blame others for his problems. One or another of his subordinates was always too slow, did not properly follow his orders or was otherwise at fault. He never acknowledged any mistakes on his own part. I had no doubt that, if our upcoming campaign did not go well, Sherman would not hesitate to point the finger of blame at me and his other subordinates.

I did not have a very high opinion of Sherman as a combat commander. He was nervous and high strung, making it difficult for him to accurately assess what was happening on the battlefield and to take steps necessary to counter unexpected enemy movements. Unlike Grant he was not a good improviser.

He was also temperamentally incapable of taking time to properly plan a battle. Perhaps in an effort to demonstrate decisiveness, he made decisions quickly, often without sufficient information about the enemy's strength or the terrain over which he would be fighting. At the time of his promotion to command in the west, he had never won more than a skirmish or led a successful attack.

Sherman and I were so unlike in temperament, and I thought his decisions so often ill-advised, that I knew it would be difficult for me to serve under him. But, as I had told Howard, I was determined to do my best to bring success to our endeavors. During the course of the Atlanta campaign, I never disobeyed any of Sherman's direct orders. However, I used every ounce of discretion contained in those orders to put my troops in a position to achieve victory and to avoid needless casualties.

During this winter of 1863-1864, I began to organize colored infantry troops for the Army of Cumberland. By the beginning of April, six infantry regiments had been mustered in and another three regiments of infantry and a battery of light infantry were being organized. I agreed with the Government's policy of enlisting black men into the army, but I admit that I had reservations about how effective the colored regiments would be in combat.

One day in March, I rode into the camp of General Thomas Morgan who was drilling the colored regiments in his command. "Do you think these men will fight?" I asked Morgan.

"Yes General," Morgan replied without hesitation. "I surely do. Do you not think so?"

"I think they might fight behind breastworks," I replied, "but I would hesitate to use them in an attack."

I stayed and watched the men drill and was impressed with their performance. I told Morgan so, and added, "Perhaps I am wrong about their ability to fight. No doubt they will have the opportunity to prove me so."

Sherman had a very low opinion of negroes and resisted the official policy of organizing colored units. After I mentioned to Sherman my visit to Morgan, he snorted and said that it was not right for the Government to promote the enlistment of negro troops.

"It's not fair to count negroes as equals. I have had the question put to me often, 'Is not a negro as good as a white man to stop a bullet'? Yes, and a sandbag is better. Can a negro do our skirmishing or picket duty? Can they improvise roads, bridges, sorties, flank movements etc. like a white man? I say no. Soldiers must do many things without orders from their own sense, as in sentinels. Negroes are not equal to this."

"I believe that the Government has a perfect right to employ negroes as soldiers," I replied. The Confederates regard them as property. Therefore, the Government can with propriety seize them as property and use them to assist in putting down the rebellion. But if we have the right to use the property of our enemies, we also have the right to use them as we would all individuals of any other civilized nation who may choose to volunteer as soldiers in our army."

"I think, moreover, that in the sudden transition from slavery to freedom, it perhaps is far better for the negro to become a soldier, and be generally taught to depend on himself for support, than to be thrown upon the cold charities of the world without sympathy or assistance."

"I am surprised to hear you, as a Virginian, say these things," Sherman responded. "Whatever the policy of our Government, I will not be persuaded to use negroes for anything beyond manual labor."

Sherman remained true to his word throughout the war. In my case, before the war was over I saw for myself that negroes could fight every bit as well as white men, not just behind breastworks, but in the forefront of assaults against fortified positions.

Upon his promotion, Sherman convened a conference with his three army commanders, James McPherson, now in command of the Army of the Tennessee, John Schofield, commander of the Army of the Ohio and me. He explained to us that Grant's mission for us was to destroy the Army of Tennessee, just as Grant, in Virginia, intended to destroy the Army of Northern Virginia. Sherman told us that he intended to set the armies in motion toward Johnston and Atlanta on May 1st.

Atlanta was about one hundred twenty miles south-southeast of Chattanooga. The terrain between the two cities was very favorable for defense, because an attacking army would have to traverse several mountain ranges and three rivers, the Oostanaula, the Etowah and the Chattahoochee.

Sherman had roughly 110,000 men in the three armies under his command. My Army of the Cumberland, numbering about 72,00 men and 130 guns, was by far the largest of the three. It consisted of three infantry corps: the IVth commanded by Howard, Palmer's XIVth and the XXth under Hooker. I also had two divisions of cavalry commanded by E.M. McCook and Kenner Garrard. A third cavalry division, under the command of Judson Kilpatrick, was temporarily assigned to the Army of the Tennessee.

I informed Sherman of our discovery that Snake Creek Gap was undefended and of my plan to take my Army to Resaca and get in Johnston's rear. He seemed receptive to the idea, but told me he wanted time to assess his options. I pressed him on several occasions, but he remained non-committal.

In Mid-April, about two weeks before the date Sherman had set for the commencement of the campaign, he called another meeting of his three army commanders and finally laid out his plan. Our forces would advance in three columns. Scofield and his Army of the Ohio, the smallest of the three armies, with about 12,800 men, would be on the left. The Army of the Cumberland, would occupy the center and McPherson's Army of the Tennessee, numbering about 24,000 men, would be on the right. Sherman's plan called for Schofield and me to move directly on Dalton, keeping Johnston occupied. The movement through Snake Creek Gap was to be made by McPherson.

I was astonished by Sherman's plan. McPherson's army was too small to take advantage of the enemy's failure to defend Snake Creek Gap. Only the Army of the Cumberland had the manpower to sever the railroad line, get in Johnston's rear, cut off his line of retreat and force him to fight against a numerically superior army. Moreover, the thirty-six-year-old McPherson was new and unproven as an army commander.

McPherson had commanded a corps in the Army of the Tennessee under Sherman and was a great favorite of Grant's. When Sherman was designated as commander of the Department of Mississippi, Grant elevated McPherson to take Sherman's place as commander of the Army of the Tennessee.

I liked McPherson and thought very highly of him. He had been one of my best students at West Point, graduating first in his class in 1853. I saw in him far greater potential than in any of his classmates, including Philip Sheridan and John Bell Hood.

After his graduation, McPherson remained at West Point for another year as Assistant Instructor of Practical Engineering. My wife and I saw a great deal of him that year and greatly enjoyed his company. He was highly intelligent, charming and well-spoken, with a becoming air of modesty. He had fought with distinction in all of Grant's campaigns beginning with Forts Henry and Donelson. During the battles around Chattanooga he commanded the XVII Corps of the Army of the Tennessee.

But McPherson had never led an independent force on a detached operation. Sherman was entrusting an inexperienced commander with the most important job of the campaign and expecting him to accomplish it with a clearly inadequate force. Moreover, Sherman's orders to McPherson were ambiguous. It was not clear whether Sherman expected McPherson to get his army in Johnston's rear and force a fight or merely to cut the rail line at Resaca and retreat to the mouth of Snake Creek Gap.

I protested to Sherman that the Army of the Tennessee was too small to succeed with the flanking movement and that the Army of the Cumberland was the right force for this task. Sherman replied that the Army of the Cumberland must remain in the center of the Federal armies in case the flanks were driven back.

The armies marched out of Chattanooga on May 1st. While Schofield and I headed straight for Dalton, McPherson slipped off to the south, heading for Snake Creek Gap. He reached it on May 8th, and the next day approached the rail line at Resaca. He got within two hundred yards of the tracks when he encountered the enemy. The forces opposing him consisted of only two brigades totaling less than 4,000 men. Johnston's army was fifteen miles to his north, completely unaware of McPherson's presence. But McPherson explained in his dispatch to Sherman that he feared that the Rebels could use the dense woods on his left to outflank him and had withdrawn to Snake Creek Gap without even cutting the rail line.

I was with Sherman when McPherson's dispatch arrived. Sherman read the message and then handed it to me. "Dense woods," I said in disbelief. "Where were their axes?"

"McPherson's timidity had cost us a victory." Sherman said disgustedly. It was not his timidity, I thought, but his lack of experience. McPherson should never have been given the assignment.

"It's not too late to salvage the situation," I said. "Hooker's corps is not too far from Snake Creek Gap. Let me send him to reinforce McPherson and he can try again." Sherman demurred. Not until two days later did he begin to send reinforcements to McPherson. Eventually the entire army, with the exception of Howard's corps, was marching through Snake Creek Gap, with Sherman personally in command. By then, it was too late. Johnston had realized the jeopardy he was in and had withdrawn to Resaca before Sherman could reach it. He was joined there by Polk with about 15,000 reinforcements.

Two days of attack and counter-attack resulted in a stalemate, leaving the Rebels firmly in control of Resaca. Then, on May 15th, General James Veatch's division, using the new hinged Cumberland Pontoons, crossed the Oostanaula River west of Resaca and got into Johnston's rear. Threatened with having his supply line cut, Johnston abandoned Resaca, withdrawing to Cassville, forty miles south-southwest of Dalton. After some skirmishing at Cassville, Johnston retreated south again, across the Etowah River to a strong position in the mountains around Allatoona Pass.

Sherman wisely decided not to try to force his way through the pass and swung wide to the west hoping to get in Johnston's rear, south of the mountains. Johnston, however, anticipated Sherman's movement and blocked our advance in the mountainous region east of Dallas, Georgia. We attempted to break Johnston's lines in a sharp engagement at New Hope Church. It was hard fighting, and my men performed valiantly, but our uphill frontal assaults against a dug-in enemy had little chance of success.

After the first day's battle at New Hope Church, as was my custom, I rode among my men to get a sense of their morale. Not surprisingly,

I discovered that the day spent making uphill assaults against strong entrenchments had made them apprehensive about the next day's fighting. Because my presence among the men always seemed to instill confidence in them, I pitched my headquarters tent near the front line where all could see me.

Sherman rode up later that evening and, concerned for my safety, ordered me to move my tent to the rear of our lines. I reluctantly obeyed, but immediately regretted it. "I will never comply with such an order again," I told one of my aides, "no matter what the consequences to myself".

Two more days of heavy fighting at New Hope Church failed to yield significant results. Sherman then ordered me to send Howard's IV Corps to Pickett's Mill, on the extreme left end of Johnston's line, to turn the Rebel's flank. After hard fighting, Howard was repulsed.

In swinging west to outflank Allatoona Pass, we had left the line of the railroad. Now, on June 1st, after a week of heavy fighting, we were running low on food and ammunition. We disengaged from the enemy and marched east, back to the rail line at a little town called Acworth, five miles south of Allatoona Pass. We were still only halfway through the mountains.

On June 10th, we began moving south again, this time keeping close to the railroad. Through a series of well-coordinated maneuvers, we forced Johnston out of several strong positions until he reached Kennesaw Mountain, where his troops dug in again.

Sherman was growing increasingly anxious. He had announced to Grant and Halleck that he would be at the gates of Atlanta by the end of May. Now, although June was rapidly drawing to a close, Sherman had failed to inflict any significant damage on Johnston's army. We were still twenty miles north of Atlanta, with Johnston strongly entrenched in our front. Sherman was anxious and frustrated.

On June 25th, Sherman issued orders for a frontal assault on Johnston's works on Kennesaw Mountain to be made in two days' time. I rode to Sherman's headquarters, hoping to convince him to adopt a different strategy. There I found him engaged in conversation with McPherson, who was evidently there for the same reason.

I said nothing, at first, as I listened to McPherson's protest against sending our men against the impenetrable enemy lines. I then suggested, as an alternative, that McPherson might swing around Johnston's right flank and threaten to cut the rail line at Marietta. This would force Johnston to send a significant force to block McPherson, thinning his lines on Kennesaw Mountain and increasing our chances of scoring a breakthrough.

Sherman would not be persuaded. "We have had enough of flanking movements," he told us. "That is what the enemy, and indeed our own officers, have come to expect. But an army, to be efficient, must not settle down to a single mode of offense, but must be prepared to execute any plan which promises success. I want to make a successful assault against the enemy behind his breastworks for the moral effect it will have. We must now locate the point where our assault has the greatest prospects for victory."

So there it was. Sherman was prepared to waste thousands of lives, with little chance of success, merely to demonstrate to the enemy, and to his own men, that his army could make a frontal assault. McPherson and I looked at each other in resigned disbelief, both of us realizing there was nothing more to say. With a heavy heart I rode back to my headquarters. There I encountered General William D. Whipple, who I had made my chief of staff prior to the battles around Chattanooga.

"Are we to attack?" Whipple asked.

"Yes," I replied. "And it is too bad."

We had two days to prepare for the assault, and I did my best in the face of what I feared would be a terrible disaster. On June 26th, Sherman called a council of his high command. He was brusque and impatient. He paced about, as was his habit, and he often appeared not to be paying close attention to the discussion. It was evident that none of his senior commanders agreed with his decision to attack. While I was riding away from the meeting, General Stanley rode up to me and addressed me in a doleful voice.

"General, I am sorry this attack has been decided on. I know it will fail."

"I fear that it will be so," I answered. "But General Sherman has decided it and we must do our best." Seeking to bolster Stanley's spirits, I added, "If we do possibly succeed, Stanley, it will lead to a great victory." Stanley nodded and rode off. My words had little effect on Stanley's dejected mood and, indeed, in speaking them, I was merely whistling past a graveyard.

Sherman's plan was for me to assault the center of Johnston's line, while McPherson, on my left, would simultaneously assault the enemy's right. Schofield, on my right, was to demonstrate against Johnston's left, holding it in place to prevent its defenders from reinforcing the center.

Sherman left it to me to choose the precise point for my attack, and on the 26th I rode as close as I could to the enemy's lines to try to find a weak point. The Rebels were dug in on the steep, heavily wooded slopes of the mountain, behind breastworks at least seven feet high. In front of their works, they had constructed two lines of abatis, rows of entangling brush and tree branches sticking out of the ground, with their tips sharpened to points. Before even reaching the abatis, the attackers would have to overrun the enemy's advanced rifle pits and behind those, a line of pickets. My field glasses disclosed the presence of strong artillery batteries behind the infantry lines.

I did not find any place in the enemy lines that appeared more vulnerable than any other. I therefore selected, as the jumping-off point, the location where we were closest to the enemy lines. Here, the men would only have to traverse six hundred yards before reaching the Rebel rifle pits. It was very little in the way of an advantage, but it was the best that could be had.

After selecting the point of attack, I instructed Generals Palmer and Howard to select one division from each of their corps, four brigades in all, to make the assault. They chose the divisions of Davis and Newton, believing them to be the freshest troops.

The next day, July 7th, began with a heavy artillery bombardment all along the line. At 9 am I gave the order for the assault to begin and watched through my field glasses as my men moved forward. At first they made good progress, overrunning the enemy's rifle pits and picket lines. As they began to claw their way up the steep slope, they were forced to pause to clear away the abatis. From behind their breastworks, the Rebels greeted them with murderous musket fire. When those who remained standing made it through the abatis, they were decimated by a hail of canister fire from the Rebel artillery.

The enemy fire was so intense that retreat back to our lines in daylight was impossible. The men who had survived the attack lay down and used their bayonets to dig shallow trenches for protection, as they waited for nightfall and the opportunity to slip back to our lines. It saddened me beyond words to see so many brave men so needlessly sacrificed.

Despite the slaughter, Sherman ordered another attack, advising me that McPherson's troops had also been repulsed and that only I was in a position to try another assault. I could not countenance it. "We have already lost heavily today, without gaining any material advantage," I informed Sherman. "One or two more such assaults would use up this army." In the face of this protest, Sherman called off the second attack. We sustained about 3,000 casualties at Kennesaw Mountain, with nothing to show for it. The enemy's losses were probably one-third of ours.

At about nine o'clock the night after the battle, I met with Sherman. He was pale and unusually subdued. I believe he was truly upset about the senseless casualties his orders had caused, but he would not admit it. "Had we broken the line today, it would have been most decisive," he told me. "As it is, our loss is small compared with some of those in the east." To me, it was no consolation that our losses in making the pointless assault at Kennesaw Mountain were less grievous than the carnage Grant's army was suffering in Virginia.

Sherman next asked me if I thought a flanking movement might be advisable. I found this an odd question since, before the battle, I had urged Sherman to send McPherson around the Rebel's flank to strike at Marietta. I could not keep the sarcasm out of my reply. "What force do you think of moving with? If it is with the greater part of the army, I think it decidedly better than butting against breastworks strongly abatised and twelve feet thick."

Sherman did not appreciate my response. I was aware that for some time, in his dispatches to Grant and Halleck, he had been blaming his lack of progress in reaching Atlanta on me for moving too slowly. "Go where we may," he shot back, "we will find the breastworks and abatis, unless we move more rapidly than we have heretofore."

With the air somewhat cleared between us, we got down to the business of discussing our next movement. Schofield occupied the position on my right, and we agreed that a turning movement by his army, south and west of Johnston's lines, offered the prospect of flanking the Rebels out of their position on Kennesaw Mountain. I asked for permission to personally inspect the ground over which the movement was to be made and to discuss the feasibility of the movement with Schofield.

I did so the next day and reported to Sherman that the flanking movement offered good prospects for success. On July 1st, Scofield and his small Army of the Ohio marched south and west opening an eight-mile gap between his left and my right McPherson made a forced march behind my lines to close the gap, and on July 2nd, Schofield was several miles closer to Atlanta than was Johnston. As we hoped, Johnston abandoned his Kennesaw Mountain entrenchments and fell back to Smyrna, a few miles north of Marietta. The success of this movement seemed to restore Sherman's equilibrium. From July 3rd to July 9th, we executed a series of additional flanking movements that forced Johnston across the Chattahoochee River to the outskirts of Atlanta.

Johnston's retrograde movement from Dalton to Atlanta had been skillfully done. Heavily outnumbered, he had stymied all of our attempts to flush him out of his entrenched positions and destroy him. In doing so, he had suffered minimal losses of men and material, while inflicting heavy casualties on us at Kennesaw Mountain. We presumed that Johnston would now have to stop retreating and defend Atlanta, but he did not get this opportunity. A few days after we crossed the Chattahoochee, one of my spies at Rebel headquarters reported that Johnston had been replaced as the commander of the Army of Tennessee by John Bell Hood.

Chapter 29

John Bell Hood had made his reputation as one of Robert E. Lee's most aggressive brigade commanders. At Gettysburg, he lost the use of an arm, and at Chickamauga, he lost a leg, amputated at the hip. Despite this devastating wound, he returned to lead a corps under Johnston.

Hood had been my student at West Point, attending my classes in artillery and cavalry tactics. He performed poorly in both classes, never, to my mind, mastering the fundamentals of either discipline. Schofield had been his roommate at the Military Academy and told us that Hood was fearless and aggressive. He forecast that Hood would disdain Johnston's strategy of retreating from one fixed position to another and would, instead, attack at every opportunity. Events were to prove Schofield correct.

On July 20th, the Army of the Cumberland formed the right wing of the Union armies. McPherson's Army of the Tennessee constituted the left wing, with Schofield's s Army of the Ohio in the center. Gaps of two miles separated each of the armies. In his haste to capture Atlanta, Sherman had spread out his forces, much the way Rosecrans had done prior to Chickamauga.

In order to fill the gap between my army and Schofield's, Sherman ordered Howard to take two of his divisions and close up on Schofield.

While this plugged the gap between Schofield's army and mine, it created a two-mile gap between Howard's two divisions that closed up on Schofield and the two that remained in their original positions. Howard believed that Sherman's order placed us in jeopardy and complained to me about it. I also recognized that Sherman's order created a potentially dangerous situation, but had confidence that the Army of the Cumberland was up to the challenge. "We must not mind the gap between your divisions," I told Howard. We must act independently."

Sherman had convinced himself that the Rebels were massed in front of McPherson and Schofield, who were threatening to cut the Western and Atlantic Railroad. On the 19th, he advised me. "You could probably walk to Atlanta, for nothing will be in your way." As he was writing these words, Hood was dispatching Generals Hardee and Stewart, with two thirds of his army, to attack me.

They attacked the next day, after we had crossed Peach Tree Creek. At about four pm, Hardee's men struck the extreme left of my line occupied by John Newton's division. Instead of rolling up this position and sweeping down our line, as the Rebels expected, their attack ran smack into stout log barricades quickly constructed by Newton, who had smelled trouble. "The situation had an ugly look," he explained to me later.

As I rode up to Newton's position, I saw that he had two artillery batteries deployed on high ground behind his infantry line. I had ridden past two other batteries on my way to this portion of the field, and I now galloped back across the bridge over Peach Tree Creek to quickly bring them up and deploy them on ground to my liking.

I took personal charge of all four of the batteries, directing them as they fired round after round of grape and canister into the oncoming Rebels. The guns had a terrible effect on the enemy, ripping great holes in their lines and, before long, sending them reeling backwards. Their attempt to turn my left having failed, the Rebels assaulted the entire length of my line. Three times they charged and three times they were repulsed. Finally, they had had enough and, at dusk, they withdrew from our front. As they retreated, my men, although exhausted, gave a great cheer, throwing their hats in the air. At Peach Tree Creek, we sustained about 1,750 casualties. Rebel casualties could not have been less than 5,000.

Despite his setback at Peach Tree Creek, Hood was determined to maintain the offensive. On July 22nd, he launched a heavy flanking attack against the Army of the Tennessee, which had swung around the Army of the Cumberland to threaten the Georgia Railroad east of Atlanta. Although heavily outnumbered, the Federal force repulsed Hood's attack, in what became known as the Battle of Atlanta. This victory was won at a high cost, however, as General McPherson was fatally wounded.

On my recommendation, Sherman placed General Howard in command of the Army of the Tennessee and, on July 22nd, sent him swinging behind Schofield and me to the west of Atlanta, where he was to support the cavalry' s raid on the Macon and Western Railroad, southwest of the city. On July 23rd, the Confederates attacked Howard near Ezra Church and were badly beaten.

Hood had lost more than 13,000 men in the span of nine days at the battles of Peachtree Creek, Atlanta and Ezra Church. At least for the moment, even his voracious appetite for battle was sated. He withdrew to Atlanta's inner ring of defenses and sat tight.

It had taken us three months to advance from Chattanooga to the outskirts of Atlanta. In all that time, my men had been engaged with the enemy in some manner on all but three days. Yet Sherman had not accomplished his stated goal of destroying the Army of Tennessee. Although we had forced the Rebels back almost one hundred twenty miles to the very gates of Atlanta, Hood's veteran army was still intact and still dangerous behind strong defensive works.

Now, in the late summer of 1864, a new consideration assumed paramount importance. Despite the high expectations entertained by the Northern population in the spring, when Grant began his campaign in Virginia, their hopes had been dashed by a string of extremely bloody and inconclusive battles, culminating in a stalemate at Petersburg. In Georgia, as well, although our losses paled beside those in Virginia, the result of three months of fighting was a stalemate outside of Atlanta. Morale among the Northern populace had plummeted to a new low, and it looked extremely doubtful that Abraham Lincoln would be re-elected in November.

Sherman recognized that only a major military success, such as the capture of Atlanta, could revive the optimism of the civilian population and provide Lincoln with a chance of reelection. Without expressly saying so, he shifted his primary objective from destroying Hood's army to capturing Atlanta.

Sherman also decided that the civilian population of Atlanta was to be punished for the sin of secession. I suspect that Sherman did not fully trust me to vigorously carry out his program of retribution, because his order to me of August 8th was unusually specific. "Orders for tomorrow, August 9th. All the batteries that can reach the buildings of Atlanta will fire steadily on the town tomorrow, using, during the day, about 50 rounds per gun, shell and solid shot." General Howard later reported to me that Sherman read the order to him before it was sent, telling him, "Let us destroy Atlanta and make it desolation."

Sherman ordered the bombardment to continue day after day. The shelling of Atlanta served no military purpose because Hood could remain behind his earthworks forever so long as the Atlanta and Western Railroad, his remaining supply line from the South, remained open. Inflicting needless destruction and hardship on the enemy population was not my idea of warfare and I hoped that, in Sherman's case, it would prove to be an isolated incident. In this hope, I was greatly mistaken. One of Sherman's first actions after occupying Atlanta was to order the forced evacuation of the city's entire civilian population.

We besieged Atlanta for forty days. On several occasions, Sherman attempted to use our cavalry to break the rail line south of the city, but these efforts failed. It was clear that only a large body of infantry was capable of breaking the rail line and forcing the Rebels out of their entrenchments.

Sherman finally realized that he could not break Hood's supply line with cavalry. Leaving a single army corps north of Atlanta, he swung his remaining forces west and south to cut the rail line at Jonesboro, south of the city. Hardee's corps attacked Howard at Jonesboro, but was repulsed. While this battle was in progress, Schofield's Army of the Ohio and a portion of the Army of the Cumberland got astride the railroad. Hood's line was now stretched to the breaking point and, on September 1st, the XIV Corps broke it, overrunning Hood's works near Jonesboro. Hood abandoned his entrenchments and retreated south in two long columns.

Hood's withdrawal from Atlanta presented us with an excellent opportunity to intercept him on the march and destroy his army out in the open, and I proposed to Sherman that we do just that. Sherman, however, was unwilling to risk a decisive battle. "I would rather you should follow the enemy as he retreats," he told me.

Accordingly, we pursued Hood for thirty miles to Lovejoy's Station, where Sherman received word from General Slocum that his troops had entered Atlanta. Sherman's goal of capturing Atlanta was now realized. He gave up the pursuit of Hood and marched back to Atlanta. Months of tension and self-doubt were lifted from his shoulders by the capture of Atlanta.

"Atlanta is ours and fairly won," he famously wired Halleck. He also made clear in the same wire that he had no immediate intention of pursuing Hood, but would remain in Atlanta for some considerable time to rest and refit his troops. Hood's army remained at Lovejoy's Station.

Our capture of Atlanta lifted the spirits of the civilian population in the North and did much to insure the reelection of President Lincoln. Shortly after we marched into Atlanta, I dictated the following message to be read to the men of the Army of the Cumberland, hoping to convey my pride in them: "Your commander now desires to add his thanks to those you have already received, for the tenacity of purpose, unmurmuring endurance, cheerful obedience, brilliant heroism, and all those high qualities which you have displayed to an eminent degree, in attacking and defeating the cohorts of treason, driving them from position after position, each of their own choosing, cutting their communications, and in harassing their flanks and rear during the many marches, battles, and sieges of this long and eventful campaign."

Chapter 30

O.O. Howard's promotion to command the Army of the Tennessee set off a chain of events that changed the entire command structure of the Army of the Cumberland. General Hooker, complaining that he should have received the command of the Army of the Tennessee resigned his commission. Although I would not have guessed it when Hooker first came west, I was sorry to see him go. He had proved himself to be an able corps commander, though his braggadocio and boorish behavior made him difficult to deal with and unpopular among his fellow generals. In his place, Henry Slocum was named as the new commander of the XX Corps. David S. Stanley replaced Howard as the commander of the IV Corps, and Jefferson C. Davis was named to command the XIV Corps, replacing Palmer, who also resigned his commission.

At the start of September, my garrisons in and around Nashville, Chattanooga and Decatur dealt a series of devastating blows to General Joseph Wheeler's cavalry, that was attempting one of its signature raids upon our supply lines. Two of his generals were captured and at least half of his command was lost. Wheeler retreated south of the Tennessee River.

We had little time to celebrate Wheeler's defeat, however, because reports soon reached us that the always-dangerous Nathan Bedford

Forrest was heading north. Forrest crossed the Tennessee River, captured the garrison at Athens and cut one of the rail lines linking Nashville and Chattanooga.

Because we lacked a cavalry force capable of contending with Forrest, Sherman asked me if I thought I could drive Forrest out of Tennessee using only infantry. Forrest was, without doubt, the most capable of the Confederate cavalry commanders. He and his men had escaped from Fort Donelson on the eve of its surrender and he had bedeviled us ever since. I told Sherman that with two infantry divisions I felt certain I could drive Forrest out of Tennessee and perhaps even capture him.

I decided to make my headquarters in Chattanooga, arriving there on September 29th. By blocking the roads that were wide enough for cavalry movements, I forced Forrest south towards the Tennessee River, where I hoped to bag him by converging my forces at his likeliest crossing points. I also enlisted the aid of naval gunboats to protect other points on the river. Forrest, wily as ever, slipped through my trap, having his men cross the river on flatboats at widely separated locations. I was greatly disappointed by our failure to capture Forrest, but at least we had driven him out of Tennessee.

While I was busy contending with Forrest, Hood was also on the move. On September 20th, he left Lovejoy's Station, heading north across the Chattahoochee River. Stanton and Halleck were very concerned that Sherman had allowed Hood to get between Chattanooga and the Federal army. Sherman, therefore, left a single corps in Atlanta and gave chase with the remainder of his forces. The Federal's advance guard battled detached elements of Hood's army south of Chattanooga, preventing Hood from damaging the Atlanta and Western Railroad.

I was not with the Army of the Cumberland during Sherman's pursuit of Hood. To ease the Administration's concern over the fact that Hood was now between the Federal Armies and Chattanooga, Sherman ordered me to Nashville to oversee the defense of the area between Chattanooga and Nashville.

Sherman attempted to chase down Hood for eight weeks. He followed him north into Southern Tennessee and then west into eastern Alabama, but could not bring him to bay. Frustrated by his inability to catch Hood, Sherman decided that the destruction of Hood's army would no longer be his objective.

He wrote to me in Nashville informing me of his plan to take 60,000 men and march across Georgia to the Atlantic Coast, abandoning his supply line and living off the land. His operations would be directed against civilians rather than enemy armies. "I propose to demonstrate the vulnerability of the South, and make the inhabitants feel that war and individual ruin are synonymous terms." If Hood followed Sherman, he and I would trap the Rebels between us. If Hood moved north toward the Tennessee River, which Sherman did not consider likely, it would be my responsibility to bring him to battle and destroy his army.

I was greatly dismayed by Sherman's proposal. Though I believed that the secessionists were traitors, responsible for bringing about a terrible conflict, I did not think that warfare should be waged against the civilian population. I wrote back to Sherman suggesting that if his purpose was to demonstrate that the government in Richmond could not defend the Southern population, a large cavalry raid from Atlanta to the coast could accomplish this.

Sherman, however, had his mind set on a march to the sea. Grant and Lincoln were initially skeptical, worried both about his army's ability to live off the land and about leaving Hood in his rear, free to march north into Tennessee and beyond.

When Halleck asked me for my opinion concerning Sherman's plan, I responded that I was confident I could defend the line of the Tennessee with the force Sherman proposed to leave me. Perhaps I was over-hasty in replying in this manner, but I was relying on Sherman's assurance that he would leave me with sufficient troops to defend Tennessee. I was also frustrated with Sherman's inability or unwillingness to bring on a decisive battle with Hood. I looked forward to exercising an independent command, confident that I could accomplish the destruction of Hood's army.

I may not have been so anxious to see Sherman march away had I known that he did not actually intend to leave behind nearly enough troops to defend Tennessee, let alone defeat Hood's army. It soon developed that Sherman proposed to leave me with only one corps of the Army of the Cumberland, Stanley's IVth. Sherman told Washington that in addition to the 12,000 men in the IVCorps, there were between 16,000 to 20,000 additional troops in Nashville. In fact, fully half of these "troops" were civilian employees of the Quartermaster Department and the rest were green recruits.

Sherman also advised Stanton and Halleck that he was leaving me with 12,000 cavalry. He did not bother to explain that about 9,000 of these men lacked horses and other equipment, some not even having firearms. Therefore, I had only 3,000 effective cavalry with which to oppose Forrest and his 12,000 veteran troopers.

Sherman also calculated that an additional 10,000 men were available in Chattanooga. Of this total, 5,000 had returned from furlough too late to join Sherman's march. Organized into a "provisional division" under General Steedman, these men were from virtually every regiment of the western armies and therefore lacked any organization or *esprit de corps*. The balance of the forces in Chattanooga were either untried colored troops or convalescents who had been deemed unfit to make the march with Sherman.

With this force I was expected to protect Nashville and East Tennessee, to guard the railroad from Chattanooga to Louisville and to defeat Hood in the bargain, a goal Sherman, with a far larger and better-trained army, had been unable to accomplish. I requested that Sherman also assign me the XIV Corps, which I considered to be the best corps in the Federal army, but Sherman refused.

Sherman's calculation of the number of troops available to me was so patently overstated that even Stanton and Halleck determined that I would not have enough troops to protect Tennessee. They ordered

Sherman to leave behind Schofield's Army of the Ohio, now restyled as the XXIII Corps. Halleck also ordered General A.J. Smith to bring two divisions of his XVI Corp, totaling 10,000 men, from Missouri to Nashville. I welcomed the addition of Smith's veterans, but it was uncertain how long it would take them to complete the riverboat journey from Missouri to Nashville. Although Sherman put the estimate of the troops he was leaving me as high as 82,000, when he began his march on November 7th, with 60,000 infantry and practically the entire mounted cavalry force in the western theater, I had only 24,000 effective infantry and 3,000 mounted cavalry at Nashville.

Chapter 31

As was true of so many things, the war had radically transformed Nashville. From a sleepy town located on the south bank of a bend in the Cumberland River, Nashville had been made into the most important transportation, supply and communications center in the entire western theater. A constant stream of trains and riverboats, carrying every manner of men and cargo, entered and departed the city at all hours of the day and night. Huge warehouses had been constructed on the wharfs, in which were stored vast quantities of foodstuffs, equipment, ammunition and the other supplies required to keep our armies in the field. From the time it was occupied by the Federal army in February 1862 to late 1864, Nashville's population had more than tripled to over 100,000.

Because the loss of Nashville would cripple the North's war effort, I had to insure that the city's fortifications were strong enough to resist attack. With few troops to spare, I assembled a construction force made up of civilian employees of the Quartermaster Department, railroad workers, other loyal civilians and former slaves who had escaped to our lines. We constructed a double line of entrenchments running west to east from riverbank to riverbank, covering all eight of the principal roads entering the city from the south. The inner line of works was approximately seven miles long and supported by twenty batteries of heavy guns. The outer line was about a mile longer, with a series of forts constructed at key locations. Having insufficient troops to man both lines of works, I manned the inner works with civilians, both employees of the Quartermaster Department and volunteers.

Railroad bridge at Nashville equipped with
sentry boxes (Library of Congress)

The river above and below the city was patrolled by ironclads from Admiral S. Philip Lee's Mississippi Squadron. These boats provided additional protection for the city, escorted the transports bringing men and supplies to the army and kept watch to assure that Hood did not attempt to cross the Cumberland River without our immediately becoming aware of his movements.

My other goal was to organize the disparate units under my command into an effective fighting force. No task was more important in this regard than procuring mounts for our cavalry troopers. Since the commencement of the war, both sides has used their cavalry largely for reconnaissance, scouting, screening infantry movements and conducting raids on supply and communication lines. Nothing was generally expected of the cavalry during pitched battles. In the aftermath of the Battles of Stones River and Chattanooga, I had begun thinking about using my cavalry in a new way.

The success of Colonel Wilder's Lightning Brigade at Stones River and Chattanooga had convinced me that cavalry could be an effective weapon on the battlefield. With a relatively small number of mounted infantry, armed with seven-shot repeating Spencer rifles, Wilder had inflicted tremendous damage on the enemy. It occurred to me that these tactics could be employed on a much larger scale. If my cavalry could employ its mobility to outflank the enemy and get in its rear, they could then dismount and fight like infantry, employing the fire-power afforded by Spencer repeating rifles. In this fashion, the cavalry's presence on the field might well prove decisive. Moreover, If the enemy was driven from the field, the cavalry could quickly remount and pursue them with a minimum of delay.

Soon after I had arrived in Nashville, James Wilson reported to me for duty. I had met Wilson, then a member of Grant's staff, at Chattanooga. Despite having only recently celebrated his twenty-seventh birthday, Wilson was assertive and self-confident, brash but not arrogant. At Chattanooga, he had impressed me by his willingness to express his disagreement with Grant when he thought his commander in the wrong.

Now, Grant had sent Wilson from Virginia to organize and command a new cavalry corps to serve with my army. He listened attentively to my plan to reshape the cavalry into what would essentially be a corps of highly mobile infantry. I explained that for my plan to succeed, I needed a commander with energy, daring and imagination. Wilson expressed great excitement about my idea and unhesitatingly assured me that he was the right man for the job, even when I told him that 9,000 of his 12,000 troopers lacked horses.

Wilson's temperament was very different from mine. While I tend to be taciturn and reserved, Wilson was voluble and outgoing. I generally kept my opinions of others to myself. Wilson was never reluctant to offer his assessments of his fellow generals or of the political powers in Washington. Despite these differences, I soon grew very fond of him. I enjoyed his spirited conversation and his unvarnished views. I also came to appreciate his energy, diligence and battlefield performance. More than this, I found myself relying more and more on his military judgment. I was never a father, but in my dealings with Wilson I came to view him almost like a son. When he was on campaign, I worried about his welfare and was always relieved when word came that he was uninjured.

James H. Wilson (National Archives)

To gather mounts for the cavalry, I gave orders that, almost without exception, every horse in Tennessee should be commandeered. Wilson's men carried out this order with relish. No one was spared our effort to mount the cavalry. Even Vice President-Elect Andrew Johnson lost his fine set of carriage horses to the army.

A large portion of my correspondence began to consist of complaints from civilians whose horses had been impressed into service. One such letter came from the owner of a traveling circus, who complained that a cavalry unit had swooped in during a performance and made off with all the circus' horses, forcing the show to close. I responded that I was certain the horses, if not the circus owner, undoubtedly felt honored to assist their country in this moment of crisis.

Chapter 32

From a spy at Hill's headquarters, we learned in late October that Hill did not intend to follow Sherman. Instead, he planned to move across Northern Alabama into Middle Tennessee and capture Nashville. From there he could move into Kentucky and perhaps even march east to join Lee outside of Petersburg. Though it proved to be a failure in the end, this may have been the best plan the Rebels could have adopted at this stage in the war.

By the beginning of November, Smith and his two divisions had still not arrived from Missouri, and Nashville's fortifications were not fully completed. Needing to buy time, I ordered Schofield and Stanley to link up in Pulaski, about seventy miles south of Nashville, to delay Hood for as long as possible.

Fortunately, Hood, who had arrived at Tuscumbia on the south bank of the Tennessee River on October 30th, was unable to cross the river into Tennessee for several weeks because we had destroyed a good part of the railroad from Corinth to Tuscumbia. Until the Rebels could repair the railroad, they could not obtain the supplies they needed to support their offensive. After the railroad was repaired and Hood was finally able to resupply his army, days of heavy rains further delayed his river crossing. It was not until November 20th that the Confederates crossed the river into Tennessee.

Schofield's corps had arrived in Pulaski on November 13th, finding Stanley's troops already on the scene. As the senior general, Schofield assumed command of their combined forces totaling about 24,000 men. Because a substantial portion of Hood's army consisted of Nathan Bedford Forrest's cavalry, I also sent Wilson to Pulaski with that portion of the cavalry we had thus far been able to remount.

Schofield was thirty-three years old at this time. I had been his instructor at West Point and originally thought highly of him, finding him bright and hard working. However, as his student career progressed, a series of disciplinary problems dogged him, culminating in his dismissal from the Academy during his fourth year.

Schofield prevailed upon the Secretary of War to order a rehearing and I was appointed to sit on the hearing board. Although the majority of the board voted to reinstate Schofield, I voted to uphold his suspension. Scofield returned to West Point and graduated seventh in his class later that year. The proceedings of the hearing board were confidential and I had no reason to believe, until much later, that Schofield was aware of my dissenting vote.

Schofield had performed competently as the commander of the Army of the Ohio during the Atlanta campaign, and I was reasonably confident in his ability to slow Hood's advance long enough for me to complete Nashville's defenses, and for Smith's two divisions and other units I was expecting to join me there. As Hood marched north, Schofield retreated to Columbia on the south bank of the Duck River.

On November 26th, the enemy reached the outskirts of Columbia, and Schofield retired to the north bank of the Duck. Hood, having learned from Forrest's reconnaissance that he greatly outnumbered the Federal forces, conceived of a plan to trap Schofield. Keeping one of his three infantry corps on the south bank of the river opposite Schofield, he sent Forrest and the other two infantry corps on a wide flanking movement, crossing the river east of Columbia and then marching north to Spring Hill. If his flanking force reached Spring Hill before Schofield, Hood could block Schofield's route back to Nashville and trap him between the two wings of his army.

It was a sound plan and almost succeeded. Although Wilson and his cavalry would later perform in exemplary fashion, at this stage they were no match for Forrest's veterans. In a series of running battles, Forrest drove Wilson's men from the field and headed north toward Spring Hill. Schofield, however, had enough experience to sense the danger he was in and sent an infantry division to Spring Hill. Arriving before the Rebels, this division established a strong defensive position.

Inexplicably, although in a good position to do so, the Rebels neither attacked the Federal division at Spring Hill nor blocked the road leading from that town back to Nashville. Schofield hurried the remainder of his forces to Spring Hill on November 29th, and that night marched them north right past the campsites of the sleeping Rebels.

Marching all night, the Federals reached Franklin, a little town on the Harpeth River, on the morning of November 30th. Schofield intended to cross the river without delay and continue north toward Nashville. However, the bridge over the river had been badly damaged and Schofield was forced to wait at Franklin while his engineers repaired it.

From Franklin, Schofield wired me that he feared Forrest would flank his present position, noting that "Wilson is entirely unable to cope with him." He suggested that he march to Brentwood, about seven miles from Nashville, and that I send reinforcements to meet him there.

This dispatch perplexed me. Schofield was well aware that I had no reinforcement to send him. The shortage of troops in Nashville was the reason I had sent him and Stanley to delay Hood in the first place. Smith and his two divisions were expected any day but had not yet arrived, nor had the provisional division of General James Steedman coming from Chattanooga. Schofield was obviously on edge, but all I could do was to urge him to delay Hood for a few more days, if possible, until the expected additional troops reached Nashville.

Schofield placed his troops in strong defensive works outside of Franklin, expecting that the strength of his position would dissuade Hood from attacking him while the bridge repairs were being completed. This, indeed, would, have been the prudent course for Hood to follow. Instead, commencing on the late afternoon of November 30th, Hood recklessly ordered a series of headlong attacks against the strongly entrenched Federal lines. The fighting continued well into the night until Hood finally ordered a cease fire.

As soon as the firing stopped, Schofield ordered a retreat back to Nashville, the bridge over the Harpeth River having now been repaired. His retreat was so precipitous that he left his dead and wounded on the field.

Hood had captured the field at Franklin but at the enormous cost of 6,000 men killed wounded or missing. Six Rebel generals and a large number of other senior officers were killed or put out of action, seriously weakening Hood's command structure. Federal losses were about 2,300, including General Stanley, who suffered a serious neck wound while personally leading a counterattack. General Wood temporarily assumed command of Stanley's corps during the march to Nashville.

Schofield was exhausted and overwrought when he and General Wood reported to me in Nashville on December 1st. He recounted to me the events that had transpired since he and Stanley had arrived in Pulaski, emphasizing that only his skilled leadership and strategic acumen had saved his army from annihilation at the hands of the far larger Rebel force. While I discounted Schofield's boasting, I told him, quite sincerely, that I, and the nation as a whole, owed him a debt of gratitude for delaying Hood and for dealing him a major setback at Franklin. I also congratulated Wood and, because Stanley's wounds rendered him unable to resume the field, placed him in command of the IV Corps.

Although the arrival of Schofield and Wood was most welcome, I remained troubled by the continued absence of General Smith and his two divisions. All during Schofield's report, I could not help interrupting him whenever one of my aides entered the room to inquire of them if there was any word from Smith. "If Smith does not get here tonight," I explained to Schofield and Wood, "he will not get here at all. For tomorrow, Hood will strike the Cumberland and close it against all transports."

My quartermaster, James Rusling, now entered the room and reported that Smith's transports had been seen very close to town. As he spoke, the door burst open and General Smith came striding in. I knew Smith to be a tough and able fighter. A graduate of West Point, he had served with distinction in Mexico and on the frontier. In the summer of 1864, at Harrisburg Mississippi, although outnumbered, he had beaten off an attack by Nathan Bedford Forrest, an accomplishment few generals in the Union army could claim. His men were seasoned and well-trained veterans.

I am not a demonstrative man, but at the sight of Smith I jumped up, ran to him and embraced him in a strong hug. "Now," I exclaimed, "I am confident that we can and will shatter Hood's army."

I asked Smith if he needed some time to refresh himself but he answered that he wished to get right down to the work of finishing off Hood. With that, I spread out my maps on the floor and Smith, Schofield, Wood and I spent the night pouring over them and discussing plans to defeat Hood. While we were thus engaged, I received more good news. The final reinforcements of my army arrived from Chattanooga, consisting of General Steedman with his provisional division of 5,000 men and two brigades of colored troops.

Chapter 33

Early the next morning I placed my forces in the outer line of defenses on the heights overlooking Nashville. Smith's two divisions took up a position on the right, Wood's IV Corps occupied the center and Schofield's XXIII Corps held the left. Convalescents, various unattached units, Steedman's division and the two brigades of colored soldiers extended the left. The inner line of defenses was manned by armed civilians. Admiral Lee's gunboats patrolled the Cumberland River both above and below the city.

It was my intention to deploy Wilson's cavalry on the far right of my line, but they had seen hard riding and fighting in their recent encounters with Forrest's more experienced fighters, and both horses and men needed time to rest and refit. In addition, several thousand troopers still remained in need of mounts. For the time being, I had to content myself with a skeleton cavalry force on the right.

After his setback at Franklin, we were unsure of Hood's intentions. We found out on December 2nd, when his army arrived on the outskirts of Nashville and began to entrench. The Army of Tennessee was composed of three infantry corps and Forrest's cavalry corps. To our surprise, Forrest did not long remain with Hood before Nashville. My scouts soon reported that Forrest's cavalry corps, together with two small infantry brigades were marching toward Murfreesboro about twenty-eight miles to the east of Nashville.

This was welcome news. While I was concerned over the damage Forrest could do to the railroad between Nashville and Murfreesboro, I did not think he posed a significant threat to the 10,000-man garrison in Murfreesboro. And by sending him away, Hood had deprived himself of his best commander and some of his best fighters. Since I planned for my cavalry to play a major role in the upcoming battle, the absence of Forrest was even more welcome.

Because of the losses he had sustained at Franklin, Hood lacked sufficient numbers to attack our defenses or to truly besiege Nashville. He had about 35,000 men, after sending away Forrest's cavalry. Southeast of the city, opposite to our lines, the Rebels constructed a line of entrenchments and fortifications stretching about four miles, end to end. General Lee's corps occupied the center of the Rebel line, astride the Franklin Pike, with Cheatham's and Stewart's corps to his right and left.

Hood's strategy was to dig in and wait for me to attack, hoping I would make some mistake that would allow him to counterattack and capture Nashville. I was determined that I would make no such mistake. As soon as my cavalry was ready for action, I intended to attack Hill and crush his army.

On the day Hill's army arrived outside of Nashville, I received two telegrams from Grant that proved to be the prelude to a series of vexatious dispatches with which Grant and Halleck bombarded me over the next two weeks. In his first communication, Grant lectured me, "If Hood is permitted to remain quietly about Nashville, we will lose all the road back to Chattanooga and possibly have to abandon the line of the Tennessee River. Should he attack you it is well, but if he does not you should attack him before he fortifies."

Later that same day, Grant wired again. "After the repulse of Hood at Franklin, it looks to me that instead of falling back to Nashville, we should have taken the offensive against the enemy where he was, but at this distance I may err as to the method of dealing with the enemy. You will suffer incalculable injury upon your railroads if Hood is not speed-ily disposed of. Put forth, therefore, every possible exertion to attain that end."

This wire puzzled me. Grant seemed to believe that I was present at Franklin with my entire army, and that I had "fallen back" to Nashville after the battle. In fact, as I had informed Halleck in a series of dispatch-es, both before and after the Battle of Franklin, only Schofield's and Stanley's heavily outnumbered corps were at Franklin. At the time of the battle, I was still awaiting the arrival of Smith's and Steedman' troops, and was defending Nashville with armed civilians and raw recruits.

I did not have the opportunity to reply to Grant's wires until after ten o'clock that night due the press of business. Although the tone and content of Grant's wires irritated me, I replied in a matter-of fact fash-ion. "The divisions of General Smith arrived yesterday morning and General Steedman's troops arrived last night. I have infantry enough to assume the offensive if I had more cavalry, and will take the field any-how as soon as the remainder of General McCook's division of cavalry reaches here, which I hope will be in two or three days." The next day, December 3rd, I sent a follow-up wire to Grant explaining that I hoped to have 10,000 cavalry mounted and equipped within a week at which time I would then be ready to take the offensive.

Two days later, I heard from Grant again, this time express-ing concern that Forrest, who was actually moving southeast toward Murfreesboro, would get in my rear by crossing the Cumberland below Nashville. "It seems to me while you should be getting up your cavalry as rapidly as possible to look after Forrest, Hood should be attacked where he is. Time strengthens him, in all probability, as much as it does you."

That evening I wired Halleck: "I have been along my entire line to-day. If I can perfect my arrangements, I shall move against the advanced portion of the enemy on the 7th instant." My specification of December 7th as the date I expected to begin my offensive was a direct result of the pressure I was receiving from Grant and Halleck. As soon as I sent this telegram, I realized I had made a mistake. My wire stated that I intended to commence my attack on December 7th if I could perfect my arrangements by that date. I realized that Grant and Halleck would ignore this qualification and expect me to attack on the 7th, regardless of the circumstances.

I attempted to clarify my intentions in a dispatch to Grant on December 6th in which I explained, "As soon as I can get up a respectable force of cavalry, I will march against Hood. General Wilson has parties out now pressing horses, and I hope to have some six or eight thousand cavalry mounted in three days from this time. General Wilson has just left me, having received instructions to hurry the cavalry to remount as rapidly as possible."

Before he even received this telegram, Grant wired me on December 6th. "Attack Hood at once and wait no longer for a remount of your cavalry. There is a great danger of delay resulting in a campaign back to the Ohio River." I immediately replied. "I will make the necessary dispositions and attack Hood at once, agreeably to your order, though I believe it will be hazardous with the small force of cavalry at my service."

On December 7th, Stanton sent a wire to Grant that, if I had seen at the time, may have led me to resign my commission on the spot. "Thomas seems unwilling to attack because it is hazardous, as if war was anything but hazardous. If he waits for Wilson to get ready, Gabriel will be blowing his last horn."

I had served my country as a soldier all of my adult life, with some distinction I can safely say. That Stanton could presume that I was reluctant to attack because I was overly-concerned with the hazards of war was the height of ignorance and arrogance, as was his cavalier dismissal of my repeated assurances that Wilson was close to completing his remounting of this cavalry. I had been a cavalry instructor at West Point and served as a cavalry officer on active duty in Texas. I knew better than Stanton, Grant or Halleck what was required to make Wilson's cavalry battle-ready.

Stanton's wire gave Grant the opportunity he was evidently looking for. His reply on December 7th stated, "You probably saw my order to

Thomas to attack. If he does not do it promptly, I would recommend superseding him by Schofield, leaving Thomas subordinate."

Grant followed up on this theme in a wire to Halleck the following day. "If Thomas has not struck yet, he ought to be ordered to hand over his command to Schofield. There is no better man to repel an attack than Thomas, but I fear he is too cautious to ever take the initiative."

Never wanting to take responsibility for any decision of consequence, Halleck placed the issue squarely back in Grant's lap. "If you wish General Thomas relieved give the order. No one here will, I think, interfere. The responsibility, however, will be yours, as no one here, so far as I am informed, wishes General Thomas' removal."

Halleck's wire made Grant pause. He withdrew his suggestion that I be relieved and sent me a rather temperate, though wholly unnecessary telegram. "It looks to me evidently the enemy is trying to cross the Cumberland and are scattered. Why not attack at once? By all means avoid the contingency of a foot race to the Ohio. Now is one of the fairest opportunities ever presented of destroying one of the three armies of the enemy. Use the means at your command and you can do this and cause rejoicing from one end of the land to the other." Reading this dispatch caused me to reflect that Sherman, for a period of six months, with a far larger army than mine, had at least as fair an opportunity as I now had of destroying the Army of Tennessee but had failed to do so.

On December 8th, the same day Grant sent this telegram, I received a report from Wilson advising me that, after conferring with his division commanders, it appeared that the cavalry could not be assembled and made ready for active duty for another three days. This news was very distressing, not because it affected our ability to defeat the Rebels or improved Hood's prospects of slipping across the Cumberland, but because of the pressure I was under to commence my attack. I immediately wired Halleck with this information and assured him that there was no indication that Hood intended to, or could attempt to, cross the Cumberland River.

On December 9th, when Grant received a copy of my telegram to Halleck, he informed Halleck that by all reports the enemy was widely scattered "and no attack yet made by Thomas. Please telegraph orders relieving him at once and placing Schofield in command. Thomas should be ordered to turn over all orders and dispatches received since the battle of Franklin to Schofield."

On the night of December 8th, the temperature plunged and a freezing rain mixed with snow began to fall. By the next morning, the ground was encased in a solid sheet of ice. I sent the following message directly to Grant: "I had nearly completed my preparations to attack the enemy tomorrow morning, but a terrible storm of freezing rain has come on to-day, which will make it impossible for our men to fight to any advantage. I am, therefore, compelled to wait for the storm to break and make the attack immediately after. Admiral Lee is patrolling the river above and below the city, and I believe will be able to prevent the enemy from crossing. Major General Halleck informs me that you are very much dissatisfied with my delay in attacking. I can only say that I have done all in my power to prepare, and if you should deem it necessary to relieve me I shall submit without a murmur."

Next I sent a similar wire to Halleck: "I regret that General Grant should feel dissatisfied at my delay in attacking the enemy. I feel conscious that I have done everything in my power to prepare and that the troops could not have been gotten ready before this. If General Grant should order me relieved I will submit without a murmur. A terrible storm of freezing rain has come on since daylight which will render an attack impossible until it breaks."

On receiving my wire, Grant sent a dispatch to Halleck: "General Thomas has been urged in every way possible to attack the enemy, even to the giving of the positive order. He did say he thought he would be able to attack on the 7th, but didn't do so, nor has he given a reason for not doing it. I am very unwilling to do injustice to an officer who has done as much good service as General Thomas has, however, and will, therefore, suspend the order relieving him until it is seen whether he will do anything."

Although I had begun to suspect that Grant was on the verge of relieving me of command, I had not received any official communication informing me of this, until Grant wired me on December 9th: "I have as much confidence in your conducting a battle rightly as I have in any other officer; but it has seemed to me that you have been slow, and I have had no explanation of affairs to convince me otherwise. Receiving your dispatch to Major General Halleck of 2 p.m. before I did the first to me, I telegraphed to suspend the order relieving you until we should hear further. I hope most sincerely that there will be no necessity of repeating the order, and that the facts will show that you have been right all the time."

Grant wired me again on December 11th: "If you delay attack longer the mortifying spectacle will be witnessed of a Rebel army moving for the Ohio River, and you will be forced to act, accepting such weather as you find. Let there be no further delay. I am hopeful of receiving a dispatch from you today announcing that you have moved. Delay no longer for weather or reinforcements."

I replied the same day: "I will obey the order as promptly as possible, however much I may regret it, as the attack will have to be made under every disadvantage. The whole country is covered with a perfect sheet of ice and sleet, and it is with difficulty the troops are able to move about on level ground. It was my intention to attack Hood as soon as the ice melted, and would have done so yesterday had it not been for the storm."

In obedience to Grant's order, I moved my army into position to commence an attack the next morning. It proved utterly impossible. For several hours I watched as men and horses slipped and slid on the solid sheet of ice covering the ground. Quite a number of cavalry troopers were injured, some seriously, when their horses fell on top of them. Infantrymen could only keep their footing if they moved at a pace little faster than a crawl. Maintaining anything resembling an orderly line proved impossible.

In the late afternoon, I summoned my corps commanders to a meeting at my headquarters at the St. Cloud Hotel. I seated myself at the head of a large oak table and watched my commanders enter one by one, each stopping in front of the fireplace to warm himself before taking a seat. I said little as they chatted among themselves, mostly complaining of the weather.

When everyone was seated, I began. "I have advised General Grant of the circumstances of this ice storm," I explained. "As anxious as we all are to get on with this war, I have recommended that an attack be deferred until the ice melts. General Grant, in turn, has ordered this army to attack the enemy and to disregard the weather. You have been in the field today and have seen things for yourself. I would be grateful for your counsel."

Although the youngest man present, and the most junior in rank, General Wilson spoke up first. "In these conditions," he said, "if I were occupying such an entrenched line as Hood's with my dismounted cavalrymen, each armed with nothing more formidable than a basket of brickbats, I would agree to defeat the whole Confederate army if it should advance to the attack." This brought chuckles and nods of agreement from the other generals.

General Wood spoke next. "The men cannot walk sir," he stated simply. "If they cannot walk they cannot advance upon the enemy." Steedman then interjected, "It might be added, that we can be assured that Hood will neither attack us nor part our company to go to the Ohio, as General Grant seems to fear he might. He will stay where he is, as we must. The fight must wait until the ice thaws." Only Schofield remained silent. Since he was not usually shy about offering his opinion on any subject, I found this odd, but said nothing about it.

I thanked my generals and dismissed them, asking Wilson to remain behind. Grant's telegrams disturbed me greatly. Since Wilson had served on Grant's staff and knew him well, I hoped that he might have some insight into Grant's thinking.

"Wilson," I said, after we had seated ourselves again, "I think, after what I have done in this war, that I ought to be trusted to decide when the battle should be fought. I certainly think I know better when it should be fought than anyone can know as far off as City Point. Do you understand why Grant has so little trust in me?"

Wilson thought a moment. Perhaps he was deciding how candid he should be in discussing the General in Chief. Perhaps he was simply reflecting on my question. Finally, he spoke. "I'm afraid Grant harbors some grudge against you, although I do not know what it is. Grant is loyal to his friends and will hear no criticism of them. But he is implacable towards those he judges to be his enemies. He bides his time and when the situation arises, he acts to destroy them."

"But I have done nothing to warrant Grant's animosity," I protested. "It is true that we do not always see eye to eye, but I have never sought to do him any harm."

"He also secs you as a rival," Wilson added. "Should you smash Hood's army, while he is still stuck in the trenches outside Petersburg, he probably fears that you will supplant him in the public's esteem. On the other hand, if the Rebels slip by us, Grant will be blamed for allowing Sherman to leave Hood in his rear."

"This whole situation is very vexing," I replied. "Sherman took his pick of the western armies and is marching unopposed through the South, while the army he should have destroyed before starting on his excursion has assumed the offensive and is now confronting us. Why should I be censured by Grant for not attacking until conditions permit, while he, with an army of over 100,000, has been confronting Lee at Petersburg for three months, and Lee shows contempt for Grant's generalship by frustrating his every move? Hood has been confronting us for only ten days. Grant is more or less ignorant of the actual condition of affairs in our front and, as you say, he and Sherman are responsible for the situation we face."

Having unburdened myself of these thoughts, which had been weighing heavily on me for several days, I bid Wilson goodnight and composed a telegram to Halleck. I gave some thought to reporting the opinions expressed by my commanders at the council of war, but concluded that Grant might perceive the council as some kind of cabal designed to undercut his authority. Instead, using the strongest language I could think of, I sent a wire to Halleck that I hoped would dissuade him and Grant from continuing to press for an attack I knew could not succeed.

"I have the troops ready to make the attack on the enemy as soon as the sleet which now covers the ground has melted sufficiently to enable the men to march. As the whole country in now covered with a sheet of ice so hard and slippery, it is utterly impossible for troops to ascend the slopes or even move over level ground in anything like order. It has taken the entire day to place my cavalry in position, and it has been finally effected with imminent risk and many serious accidents, resulting from the numbers of horses falling with their riders on the road. Under these circumstances, I believe an attack at this time would only result in a useless sacrifice of life."

I knew of no more direct way to express my view. I believed that no commander, at a distance of five hundred miles away, could continue to insist on an immediate attack in the face of a warning such as this from the commander on the scene. In this, I was greatly mistaken.

The next morning there was no break in the weather. As I worked at my desk, my chief of staff, General Whipple, and Generals Wood and Steedman, knocked on my door and asked to speak to me. I told them to come in and they did so, closing the door behind them.

I bid them to be seated and asked what was on their minds. General Whipple spoke first. "General, did you notice how reluctant General Schofield was last night to express his view on making an immediate attack"?

"Yes, of course. I thought it quite odd. Schofield does not usually hesitate to express his opinion on whatever subject is on the table. What did you make of it?"

They exchanged glances and Steedman spoke. "If I may speak frankly, General?"

"Yes, yes."

"It is no secret that General Grant is no friend of yours. We believe he may be looking for an excuse to bring you down and replace you with one of his friends. Schofield is such a man. We think he is working to undermine you. Shortly after we returned from Franklin, he engaged me in a conversation obviously designed to ascertain whether I was dissatisfied with how you were conducting present operations. When I realized what he was up to, I told him that I had complete confidence in you and terminated the discussion."

Wood now spoke. "Schofield cornered me after last night's council of war. He was fishing to see if I would say something critical of your generalship. I told him that you were conducting affairs in the best possible manner and walked away from him. I would not be surprised if he has had similar conversations with Smith and others."

Whipple then added, "We think it possible, even likely, that Schofield is communicating directly with Grant and the War Department, raising questions about your conduct of affairs."

My immediate reaction was one of shock and disbelief, but as I considered the matter, it began to make sense. I knew that Schofield was very ambitious and that he believed he was qualified for more than command of a corps. I also reflected that he may have learned that I had voted to uphold his expulsion from West Point, though the votes were intended to be kept confidential. It was therefore entirely possible that he was plotting against me from a combination of revenge and ambition.

"Steedman, I want you to search the telegraph office for any wires Schofield may have sent to Grant or Halleck," I said. "Let's find out for certain what he is up to. We will reconvene here at four o'clock. That should give you time to make your inquiries, and I have work to attend to in the meantime."

We met in my office at the appointed time. Without a word, Steedman handed me the draft of a wire to Grant in what I recognized as Schofield's handwriting. Dated December 8th, it contained a very gloomy appraisal of our situation and ended with the words, "Many officers here are of the opinion that General Thomas is certainly too slow." Steedman next showed me several wires from Schofield to the War Department express-ing his doubts about whether we could prevent Hood from crossing the Cumberland.

After reading these messages, I thanked the three generals and dis-missed them, indicating that I needed time to consider how to proceed. In truth, there was not much I could do, at least for the moment. We were on the eve of fighting what I expected would be the decisive battle in the western theater, if not of the entire war. Schofield, whatever his faults, was an experienced corps commander. I could not afford to re-place him now with someone inexperienced in command at the corps level. I could, however, let him know that I was aware of his intrigues, and this I determined to do without delay.

John M. Schofield (Library of Congress)

I asked Whipple to have Schofield report to my headquarters and he arrived a few minutes later. I told him to be seated.

"General," I began, "At last night's council of war, you did not express an opinion on the question of whether we should attack immediately despite the weather or wait until the ice melts. I am anxious to hear your view."

Schofield paused, no doubt to compose his thoughts. He had not expected this question. "Whatever decision you make, General, he cautiously replied, "I will support you to my utmost".

"But what is your own view, Schofield? Do you think that I have perhaps been-- too slow?" I used the last two words deliberately.

"General, I have the utmost confidence in you and would not venture to second-guess your decisions."

"Then, General, "I said. "Can you explain the meaning of this?" I produced a copy of his draft dispatch to Grant and slid it to him across the desk. He recognized it at once and the color drained from his face.

"This is not what it appears," he stammered. "I sent it at the request of General Grant. You note that I did not express it as my own view that you have been slow."

"Yes, you describe it as the view of many officers. Is this, in fact, so?"

"No, no. Grant informed me that he thought you were being too deliberate and asked me to confirm his opinion."

"Yet you have been sounding-out other generals about my performance."

"Only at General Grant's request. You must believe me."

I was not certain I did believe him. There was no doubt that Grant was not my friend, but I found it difficult to attribute to him an active intent to ruin me. I thought it more likely that Grant had made some critical comment about me in Schofield's presence and that Schofield had interpreted this as a license to undermine me.

"I'm not certain that I do believe you," I replied. "But for the time being there is nothing more to be said about this. We have a battle to fight. I trust, however, there will be no further wires to Grant."

"No, sir. You have my word."

I did not think his word meant very much, but I let this go. I dismissed him and attempted to put the whole matter aside and to focus instead on the upcoming battle. But I could not help wondering what the response would be to my most recent wire, warning that an attack before the ice melted could only result in the useless sacrifice of life.

In fact, neither Grant nor Halleck bothered to reply. Instead, on December 13th, Grant ordered General John Logan, the commander of the XV Corps in Sherman' army, who was visiting Grant at City Point, to board a train to Nashville and relieve me of my command, if I had not engaged with Hood by the time he arrived.

At some point after sending Logan west, Grant decided that the situation in Nashville required him to assume personal command and, on the evening of the 14th, he boarded a steamboat for Washington, with the intention of traveling by train from there to Nashville. Before he boarded the train, Grant received my telegram announcing my success on the first day of the Battle of Nashville. He did not board the train west.

Chapter 34

Unaware of Grant's activity, I waited anxiously for a break in the weather and, on December 13th, the cold snap finally broke and the ice began to melt. That evening I wired Halleck: "At length there are indications of a favorable change in the weather, and as soon as there is I shall move against the enemy, as everything is ready and prepared to assume the offensive."

By the morning of the 14th conditions had improved to the point that I determined to make my attack the next day. I summoned my commanders to review with them, once again, my plan for the battle.

Wilson's cavalry corps, on the extreme right of my line would sweep around the enemy left flank, getting into his rear. This attack would be the culmination of my plan to use my cavalry as a powerful assault force. The troopers would fight dismounted, using their seven-shot Spencer's to pour devastating fire on the enemy. Smith's and Wood's corps, next in line, would also sweep right, hitting the enemy's left flank and then proceed to roll up the Rebel line. I expected this powerful three corps attack to shatter the enemy line and cut its communications to the south.

As originally drawn up, Schofield's corps was to remain in the center of the line as a reserve to be sent where most needed. Schofield, however, no doubt wishing to atone for his duplicity, asked to be involved in the attack. I acquiesced and directed him to join in the attack against Hood's left. This increased the attacking force to four full corps.

Steedman with his Provisional Corps, including the negro regiments, occupying the left of my line, would initiate the fighting by attacking the enemy right. This attack would, if all went well, cause Hood to send reinforcements from his left, where my main blow was to fall. At the very least, Steedman's assault would prevent Hood from reinforcing his left.

That evening I dictated the following telegram to Halleck: "The ice having melted away to-day, the enemy will be attacked tomorrow morning. Much as I regret the apparent delay in attacking the enemy, it could not have been done before with any reasonable prospect of success."

I then composed the letter to my wife with which I began these memoirs. It was a great relief to share my feelings with her even though my letter would not reach her until well after the battle. Once I had finished the letter, I lay down and managed to get a few hours' sleep.

I awoke before dawn on December 15th to find a heavy blanket of fog covering the ground. Dawn did little to dispel the fog and brighten the surroundings. In the gloom, I set out from my headquarters at the St. Cloud Hotel and headed for a high hill east of the Hillsborough Pike that I had selected as the site for my headquarters. This location was near the center of our lines, which would facilitate communications with my commanders while also affording me a panoramic view of the battlefield, if and when the fog lifted.

One's thoughts on the precipice of monumental events are very curious. By mid-December, as the cold weather had closed in upon Nashville, I had used up my entire monthly coal allowance and been forced to borrow a supply from one of my neighbors, a Mr. Harris. Now, as I rode along the Hillsborough Pike, it suddenly occurred to me that I had not replenished Mr. Harris' coal supply. I called over one of my aides and instructed him to send fourteen bushels of coal to Mr. Harris. That being accomplished, I continued toward the vantage point from which I would conduct the most important battle of my career.

Steedman's attack was set to commence at six am, but the combination of heavy fog and muddy roads delayed him. Finally, about eight am, the sun broke through and the entire landscape was suddenly illuminated. Steedman moved forward to engage Cheatham's corps on the Rebel right. Cheatham's troops were well-dug in and Steedman's men made little progress and suffered relatively heavy losses. They did, however, manage to keep Cheatham's corps engaged for several hours that morning, preventing Hood from shifting any forces to the left of his line, the site of my main attack.

The negro regiments in Steedman's command were in the forefront of the attack and bore the brunt of the casualties. I watched their attack observing that they fought bravely and well. Their performance that morning dispelled all my doubts about whether black soldiers could fight effectively.

The attack on the Rebel left was to be initiated by Smith's XVI Corps of 12,000 men, assisted by the 4,000 troopers of Hatch's cavalry division, and Wood's IV Corps, containing about 13,500 men. As these troops moved out of their fortified lines at around six am, General Donaldson's force of quartermaster employees and armed civilians took their place in the outer line of earthworks, freeing all 25,000 of Wood's and Smith's men to make the attack.

The attack was slow to get under way due to the fog and some lack of coordination among the various units. However, at about ten am, Smith and Wood moved forward. Hatch's cavalry division ranged far to Smith's right, moving beyond and behind the enemy left, powerfully supporting Smith with their seven-shot Spencer repeaters. By noon, the attackers had overrun the two Confederate earthen forts, or redoubts, that were defending the enemy left flank, and Smith's and Wood' veterans were surging forward, rolling up the Confederate line.

At this point, seeing that victory was within our grasp, I issued orders to have Schofield come into action on Smith's right and for V
in what was to be the largest cavalry movement of the war
the remainder of his 12,000 cavalry and sweep wide

left flank to get into his rear. Here his troopers would dismount and advance on the Rebels from the south.

The combination of our hammer blows on the enemy's front and Wilson's attack from the rear caused the collapse of the enemy left and forced Hood to abandon his defenses and retreat southward. We continued to drive the Rebels back until darkness put an end to the first day's fighting.

While I was pleased with the day's results, I knew that our job was not finished. My goal was not simply to win a victory, but to destroy Hood's army. As I rode along the lines, I was already contemplating the next day's battle. Whipple, who had been busy throughout the day carrying my instructions to far-flung parts of the battlefield, rode up and greeted me.

"Well, General, "he said, "a fine day's piece of work, don't you think?"

"Yes." I replied, "So far we have done pretty well. Unless Hood decamps tonight, tomorrow Steedman will double up Hood's right, Wood will hold his center, Smith and Schofield will again strike his left, while Wilson will work away at his rear. I have some fear that Hood will not stay to fight another day, but if he does not, we are in a good position to pursue him."

"From what we have seen of Hood," said Whipple, "I do not think he will seek to avoid another fight."

"Yes, I suspect you are correct, Whipple. I certainly hope so, for if he stays to fight, we will finish tomorrow what we began today."

A few minutes later, I came across a group of Rebel prisoners being escorted back to Nashville by black troops. One of the prisoners called out to me. "General, can you help us out? We would rather die than be made prisoners by these niggers."

Having seen so many brave black men perish that day, I was in no mood for such sentiments. "Well then," I said "You had better say your prayers and get ready to meet your maker." The guards could not suppress their smiles. I returned their salutes and rode off.

The first thing I did when returning to headquarters was to send a wire to my wife, informing her that we had whipped the Rebels and that I expected to deal them an even more crushing blow in the morning. Next, with great satisfaction, I dictated the following dispatch to Halleck: "I attacked the enemy left this morning and drove it from the river, below the city, very nearly to the Franklin Pike, a distance of about eight miles. Have captured General Chalmers' headquarters and train, and a second train of about 20 wagons, with between 800 and 1,000 prisoners and 16 pieces of artillery. The troops behaved splendidly, all taking their share in assaulting and carrying the enemy's breast-works. I shall attack the enemy again to-morrow, if he stands to fight and, if he retreats during the night, will pursue him, throwing a heavy cavalry force in his rear, to destroy his trains if possible."

The first response to this wire came from Secretary Stanton: "I rejoice in tendering to you and the gallant officers and soldiers of your command the thanks of this Department for the brilliant achievements of this day, and hope that it is the harbinger of a decisive victory, that will crown you and your army with honor and do much toward closing the war. We shall give you a hundred guns in the morning."

A wire from Grant followed soon thereafter. Congratulating me on what he termed a "splendid success," he confirmed the rumors that he had been planning to come west to take command: "I was just on my way to Nashville when I received the news of your victory, but I shall go no farther."

Still unable to refrain from giving me unneeded advice from five hundred miles away, he added, "Push the enemy now, and give him no rest until he is entirely destroyed. Your army will cheerfully suffer many privations to break up Hood's army and render it useless for further operations. Do not stop for trains or supplies, but take from the country as the enemy have done. Much is now expected."

The next morning, President Lincoln telegraphed his congratulations, coupled with an exhortation to keep after Hood: "Please accept for yourself, officers and men the Nation's thanks." Lincoln had been sorely disappointed on many occasions, notably after the battles of Antietam and Gettysburg, over his commanding generals' inability or unwillingness to follow up a victory by pursuing the enemy and dealing it a decisive blow. Thus, I understood the concern expressed in his concluding sentences," You have made a magnificent beginning. A grand consummation is within your reach. Do not let it slip." I did not intend to.

One unavoidable consequence of the day's fighting was that our forces were widely scattered and units had become intermingled. I spent a good deal of the evening supervising the repositioning and untangling of our troops in preparation for the renewal of my attack in the morning. Once the regiments were reformed and repositioned, the men slept on their guns in line of battle.

Early the next morning, I rode out along our lines. The men greeted me with cheers and shouts. It was apparent they were in high spirits over their success of the previous day and shared my confidence that today they would finish the job.

The arrival of dawn brought reports that Hood had not retreated but had taken up a new position about two miles south of his previous line. This position was in some respects stronger than that of the previous day. It was about two miles shorter than on the 15th, allowing Hood to mass his troops closer together for greater firepower, and was anchored by heights on both flanks, Overton Hill on the right and the especially formidable-looking Compton Hill on the left.

Once our reconnaissance developed the enemy's position, I issued orders to my corps commanders. I saw no reason to alter the strategy that had worked so well the previous evening. Steedman and Wood would attack the Rebel right, now defended by General Stephen D. Lee, hoping for a breakthrough but, at minimum, keeping Hood from shifting any of Lee's troops from his right to his left flank, where the main attack was to be directed.

Wilson's cavalry was again to sweep around the Rebel's left flank and gain his rear. This would be the signal for Schofield to attack the left of the Rebel position. Once Schofield's attack commenced, Smith, on Schofield's left, would add the weight of his two divisions to the attack.

The day's action began with an artillery barrage all along the Confederate line. When the barrage ceased, Wood and Steedman launched their assault on Overton Hill that anchored the Rebel right. This position was heavily defended by troops of General Lee's corps who were well dug in. Twice they hurled the attackers back with heavy artillery fire of grape and canister.

Wilson also ran into stiff resistance from Cheatham's corps defending the Rebel left. Between nine and ten am, I rode out along the Hillsboro Pike to meet with Wilson and assess the situation for myself. Wilson was discouraged with his lack of progress, and suggest that he shift his corps to the other end of our line to assist Steedman and Wood with their stalled attack against the enemy right. I rejected this suggestion, telling Wilson to continue his attempt to get into Cheatham's rear.

Finally, around noon, Wilson sent word that he had gotten around the enemy's flank and was in position to attack Cheatham's rear as soon as Schofield began his assault on Cheatham' front. The Rebel defenders were now in grave jeopardy. A captured dispatch from Hood to General Chalmers, Hood's cavalry commander, was brought to me. I smiled as I read Hood's frantic message: "For God's sake, drive the Yankee cavalry from our left and rear or all is lost."

Now was the moment for Schofield to attack. I sent orders to him to immediately commence his assault on the enemy left, but waited in vain for the sounds of his attack. Instead, Schofield sent a dispatch requesting reinforcements from Smith's corps. I saw no reason why reinforcements were needed, Schofield's entire corps being in excellent position to make a massed assault. However, thinking that perhaps I was unaware of some development on Schofield's front, I sent Whipple to evaluate the situation. He soon returned with his assessment that Schofield did not require reinforcements.

I immediately mounted my horse and set out to see Schofield. On the way, I stopped to speak with General Smith who told me that the commander of his First Division, John McArthur, tired of waiting for Schofield, was requesting permission to commence an assault on Compton Hill that anchored the enemy left. I told Smith that I was on my way to see Schofield to get him moving, and that McArthur should wait until Schofield's corps went into action.

By the time I reached Schofield it was close to three pm. "General," I said as I dismounted, "the whole army is awaiting your attack. Why do you hesitate?"

"The enemy is strongly entrenched," he replied, "I fear that an attack now will cause the death of many brave men."

I was rapidly losing patience, seeing our prospects for victory being jeopardized by Schofield's unnecessary caution. I surveyed the field and could clearly see Wilson's troopers already beginning to storm the Rebel works from the rear.

"The battle must be fought now, even if men are killed." I replied, my annoyance showing in my tone and expression. "Order your entire corps forward."

Just then, I heard the sound of heavy musket fire coming from in the direction of Smith's corps. I abruptly terminated our conversation, remounted and rode to the sound of the guns. I encountered Smith, who was surveying his front with his field glasses.

"General Smith," I called to him before even dismounting. "What is going on here?"

"It is McArthur," he replied. "He has commenced his attack without waiting for orders."

"You had better send in your other division at once then, General," I said.

In my haste to reach Schofield, I had left my field glasses at my headquarters. I borrowed Smith's glasses and surveyed the field. Thick smoke made observation difficult, but occasionally a gust of wind would blow the smoke away making it possible to see the progress of Smith's troops. As I watched, McArthur's men broke through the Confederate defenders and stormed Compton Hill. Spurred on by this success, Smith's other division and Schofield's troops, who had finally been ordered forward, stormed the rebel works all across the line. On the right, Steedman's troops, black and white, finally reached the summit of Overton Hill, driving the Rebels before them. All along the line, the Rebels were now in full flight, leaving behind their guns, baggage and everything else that that might impede their headlong stampede.

A great cheer went up from our army as this scene unfolded. Overcome with emotion, I shouted to no one in particular, "Hear that? It is the voice of the American people."

I rode up Overton Hill and reached for my field glasses. They were Smith's. In my excitement I had failed to return them. From this vantage point, I could see my troops, shouting and cheering as they chased after the fleeing Rebels. I shouted out to them, "What a grand army I have! God bless each member of it."

As darkness began to set in, Wilson's troopers were in the process of remounting in order to fulfill the second part of their mission, pursuit of the retreating enemy. I rode out along the Granny Hill Pike and saw a familiar figure in the gathering darkness.

"Is that you, Wilson?" I shouted. "Dang it to hell, didn't I tell you we would lick them, didn't I tell you?" Before he even had time to respond, I turned to business, "Follow them as far as you can tonight and resume the pursuit as early as you can tomorrow morning," I told him. He saluted and rode off down the Pike. I turned my horse and headed back to headquarters.

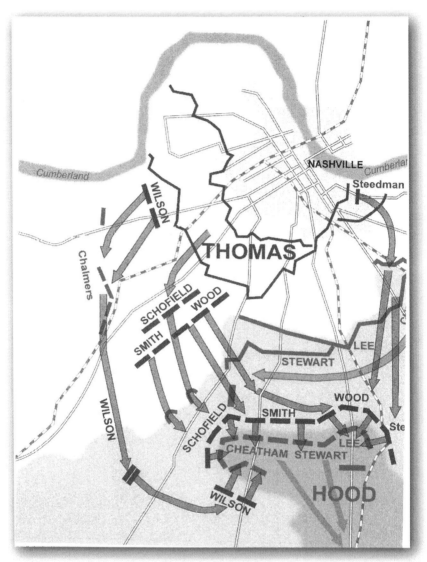

Battle of Nashville

We chased the retreating Rebels in a continuous running battle from Nashville to the Tennessee River. In the midst of our pursuit, Grant and Halleck persisted in admonishing me to keep after Hood's army and not let it escape. Their hectoring culminated in a dispatch from Halleck on December 21st: "Permit me, General, to urge the vast importance of a hot pursuit," it stated. "Every possible sacrifice should be made. If you can capture or destroy Hood's army, Sherman can entirely crush out the rebel military force in all the Southern states. A most vigorous pursuit on your part is therefore of vital importance. No sacrifice must be spared to attain so important an object."

Up to this point, I had made it a point, throughout the Nashville campaign, to keep my temper in check and reply to all of Grant and Halleck's messages in a matter-of-fact manner. Now, with my army enduring every hardship of terrible roads and worse weather in undertaking a pursuit of the enemy unequalled in the history of the war, I lost patience with Halleck and was tempted to remind him of his own snail's pace in pursuing this same Rebel army after the battle of Shiloh and allowing it to slip away unscathed.

I might also have pointed out that I did not understand what military force Sherman intended to destroy, since he had not faced, let alone destroyed, any Rebel armies on his march to the sea. Even in capturing Savannah that very day, Sherman had let the 10,00 defenders of the city escape, contenting himself with occupying the city and sending one of his self-aggrandizing telegrams to Lincoln, presenting the President with the city as a Christmas present. Of course, I did reply in this fashion, but nevertheless made my irritation plain.

"General Hood's army is being pursued as rapidly and as vigorously as it is possible for one army to pursue another. We cannot control the elements, and you must remember that to resist Hood's advance into Tennessee I had to reorganize and almost thoroughly equip the force now under my command. I fought the battles of the 15th and 16th inst. with the troops but partially equipped, and notwithstanding the inclemency of the weather and the partial equipment, have been enabled to drive the enemy beyond Duck River, crossing two streams with my troops and driving the enemy from position to position, without the aid of pontoons, with but little transportation to bring up supplies and ammunition."

"I am doing all in my power to crush Hood's army, and, if it be possible, will destroy it, but pursuing an enemy on mud roads, completely sogged with heavy rains, is no child's play, and cannot be accomplished as quickly as thought of. I hope, in urging me to push the enemy, the department remembers that General Sherman took with him the complete organization of the Military Division of Mississippi, well equipped in every respect as regards ammunition, supplies, and transportation, leaving me only two corps--partially stripped of their transportation to accommodate the force taken with him--to oppose the advance into Tennessee of that army which had resisted the advance of the Military Division of Mississippi and which is now, in addition, aided by Forrest's cavalry. Although my progress may appear slow, I feel assured that Hood's army can be driven from Tennessee and eventually driven to the wall, by the forces under my command. This army is willing to submit to any sacrifice to crush Hood's army or to strike any other blow which may contribute to the destruction of the rebellion."

Neither Halleck nor Grant replied to this wire, that contained truths they were, no doubt, reluctant to acknowledge. Stanton, however, apparently recognized the insulting nature of Halleck's message and the irritation evident in my reply. The morning after my wire to Halleck, he telegraphed me.

"I have seen today General Halleck's dispatch of yesterday and your reply. It is proper for me to assure you that this Department has the most unbounded confidence in your skill, vigor, and determination to employ to the best advantage all the means in your power to pursue and destroy the enemy. No Department could be inspired with a more profound admiration and thankfulness for the great deed which you have already performed, or more confiding faith that human effort could do no more, and no more than will be done by you and the accomplished, gallant officers and soldiers of your command."

On Christmas eve, I received another wire from Stanton informing me that President Lincoln had nominated me for promotion as a major general in the regular army. Though a major general of volunteers, I had held the rank of brigadier general in the regular army for the past fourteen months.

I had been so worn down by Grant and Halleck's continuous stream of critical telegrams that the news of my promotion failed to generate any joy or satisfaction. My immediate reaction was to reflect that, despite my successes at Mill Springs, Stones River, Chickamauga, Missionary Ridge and Peach Tree Creek, I had been passed over for promotion, while Grant had seen to it that Sherman, Meade and even Sheridan were promoted to major general while I remained a brigadier. I learned after the war that, even at this point, Grant had proposed delaying my promotion to assess the full extent of the damage we had wrought on the Army of Tennessee, but that President Lincoln had overruled him.

I happened to be chatting with the chief army surgeon, George E. Cooper, when Stanton's telegram arrived. After reading it, I handed to him, asking: "What do you think of that?"

"Thomas," he replied, after reading it, "It is better late than never."

"I suppose it is better late than never, but it is too late to be appreciated. I earned this at Chickamauga."

Putting aside personal considerations, I turned my attention back to the pursuit of what was left of Hood's army. We chased the Rebels for ten days and nights after the battle of Nashville, battling his rear guard as well as freezing temperatures, rain, snow and sleet. Wilson's cavalry led the way and when their horses needed rest, Wood and his rapidly moving IV Corps overtook the troopers and took up the chase. So relentless was the pursuit that 6,000 cavalry horses were disabled or had to be destroyed.

With the exception of the Confederate rear guard, Hood's army became a disheartened and disorganized rabble of half-armed and barefooted men. The rear guard, however, especially when Forest and his cavalry returned to take up this role, was undaunted and firm and did its work bravely to the end.

On Christmas morning, the shattered remnants of the Rebel army managed to cross the Tennessee River over a bridge at Muscle Shoals, Alabama. Forrest fought his final rear guard action on the 26th, and on the 27th crossed the river to join Hood. In the last act of our pursuit, Wilson managed to get a detachment across the river at Decatur, Alabama and destroy Hood's last wagon train. On December 29th, I called off the chase.

As my men returned to Nashville, I at last had a full opportunity to assess the extent of our victory. I was sorely disappointed that we had not been able to break through the Rebel rear guard and completely decimate or force the surrender of Hood's army. Nevertheless, our victory was overwhelming.

Chapter 35

In the Battle of Nashville, and the many rearguard actions that followed, we had captured over 13,000 prisoners, one third of the army that faced us at Nashville. In addition, as Hood's army retreated, an additional 2,000 deserters came into our camps. Given the precipitous Confederate retreat, it was impossible to estimate the number of Rebels killed and wounded. However, of the 55,000 men Hood took with him for his invasion of Tennessee, less than 8,000 were still armed or could be considered effective when Hood's retreat finally came to a halt in Tupelo, Mississippi.

Since we had captured or destroyed all of the enemy's supply wagons, the Rebel troops lacked food, clothing, supplies and ammunition. We had also captured 72 guns, leaving Hood with virtually no artillery. In short, the Army of Tennessee, one of the two major armies of the Confederacy, had virtually ceased to exist as a fighting force.

In contrast, our own losses were relatively modest. We suffered just 3,057 casualties, of which only 380 were killed. On the offensive and attacking fixed works, we suffered fewer casualties than did Schofield at Franklin, although, in that battle, our troops remained on the defensive throughout.

To me, the achievement of so much, at a relatively low cost, was a vindication of the time I had taken to prepare my army for the battle. Had I listened to Grant and Halleck and gone on the offensive before my army was properly equipped and trained, we might still have prevailed, but would not have won such an overwhelming victory, while our casualties might have resembled Grant's staggering losses in his Virginia campaign.

These reflections led me to consider why Grant had practically become unhinged at my short delay in commencing my attack. No doubt a good part of this was based upon the personal animus be bore towards me for reasons I still do not understand. I also believed, along with Wilson, that Grant saw me as a rival, and was concerned that if I succeeded on my terms at Nashville, the public would draw unflattering comparisons between my success and the stalemate he had achieved in Virginia at so high a cost. The critical messages Schofield was sending Grant undoubtedly fueled Grant's concerns.

My approach to warfare was alien to Grant's way of thinking. To Grant, the key to success was to find the enemy and attack him, hammering away, whatever the cost in men and material. Preparation and planning were less important than seizing and keeping the initiative. At Chattanooga, Grant had ordered me to attack the north end of Missionary Ridge, an attack I knew would result in the wholesale slaughter of my men. I was only able to head off Grant's order by convincing Baldy Smith to persuade Grant to call off the attack. In Virginia, Grant's repeated hammer blows against Lee's army had practically wrecked the old Army of the Potomac. To give Grant his due, however, he had limited Lee's ability to maneuver and eventually bottled him up at Petersburg.

In contrast, I believe in meticulous planning and preparation before committing my army to the attack. While it was never possible to foresee every contingency, a well-trained, fully equipped army, following a well thought out battle plan, maximizes the prospects for success, while avoiding unnecessary losses of men and material. I was therefore determined not to move against Hood until the green units in my command had been trained and equipped and I had procured a sufficient number of horses to enable my cavalry to perform the role I had designed for them.

Grant and Halleck never understood how I planned to use my cavalry and therefore disparaged the need to mount as many of Wilson's troopers as possible. The decisive role played the cavalry in the victory at Nashville vindicated my decision.

It was also evident that Grant misapprehended the actual situation we faced in Nashville. I was regularly reading the Southern newspapers in hopes of gleaning useful information about Hood's plans and dispositions, but what I mainly found were wildly exaggerated accounts of Hood's strength and the success of his campaign. Grant was reading the same newspaper articles and apparently crediting their accuracy, even though they were wildly at odds with the dispatches I was sending him.

Grant was fixated on the idea that Hood would move around Nashville, cross the Cumberland River and reach the Ohio River. He simply refused to believe my repeated assurances that Hood's army lacked the food and supplies necessary for a campaign north of Nashville, at least while my army stood in the way, or that Admiral Lee's gunboats, and my own patrols up and down the river, were sufficient proof against a river crossing.

Grant's view that a delay in my launching an attack benefitted Hood as much as it did me was contrary to the self-evident facts. Far from time working to Hood's advantage, every day that passed increased our chances for success. Hood had no prospect of receiving reinforcements and his men were cold, hungry and demoralized, lying out in the bleak hills south of Nashville, being continuously thinned out by sickness and desertion. The longer we held them at bay, the weaker they became, while my men in Nashville were comfortable, sheltered, well fed and gaining every day in strength.

Grant's anxiety that Hood would escape me and invade Kentucky was also based on his realization that should this happen, he would bear the ultimate blame. As success followed success for Grant and he rose in rank and stature, he became increasingly conscious of the opportunities that would present themselves should he preside over a Federal victory. Conversely, should he fail, all his accomplishments would no doubt be forgotten and he might well return to the anonymity of his pre-war years.

When Sherman had broached his idea of marching to the sea and leaving Hood in his rear, Grant's instincts were against it. His view, like mine, was that the key to victory was the defeat of the Confederate armies. Sherman's proposal was the antithesis of this strategy. But Sherman assured Grant that it was unlikely that Hood would move north and that, if he did, I had more than enough troops to stop him. Based on these assurances, Grant approved Sherman's proposal and Stanton and Lincoln deferred to Grant' judgment. Grant thus became responsible for the outcome of Sherman's strategy, both to the Administration and to the public.

Contrary to Sherman's assurances, Hood had moved north and the troops Sherman proposed to leave with me were clearly insufficient to insure that Hood could be repulsed. Grant saw that if the Army of Tennessee was able to reach the Ohio River, he would be held responsible for not insisting that Sherman bring Hood to battle. Grant's reputation, already damaged by the unprecedented casualties incurred in his campaign against Lee, might well suffer a fatal blow. This concern so worried Grant that the defeat of Hood at the earliest moment became an obsession.

Chapter 36

Now that the once-mighty Army of Tennessee had been shattered, I hoped that my relationship with Grant would improve. I was sorely mistaken. It was my intention to move south as soon as possible, with the aim of capturing Selma and Montgomery and putting these cities' considerable industrial facilities out of commission. But when I advised Grant and Halleck of my need for some time to refit before making this movement, Grant began stripping my army from me.

Schofield, at his own request, and with my tacit blessing, took his XXIII Corps east to North Carolina. Smith and most of Wilson's splendid cavalry were ordered to the assistance of General Canby, outside of Mobile. By the end of January, I was left with little more than Wood's IV Corps, some detached units and a skeleton cavalry force. At the same time, the size of my Department of the Cumberland was significantly increased by the addition of the Department of the Ohio. I was therefore expected to protect a much larger territory with far fewer troops.

An infantry movement against Selma and Montgomery was now out of the question. However, it occurred to me that, with the cavalry's new-found offensive capability, Wilson was quite capable of sweeping aside any opposition and capturing these cities. I broached this possibility to Wilson, who readily accepted the assignment. Grant, still stalemated outside of Petersburg, assented to my plan, specifying however, that Wilson was to exercise his independent judgment in executing the campaign. I was so used to Grant's slights that I refused to let this latest example bother me. At any rate, Wilson let me know that he fully intended to follow my instructions. By the first week in March, Wilson had 20,000 mounted men under his command, most of whom were armed with the Spencer repeaters,

On March 22nd Wilson's cavalry crossed the Tennessee River at Chickasaw and proceeded to inflict massive damage on Alabama's warmaking capability. Then, on April 4th, he wired me that he had defeated Nathan Bedford Forrest's cavalry outside of Selma and had captured the city. The victory over Forrest was particularly gratifying, given the problems he had caused us throughout the war. A week later Wilson captured Montgomery.

The war was now rapidly coming to a close. At long last, on April 2nd, the Army of the Potomac broke through Lee's lines at Petersburg and entered Richmond the following day. Lee fled west with what was left of his army, hoping to entrain at Appomattox Station and join up with General Johnson's small army facing Sherman in North Carolina.

On April 9th, the eagerly-awaited telegram arrived announcing the surrender of the Army of Northern Virginia. I sent dispatches to all my commanders informing them of the news and instructing them to "Fire a salute of two hundred guns at Meridian tomorrow at each post within your command in honor of the capture of the rebel Army of Northern Virginia and of the raising of the old flag over Fort Sumter."

During the next week, while my commanders were forcing the surrender of various small armed bands of rebel guerillas, I decided to organize a grand review of the IV Corps. On April 15th all was in readiness, with the men drawn up in ranks and a reviewing stand constructed for the high command to greet them as they marched by. My staff and I were passing in front of the assembled troops, with their cheers ringing in our ears, when a messenger on horseback came racing up to me. Without a word, he saluted and handed me a dispatch from the War Department.

The contents of the wire put an immediate end to the celebration. President Lincoln was dead, murdered by an assassin the previous evening. I informed my staff and, as the news was passed from unit to unit, the regimental banners and American flags were lowered to half-staff and the men were dismissed to their quarters.

I felt a deep sense of loss over the President's death. I had not agreed with every decision President Lincoln had made. However, unlike most politicians, he seemed indifferent to personal power and acclaim. His sole motivation was the salvation of the Union and in this, despite numerous disappointments and setbacks that would have broken the determination of a lesser man, he never wavered.

As heart-sore as I was by the President's death, I was somewhat consoled by the fact that he had lived to see the destruction of Hood's army and Lee's surrender, meaning victory for the North. I worried that his death at the hands of a Southern sympathizer, coupled with the attempted assassination of Secretary of State Seward, was part of a last-ditch Rebel plot to achieve victory through acts of terrorism and violence. This concern dissipated over the following days and weeks, as it became clear the John Wilkes Booth and his small group of conspirators had not acted in concert with Jefferson Davis and the Confederate government.

As to Lincoln's successor, I had come to know Andrew Johnson quite well during his tenure as wartime governor of Tennessee. We had not always seen eye-to eye, but I respected him as an honest man and a strong advocate of the Union. I was hopeful that he could oversee the peaceful reintegration of the Southern States, and sent him a wire assuring him of my esteem and support.

A few days after Lincoln's assassination, General Sherman accepted the surrender of General Joseph Johnson who had been opposing him in North Carolina. Sherman, however, exceeded his authority to only negotiate surrender terms by including political provisions in the surrender document, including, among other things, the recognition of the existing Southern state governments and the guarantee of virtually all pre-war civil rights to all Confederate soldiers and office-holders. President Johnson repudiated Sherman's terms and ordered Grant to North Carolina to rectify Sherman's blunder. This was quickly accomplished and new, strictly military, surrender terms, consistent with the terms Grant had offered Lee, were agreed upon.

For all intents and purposes, the war was over. On May 1st, I ordered all my department commanders to cease hostilities and to insist that all remaining Rebel armed bands surrender under the terms agreed upon by Grant and Lee. Most of the Rebels accepted these terms, but a few groups of armed men, claiming allegiance to the South, chose to prey on civilian Union sympathizers. I considered these guerillas to be nothing more than common outlaws and ordered my commanders to hunt them down and show them no mercy.

Chapter 37

As the Confederacy collapsed, a final step remained to signal its demise. Jefferson Davis was still at large, having slipped through Grant's army. His capture now became my primary focus. It was rumored that Davis was heading toward Texas, perhaps to attempt to rally the small Rebel army there that had not yet surrendered, or perhaps to make his way to Mexico.

Wilson's cavalry corps was the logical choice to mount a pursuit. At my request, General Canby's infantry replaced Wilson's troopers occupying Selma and Montgomery, freeing Wilson's men to search out and capture the fleeing Davis. Wilson's horsemen fanned out across the southern countryside in hot pursuit, tracking down the numerous rumors of Davis' whereabouts. I was confident that Wilson's men would apprehend Davis, telling Admiral Lee that if Davis managed to escape, he would prove to be a better general than any of his subordinates.

The chase left Wilson far from any telegraph lines so that I did not hear from him for almost a week. Finally, a dispatch arrived from Wilson advising me that, on the morning of May 10th, a detachment of his cavalry had captured Davis near the town of Irwinville, Georgia. I immediately wired Grant this news and requested instructions on where to send the prisoner. Curiously, Grant did not reply. I directed Wilson to bring

Davis to Nashville while I waited for the Administration to inform me what it wanted done with him.

Davis had been captured with his wife, as well as several other Rebel officeholders. I had no sympathy for Davis, believing that he bore a major responsibility for the terrible war we had just endured. Because he was with his wife, however, I did not order him imprisoned in the Nashville jail, but had him and Mrs. Davis taken to the basement of the St. Cloud hotel, where I maintained my headquarters. There was nothing I wanted to say Davis, and I had no intention of meeting with him, being content to send him on his way as soon as I received instructions. On the afternoon of his arrival in Nashville, however, Davis asked to see me.

I had him brought upstairs to the room I used as my office and told the guards to wait outside. I had not seen Davis since our service together in Mexico and hardly recognized him. He was thin and frail, his face gaunt and ashen. With an obvious effort of will, he held himself firmly erect, although his movements were slow and deliberate, as if each step was a burden. Although he attempted to present himself as proud and unbeaten, I sensed underneath this facade a weary and thoroughly defeated man.

I did not offer him my hand and he did not extend his own. Instead, I asked him to be seated on one of the chairs opposite my desk. He lowered himself into the chair and addressed me in a quiet, steady voice. "General Thomas," he said, "Much has transpired since we last met. That was in Mexico, I believe, when my Mississippi Volunteers rode to your defense at Buena Vista."

"Yes," I replied. "You were doing your duty to your country on that occasion."

This caused him to pause. "I have never ceased doing my duty as I saw it," he responded.

"Yes, well we have a different view of that matter, I dare say."

"You know, General Thomas, aside from Lee and Jackson, none of my commanders had my full confidence. Had you fought for our country and led one of our armies, I believe the outcome of the war might have been different."

"Mr. Davis, I did fight for my country and I am happy that it will remain a single nation."

"I will not argue the point with you, General. I have come to ask a favor."

"I am not certain that I am in a position to do you any favors, but what is it you wish?"

"I do not know what Washington intends for me…" he began.

"Nor do I," I interjected. "I have no authority on that question."

"You misunderstand me. I am not here to ask anything for myself. I suppose I will hang," he said without emotion. "It is my wife for whom I am concerned. You have the reputation of being an honorable man. I would ask you, for the sake of our old acquaintance, and out of a sense of decency, to do what you can to make sure that she is not ill-treated."

"Certainly while you are in my custody, you need have no concern on that score. I am also quite confident that no one in the army high command or in the national administration wishes your wife any ill-will. I will certainly do whatever I can to assure that she is treated kindly and with respect."

"Thank you, General. That is much appreciated."

Despite myself, I was moved by his concern for his wife and his resignation over his personal fate. "Is there anything else, I can do for you, Mr. Davis?" I asked.

"No, nothing."

"Well, then, I will say goodbye. I do not expect that I shall see you again while you are here in Nashville." This time he extended his hand and I took it. I summoned the guards and Davis was led away.

Still having heard nothing from Washington, I determined to send Davis to Washington on my own authority. On May 15th, I wired Grant, "Wishing to forward Jeff. Davis and party without delay and having received no instructions to govern me, I have directed that he be placed on board a steamer at this place, forwarded to Parkersville, Virginia, thence by rail to Washington to be turned over to the Provost Marshall General, U.S.A. This arrangement appears to me to be not only the safest but most expeditious. He will be under an ample and efficient guard."

I gave orders to his guards and sent word to all the commanders en route that Davis and his wife were to be treated with courtesy and kindness. They were put on the steamer *Shamrock*, which transported them from Nashville to Parkersville, where a special train took them to Washington.

Chapter 38

With the end of organized opposition, the army's role shifted from fighting the Rebels to aiding the process of reconstruction. The Southern states were organized into military divisions, each commanded by a major general of the regular army. On June 7th, I received official word that I was to command the Division of Tennessee. This division covered an enormous territory, encompassing Tennessee, Kentucky, Alabama and Florida. I determined to keep my headquarters in Nashville.

Each of the states in my division was designated as a military department under the jurisdiction of one of my subordinate commanders. Military rule was to continue until the seceding states were permitted to re-establish their own state governments and send Representatives and Senators to Washington according to procedures to be established by the President and Congress.

The end of the rebellion also brought with it the dismantling of the huge volunteer armies that the Federal government had put into the field. Having done all that was asked of them, the troops, many of whom had served for the full four years of the war, were understandably anxious to return to their families and their civilian pursuits. By the end of

1865, only about 25,000 troops remained in my division and the number continued to decline throughout 1866.

I was initially optimistic that the former Rebel soldiers and the secessionist sympathizers would peacefully acquiesce in the social and political changes brought about by the war. In this, I was greatly mistaken. While some areas enjoyed peace and order, in many others, generally the less-settled regions, lawless bands began to harass and intimidate freedmen, whites who had remained loyal to the Union and recent immigrants from the North. Threats and acts of violence, including murder, were reported to me from all parts of my division. Blacks and loyal whites were being murdered or driven from their farms. Scattered detachments of federal troops were themselves targets of shootings and assaults. This was especially the case with the many former slaves who had remained in the army.

Apprehending those responsible for these acts of violence proved difficult, as the perpetrators melted into the local populations that were usually sympathetic to the malefactors. The local police forces were no help. Indeed, their ranks often included those responsible for the violence.

In areas where repeated acts of violence occurred, I began to station larger semi-permanent garrisons. I was hindered in this effort by the continued demobilization of the army. Indeed, because of the high cost of feeding and maintaining horses, the cavalry, that proved most effective in quelling violence, was the particular target of the Government's effort to reduce the size of the army.

In May, 1866, tensions between whites and discharged negro soldiers in Memphis erupted into violence. The local authorities made no attempt to curtail the violence and only the arrival of a cavalry detail from Nashville put an end to the rioting. Three days of rioting left forty-six blacks and two whites dead and scores injured. Grant ordered an investigation and after conducting extensive interviews, I had no hesitation in reporting that the whites were to blame, having launched what amounted to an assault on the colored population.

Shortly after the Memphis riot, I sent General Whipple on an inspection tour through Mississippi, Alabama and Georgia to ascertain the best places to station troops. His report confirmed my own conclusion that, despite protestations of loyalty, the white population was deeply antagonistic toward the Federal government and was determined to resist all efforts to grant the freedmen economic advantages or political rights.

Faced with this reality, my personal views became more and more aligned with the program of the Radical Republicans in seeking to promote economic and political justice for the freedmen. While the physical safety of the colored population was my paramount concern, I began working closely with the Freedmen's Bureau to assist its efforts to promote economic self-sufficiency for former slaves.

Many large plantations located throughout my Department had been abandoned during the war, and I commenced a program of carving up these large holdings and giving individual farmsteads to the freedmen. I also saw to it that they were provided with the necessary tools to work the land. I was careful in all such cases to locate the owners of the plantations and compensate them for the loss of their property. I wanted no charges of illegal confiscation to jeopardize this program.

On the political front, I began to closely monitor local elections to prevent violence and intimidation from discouraging black voters. In certain cases, where abuse of the voting process seemed evident, I oversaw the establishment of voting procedures to assure fairness. Although I faced criticism that I was disobeying my orders to stay out of civil affairs, in my view my actions were essential to prevent violence and to maintain order.

As 1866 wore on, despite my best efforts, acts of intimidation and violence against blacks and loyal whites continued to increase. Particularly worrisome was the formation of permanent gangs of armed brigands, most notably the Klu Klux Klan, headed by my old nemesis Nathan Bedford Forrest. Because their membership was secret and they had the tacit, if not open, support of the civil authorities, it was difficult to predict where these criminals would strike. I also lacked sufficient troops to effectively combat them.

Testifying before Congress, I warned of the Klan's growing strength and advocated a larger army presence in the locations where the Klan and similar gangs were active. Congress failed to take any action

Chapter 39

As the election year of 1868 approached, it was obvious that Andrew
Johnson would not be nominated for another term. Indeed,
the Radical Republican's antagonism toward the President over his
Reconstruction policy eventually led to the Johnson's impeachment.
With the Republicans seeking another presidential candidate, I began
to receive letters from politicians, friends and fellow officers, requesting
permission to float my name as a potential candidate.

My friend, James Garfield, still serving as a member of Congress
from Ohio, went so far as to assure me that he could make me the next
President, if only I would indicate my willingness of serve. Nothing that
had transpired during the course of the war or its aftermath had improved my opinion of politicians. It has always been my view that many
politicians are corrupt, and that even the more-or-less honest ones are
primarily interested in attaining personal power. Very few, with certain
exceptions such as the late President Lincoln and my friend Garfield,
were men of principle and integrity.

My response to one of the many letters urging me to seek the presi-
dency was typical of the answers I made to all such letters. "I am a soldier
and I know my duty," I stated. "As a politician, I would be lost. Besides,

I want to die with a fair record and this I will do if I keep out of the sea of politics."

Meanwhile, the power struggle between the President and the Radical Republicans in Congress continued to intensify. By this time, either because he had become bitten by the presidential bug or because he had developed a genuine concern for protecting the rights of the freedmen, General Grant had openly taken the side of the Radicals. As the victor in the late war, Grant's views held great weight with Congress and with the public. President Johnson felt that Grant owed his allegiance to the Commander in Chief, not to Congress, and became increasingly dissatisfied with Grant's very public opposition.

In February, 1868, I learned that the President had forwarded to the Senate my nomination as Brevet Lieutenant General and Brevet General, with the intention that I was to replace Grant as General in Chief. I must admit that after the many humiliations I had suffered at Grant's hands, the idea of replacing him as General in Chief held some initial attraction for me. However, on reflection, I realized that Johnson was merely attempting to use me as a pawn in his political contest with the Radical Republicans. I was unwilling to become embroiled in this political struggle.

Therefore, as soon as I learned that Johnson had submitted my nomination, I sent similar letters to the President and to Senator Ben Wade, the President of the Senate, asking that my nomination be withdrawn. To both, I explained: "For the battle of Nashville, I was appointed a Major General in the United State Army. My services since the war do not merit so high a compliment as promotion to General of the Army; and it is far too late to be regarded as a compliment if conferred for services during the war."

Grant, though obviously aware of these developments, said nothing to me about them. After his election as President, he promoted his friend Sherman as the new General of the Army and made Sheridan a Lieutenant General.

In early 1869, while in Washington on official business, I paid a courtesy call on President-Elect and Mrs. Grant, accompanied by one of my staff, Alfred Hough. Grant greeted me with unaccustomed friendliness. While seated with him and his wife in their parlor, he suddenly said, "Thomas, there has got to be a change on the Pacific Coast and either you or Sheridan will have to go there. How would you like it?"

"As for myself," I replied, "I would have no objection to serving there, but on Mrs. Thomas' account, I would not want to take her any further away from her friends in the East."

Mrs. Grant then interjected. "Ah, General Thomas, that is the point. Since you are already married and General Sheridan is not, do you not think the prospects for Sheridan's chances of matrimony dictate that he ought to remain in the East instead?"

This observation was made lightly and the Grants' chuckled, but I had no doubt of the significance of Mrs. Grant's comment. As we entered the waiting coach outside the Grants' front door, I turned to my aide and said, "Hough, we are going to California. That was settled tonight."

My prediction to Hough proved correct and shortly after President's Grant's inauguration, I received orders to take command of the Division of the Pacific and have now established my headquarters in San Francisco. I have no doubt that this will be my last command.

CONCLUSION

I have spent my entire adult life in the army and have served on many bat-
tlefields, fighting the Seminoles, the Mexicans, the Comanches and the
Southern Rebels, when they sought to tear this country apart. I have always
done my duty as I understood it, and I believe that my service in the War of
the Rebellion contributed, not inconsiderably, to the success of our arms.

The late war was perhaps the most terrible ever fought. The victory of Northern Arms changed the nation forever in ways that no one
dreamed of when the war commenced.

I had grown up in Virginia and, as a boy, I viewed slavery as the natural order of things. When negro soldiers were originally enlisted in our
ranks, I doubted that they could be counted on as combat troops. Yet at
Nashville, I saw first-hand that their bravery and commitment to duty were
equal to the best white troops. Witnessing their valor and self-sacrifice, I
had no tolerance, after the war, for the attempts, often violent, by Southern
whites to keep the freedmen in political and economic subservience.

The white Southerners in my Department of Tennessee complained
that I supported the policies of the Radical Republicans and, in truth,
I found myself siding with the Radicals' agenda to an ever-increasing
degree, as the Southern whites escalated their campaign of intimidation
and violence. The enactment of the 14th Amendment, granting citizen-
ship to the colored population, was a welcome and necessary step to

procure the freedmen the economic and political justice they deserve. By itself, however, it is not enough. As long as required, the army must remain in the Southern states to ensure that the freedmen's rights, both economic and political, are protected.

My first experience in combat was in Florida, fighting the Seminoles. For transportation, we traveled on foot or paddled the rivers in canoes. Our weapons were flintlock muskets, swords and tomahawks.

In the Civil War, we rapidly moved whole armies over vast distances by railroad. The troops were armed with deadly rifled muskets and, in the closing year of the war, even deadlier breach loading repeating rifles. Rifled artillery was able to rain destruction on the enemy from miles away.

These new ways of making war required new strategies and tactics. I therefore determined early in the war to master these new technologies to create a truly modern army. I realized this goal at Missionary Ridge, in the Atlanta Campaign and at Nashville. I fear no contradiction in stating that the Army of the Cumberland was the finest fighting force on either side in the late war.

Throughout four years of bloodshed, the bravery and self-sacrifice of our volunteer soldiers never ceased to amaze me. When properly trained and equipped, they proved themselves to be the equals of any fighting force in the history of the world. It was always my first concern to make sure that my men were properly fed, clothed and equipped, and that in battle their lives were not unnecessarily put at risk. For this, I believe I earned their trust and, I think, even their affection. I reciprocated these feelings tenfold. While I suffered my share of personal disappointments and frustrations during the war, these pale beside the pride I feel in my men and what we were able to accomplish together. I made my army and my army made me.

June 1, 1869
San Francisco, California

THE END

AFTERWORD

On March 12, 1870, a letter appeared on the front page of the *New York Herald* highly critical of Thomas' generalship at the Battle of Nashville and claiming that General John Schofield was the true author of the Northern victory. The letter was anonymous, containing only the signature. "One Who Fought at Nashville." The author of the letter was, in fact, Jacob D. Cox, who had led a division in Schofield's corps at Nashville and had recently been named as President Grant's Secretary of the Interior. There is no doubt that Schofield knew of the letter prior to its appearance in the *New York Herald* and encouraged Cox to publish it.

The letter incensed General Thomas and on March 28th, he began to compose a detailed response at his office in San Francisco. As he was writing, he suffered a major stroke and collapsed at his desk. He died that evening with his wife, Frances, at his bedside. He was fifty-three years old. It seems probable that the stress caused by Cox's public disparagement of his reputation, and Thomas' anxiety to set the record straight, contributed to his stroke.

Thomas' body was carried by train to Troy New York, his wife's home town, where he was buried on April 8, 1870. President Grant and General Sherman were among the many dignitaries in attendance. The pall bearers included Generals Meade, Hooker, Rosecrans, Granger and, ironically, Schofield, who was selected because of his rank of major general.

Shortly after his death, the Society of the Army of the Cumberland commissioned an equestrian statue of Thomas, to be cast in bronze, melted down from captured Confederate cannon. The statue was unveiled on November 20, 1879 in Washington D.C. where it still stands today at Thomas Circle.

AUTHOR'S NOTE

I consulted many sources in the composition of this book. Particularly helpful were the following books: *Education in Violence* by Frances F. McKinney; *George Henry Thomas, As True as Steel* by Brian Steel Wills; Civil War Generalship, *The Art of Command* by W.J. Wood; *The Decisive Battle of Nashville* by Stanley F. Horn; *The Warrior Generals, Combat Leadership in the Civil War* by Thomas B. Buell; *Master of War: The Life of General George H. Thomas* by Benson Bobrick; and the paper entitled *Grant and Thomas: December 1864* by Stephen Z. Starr, presented to the Cincinnati Civil War Round Table on April 27,1961. All of these sources are highly recommended to anyone interested in learning more about General Thomas and the Civil War in the western theater.

Made in the USA
Middletown, DE
13 November 2016